Alexis

Double Life

S. Usher Evans

ISBN: 1499198604
ISBN-13: 978-1499198607

DEDICATION

This book is dedicated to
Anyone who has ever read anything I've ever written
And the people who have supported me in my journey of self-discovery
(I know that's a big group).

CONTENTS

PROLOGUE

She let out a quiet, bored sigh.

They had been here for hours—or what felt like hours anyways. Time seemed to stand still in the center of Leveman's Vortex.

It was hard to describe this place, even though she had been here more times than she could remember. There was nothing but white mist for as far as her young eyes could see; it covered the ground and filled the sky. In fact, the only discernible landmark in this entire place was this oasis. Giant boulders jutted out from the misty ground, forming a small hill to a raised dais, atop which an old, weathered stone arch stood tall.

The arch itself was strange—it was here the very first time she had arrived, and it was here every time her father had brought her back here. There was nothing to the side of it, nothing behind it, but a thin silvery curtain that was nearly invisible fluttered ever so often, as if pushed by the wind.

She'd learned in Temple that this white, misty place was called Lethe, and it was the beginning and end of life in the universe. Souls were created and given purpose by the Great Creator and shot out to the far reaches of the universe, where they were born as people. People, unlike souls, had free will, and could choose whether to be good or bad. But the souls eventually returned to the Vortex, passing through this arch, called Arch of Eron in Temple. In the scriptures, it was said that once a soul returned through the arch, it would be judged on the goodness and piousness of the life it had led. If the soul had been truly benevolent, then the Great Creator would allow it to ascend to heaven, and reap the rewards of a life well lived.

But, if the soul was too heavy, weighed down from years of maliciousness and evil deeds, it would be damned to spend all eternity in a river of fire, cursed to burn for their sins. This was the fate that had befallen

1

many of the icons in the scriptures. They had tried everything, hiding behind their more pious brothers, using magic to transfigure themselves, bartering, pleading with the Great Creator. Each one got just as far as the Arch of Eron before their judgment was meted out. Cursed to the river of fire, called Plegethon, every one.

Her father did not believe what the priest said in Temple—in fact, they had stopped attending regular services some years ago. He believed there was a scientific explanation for everything in this holy place, and he was obsessed with demystifying the mystical. He was a scientist, a Deep Space Explorer, charged with exploring undiscovered planets, analyzing plants and sketching animals, to determine if a planet was suitable for human life. But instead, he used his considerable DSE talents here in the center of Leveman's Vortex, trying to understand why this phenomenon even existed—the physics, the chemistry, all of it.

The vortex itself was gigantic; white arms extended from the center, stretching out as wide as some small solar systems. It was beautiful, but also deadly—ships, comets, even whole planets that orbited too close would be evaporated by the intense gravity. It was no wonder that some people, including her Mother, believed that some all-powerful deity lived here, judging souls that were sucked into it and damning them to a fiery end.

Although, to be honest, she had never seen much of anything here, so she was inclined to believe her father's opinions. They were the only two souls here, after all, as he had brilliantly discovered the precise mathematical formula to calculate the trajectory of entry without getting pulverized. It was a complex set of numbers and calculations, based on the weight of the ship, counter-propulsions, and other factors.

He had been bringing her here since she was a small child, but no matter how many times they came to and from this place, the journey was still terrifying. The ship would shake like it was going to explode at any second; the gravitational pressure would grow so intense that she could barely keep her eyelids open. She wanted to be like her father—unfazed, calm and collected—but she couldn't help the terror that ate at her and wouldn't quiet down until they had landed in the white nothingness.

Although it wasn't always nothingness—more recently she had begun to see things. Not real things, but in her mind. Her father had said there was a powerful magnetic field in this place, which cause the hallucinations and messed with his equipment-

"DAMN IT!"

She jumped three feet, watching her father angrily throw the small sensor to the ground in fury. He was tall, with thick brown hair and a thicker brown beard, which he was stroking, deep in thought. He seemed to have changed his mind about the offending instrument, walking over to where it lay and starting to tinker with it. She watched him pull a small leather-bound journal from his pocket and jot down a few thoughts, before stuffing it back in his pocket. As always, he said nothing to her.

He never looked like he was affected by any magnetic field, always so focused on what was in front of him, and never on her. She longed to help him—to know what he was thinking and to do more than just sit quietly and wait for his patience to run out. She watched him smile, opening the back of his machine and pulling out a screwdriver to move around some wires. He had such an incredible mind, and she longed to figure out what was inside of it.

"Father, what's wrong with it?" she asked, curiosity getting the better of her.

Her voice startled him and the machine slipped from his hands, loudly clanging on the stone below him.

"GOD-DAMNIT!" he screamed, whirling around to look at her. There was a violent anger in his eyes, and his face flushed red. "WHAT HAVE I TOLD YOU ABOUT INTERRUPTING?"

She immediately hunched down, desperate to disappear, his angry words echoing in the empty air and in her head. He was always cross with her—she was either careless with his equipment or interrupting his experiments.

Out of the corner of her eye, she saw him angrily snatch up the machine and turn it over, shaking his head irately.

"Well, it's broken," he said, the anger still in his voice. "There goes five hours of research. Are you satisfied?"

"No sir," she whispered, trying to keep herself from crying. It just made him angrier when she did.

He walked around the space, picking up his instruments scattered around the archway, muttering angrily to himself. Every so often, he would speak up to berate her again for interrupting him.

"You're so careless."

"Don't listen to me, don't listen to your mother."

"Never do as you are told."

She pulled her knees up to her chest and wrapped her arms around them, his words stinging her like hot pokers. This was par for the course—she would make some mistake, he would begin the diatribe, and it would go on for hours sometimes until he was no longer angry with her. But he wouldn't simply chide her for what she did wrong; he would start listing all the things wrong with *her*.

"Impatient, petulant. Selfish."

"Don't know when to shut up."

"I don't even know why I bring you sometimes."

"I am about finished with you."

She looked up at him, his last barb stinging more than they usually did. She was only here—she was only his chosen assistant—because he allowed it, because he needed her for some reason. She was terrified at the thought that he would ever decide he had no use for her, and leave her to the mercy of the rest of the family whose jealous hatred of her had grown over the years. For as much as her father had no patience for her, at least he showed her some level of attention. The rest of her siblings, as well as her mother, were not so lucky.

"I tell you to be quiet, and you can't even do that."

"Can barely even handle a simple task of excavating a planet."

"Cannot follow simple directions."

An angry feeling surfaced in the back of her mind, as she watched him. She had always been made to feel like there was something wrong with her, from her father's angry rants to the way her Mother would speak to her to the way her siblings tortured her when neither was around. She had even gone to the family priest once, seeing as he was the closest thing to the Great Creator, but he had the same opinion. She needed to become more subservient, more pious, less…her.

The more she thought about it the angrier she became. She was who she was—she was born this way. Why should she have to change who she was to satisfy someone else?

She sat up, looking at the arch behind her, watching the silvery curtain shimmer and wave lightly. In all the years they had been coming here, he had never once even come close to this thing. She had always thought he would make his way over here, as soon as he finished understanding the rest of this place. But perhaps, even he believed that there was something mystical going on behind this old, old arch. Maybe the Great Creator could provide His opinion…

Silently, she pushed herself upright and stood facing the arch, her eyes searching the other side for any sign of a god, or even anything. But the harder she looked, the more the curtain seemed to become more opaque.

"What are you doing?" she heard him say.

She ignored him with reckless abandon as she inched closer to the passage way. Her heart beating out of her chest, she reached up to touch the silver curtain-

"GET AWAY FROM THERE!"

She felt softness between her fingers, before she was jerked backwards by the back of her shirt, tumbling off of the dais and roughly onto the boulders below. In an instant, her father was down at her level, searching her face. It was the first time she had ever seen him frightened.

"What are you doing?" he gasped.

"I— she said, but she stopped when the ground began trembling. Beside her fingertips, pebbles shook, dancing across the surface of the boulders before disappearing beside them. A loud crack echoed across the land—a large piece of the arch broke off, loudly tumbling down and nearly missing them.

"What did you do?!" he yelled at her, fear like she had never seen in his eyes.

She turned to look at the arch, horrified as the beautiful silver wisps that hung from the arch had turned inky black, slinking to the ground almost like liquid, and the arch began to crumble. She could feel her father yanking her out of the huge rocks that came thundering off the dais.

But they didn't just fall to the ground, they fell through the ground. Steam and red heat burst through the holes—she could feel her cheeks burning. Looking down, she saw a coursing river beneath her—ablaze with a coursing inferno.

The river of fire, Plegethon—the place where bad souls went.

It was all true—the Great Creator, the Arch of Eron. It was all true.

Her father was screaming at her from afar, waving at her to follow him as he ran. She stood, unable to move, as the world disintegrated around her.

She could hear a thousand voices in her head, all telling her the same thing.

She had a terrible, bad, evil soul.

And then the ground beneath her cracked and she was falling...falling...falling...

CHAPTER ONE

Lyssa jerked awake, a lingering chill running down her spine. Her hands instinctively grasped at the grass, and slowly she came to remember that she was seated very safely against a large tree next to a stream on a relatively harmless planet in the farthest reaches of the known universe.

The sunlight was streaming through the lush green jungle and cascading on the mossy ground. Nearby, a rushing stream was gurgling, and an obnoxious beeping sound was coming from a metal sensor that was testing the water for any known toxins and overall drinkability.

She rubbed her face sleepily. She couldn't remember what she'd been dreaming about now; only that she had that sleepy, lethargic feeling in the back of her throat when she'd slept too long. Also, there was a tingle in her back from sleeping awkwardly against a tree. Yawning, she reached down and unhooked a small black computer with a single touch screen from her belt.

She unlocked the screen, bringing up a page of different application buttons. She flipped through the list for a moment, and tapped the button linked to the sensor in the water. She scrolled through the composition, not particularly interested in what the analysis had to say, only that the water was relatively clean and most likely drinkable to 98% of all known life in the universe.

She exited the application and thumbed through the list of other applications, still groggy from her unintended nap. She'd been wandering around on this planet all day, hacking her way through dense flora, and trying to ascertain if there was any other life on this planet except for her, a few birds, and one lizard.

So far, this planet seemed rather ordinary – jungle, desert, plains, and nothing out of the ordinary. It wouldn't be the most money she'd ever made, but it would fetch a fair-

Grrrr.

Lyssa's ears jumped to attention. That could have been the wind, but she didn't think so. She had developed a good sense for when she was being watched (or hunted). Slowly rising to her feet, she snatched her sensor out of the water and stuffed it into her backpack, slinging it over her shoulders. Just in case, she pressed the emergency call button on her mini-computer.

Grrr.

The leaves were rustling all around as a breeze blew through the trees. She scanned the tree line for any signs of-

There it was. She didn't know what it was; only that she could see two shining eyes and a couple of gleaming white teeth.

This could put a damper in her sale.

The giant cat jumped out of the bushes, mouth open, teeth bared, drool dangling, just as Lyssa turned on her foot and leapt towards the swath of jungle that she had cleared earlier.

The cat was fast, but this was not the first bloodthirsty animal that had ever chased Lyssa. She deftly sprinted through the jungle, flying over roots and making sharp turns around the path that she had cut.

And then, all of a sudden, she found herself at the edge of a deep ravine. She looked behind her and saw the cat flying towards her. Without much choice, she realized what she had to do next.

With a small whimper and closed eyes, Lyssa leapt into the crevasse.

The wind in her ears and her heart in her throat, she kept her eyes glued shut, waiting for what was coming next.

Instead of hitting the ground, she was yanked upwards roughly. A cord, hanging from her ship, had been magnetically connected to a clip on her utility belt. She looked up at her ship as she was reeled in. It was a small, oblong hypermile vehicle that glinted silver in the sunlight.

She was close enough to grab hold of the open hatch at the bottom of her ship, pulling herself up and unhooking the cord from her belt and closing the hatch. The lower level on her ship contained a small bedroom and this room filled with steel cabinets. Wiping the sweat from her forehead, she pulled off her backpack, tossing it uncaringly on the floor. Just above the now closed hatch, ladder rungs lined the back wall. She trotted over and hoisted herself up to the second level. The second floor was much like the first, with gleaming stainless steel cabinets. She walked through an open door on the opposite side of the room, into a small bridge with one plush leather chair, a dashboard, and large open windows.

Bypassing the chair as she was covered in sweat, she hovered over the dashboard, lightly touching it. A rainbow of buttons appeared under her fingertips. The windows in front of her dimmed, and panes of application windows appeared, displaying all manner of different content. With a wide swipe across the screen, the applications collapsed.

Her fingers danced over the dashboard, pulling up new application windows. These applications were navigational: star maps, fuel and energy gauges, and other status screens. She looked up for a second to examine the star maps and analyze the best route to get back to civilization, taking into account her hypermiling fuel was about halfway empty. She reached up to the screen and, with her finger, redirected the route to a straighter line, almost overlapping with a bright white ball on her star map.

WARNING: THIS ROUTE WILL TAKE YOU NEAR LEVEMAN'S VORTEX. BE AWARE OF SEVERE GRAVITATIONAL PULL.

"Yes, I'm aware," she muttered, clicking out of the warning banner. She hated taking this route, but she hated having to pay for fuel more. She checked the clock widget on the top of her dashboard – she'd probably be back in six universal hours.

The ship turned upwards and headed towards the atmosphere of the planet. Lyssa leaned the back of her legs against the chair, balancing until the pressure and gravity stabilized. The blue sky faded quickly to pitch black, dotted by a billion stars. She locked the dashboard and walked back towards her ladder and climbed downstairs.

Kicking her backpack out of the way, she headed to the bedroom, a small room with a closet and bathroom, a bed and a small porthole window, currently filled with the streaks of stars flying by.

Lyssa stepped into the bathroom and turned on the shower, taking a moment to look at her reflection in the small mirror.

She was twenty-one years old, with dark brown hair pulled high in a ponytail and tired brown eyes. Her skin was dotted with freckles and odd tan lines from being on planets in different shirts. She was small, but fit, with runners legs and a pair of arms that could do at least fifteen push-ups and maybe a pull-up if she really, really, really wanted to.

Lyssa held her doctorate in Deep Space Exploration from the Planetary and System Science Academy, and was fully licensed to discover, excavate, and sell planets. Most of them were the same kind of planet—temperate climate, no sentient animal life, plenty of potable water. These kinds of planets always sold to prospectors—easy to turn into residential planets for large swaths of the growing population. But even better, they weren't that complex, so she only had to spend about a day and a half (versus two or three weeks) gathering they key information about the planet, such as chemical makeup of the plants, water quality, and a general sense of the animal life.

Which meant she could spend the rest of her time doing what she actually wanted to do.

Realizing that she had been staring at herself for a good five minutes, she finally began peeling off her sweaty clothes.

***

Sometime later, she walked back into the bridge of her ship, toweling her long hair. She was now wearing a black tank top and baggy black pants, complete with a pair of boots with running treads on the bottom. She tossed the towel on one of the jump seats that lined the wall of her bridge and sat down on the squishy black chair.

She leaned forward onto the dashboard and began typing into the keyboard in front of her, moving her fingers along a pad to manipulate the screen in front of her. The star maps and gauges moved out of the way, and a list of applications came up in its place.

She scrolled down to the third application in the list and clicked on it to open. The application displayed a list of pictures of unsavory-looking characters, along with small stories about the latest crimes each had perpetrated:

	7) Lee, Linro Wanted in connection with hijacking of transport ship. Estimated cost of stolen materials: 100,000C
	10) Sloan, Flynn Captured by Santos Journot
	35) Journot, Santos Wanted in connection with piracy (bounty hunting)
	11) Teon, Sage Wanted in connection with the break-in at the Academy of Geological Sciences. Estimated cost of stolen artifacts: 2,700,000C

Her eyes lingered on the last line—Sage Teon. But not because the man pictured was young and handsome, with shaggy blonde hair and green eyes, but rather because the very thought of him made her want to punch something.

Her eyes snapped back to the top, as a new story had just appeared.

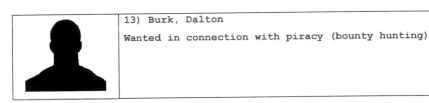

	13) Burk, Dalton Wanted in connection with piracy (bounty hunting)

She narrowed her eyes and clicked on his name, displaying his full wanted information.

	13) Burk, Dalton
Wanted For	Engagement in piracy, bounty hunting, grand larceny, theft
Reward	18,573,900C
Known Alias	Yasun Ari, Bowie Bovenizer, Followill Galafassi…
Known Accomplices	Cecil Giersch, Kaiis Thien, Dreavin Thoas…
Pirate Web affiliation	Contestant

She looked at the list of known aliases and pursed her lips thoughtfully. Flipping back to her application list, she opened an app that displayed the logo and log-in information for the Universal Bank—the central banking organization for the Universal Beings Union. Because the reach of civilization was so widespread, the UBU was established to provide a standard set of laws, trading partners, and—most importantly—currency system. The currency—known as universal credits, or "C"—was the only money accepted and used across the universe.

Even pirates used this currency, which was how bounty hunters tracked and captured them. To compensate, pirates, who were already forming groups to pool money to pay off the police, began to pay off the bank to be able to create more than one alias. The groups then began to rank who had better pirates in their web—based on the most wanted list the police released.

There were four main pirate "webs" now, each still in competition with each other. When bounty hunting was added as a punishable offense under the piracy laws, the webs began using bounty hunters to seek out and capture the top pirates in the other webs. Lately, most pirates did some bounty hunting, although not all bounty hunters were traditional pirates.

Snapping from her thoughts, she logged into the Universal Bank to check on Dalton Burk's aliases. Along with the ability to create multiple aliases, the pirate webs also paid for the ability to search for the profile of anyone in the system and look at every transaction they had ever made. Pirates sometimes would use five or six alias C-cards in one sitting, just to throw bounty hunters off their trail.

While her ship was connecting, she brought up a third window—this was a custom program she had created to keep track of pirates she was hunting:

Hit List	
Relleck	Kodah Mottola, Owen King, James Nolte, Alfie O'Hara
Burk	Zuma Davi, Daigle Cypheridge, Soren Gonzalez
Lee	Bawley King, Jesse Opal, Oliver David, Boo Jameson
Brendler	Koa Fascinelli, Ellington Nixon
Needler	Jackson Money, Jack Oscar, Aleph Miller

Momentarily distracted, she began to click on the first set of names—Relleck. She smirked—all of the accounts were actively in use, at casinos, with prostitutes, and hotel rooms. It looked like he had lost a fair amount of money at the casino last night. She calculated the time between transactions, based on the average purchase patterns, just to make sure he didn't have a fifth she didn't know about. She was satisfied that he was still unaware she had his number.

Turning back to the second pirate on the list, she tapped on the first of three of Burk's aliases, and it took her straight to their transaction histories in the Universal Bank:

Davi, Zuma		
Time of Transaction	Location	Amount
UT20014-95-81-12:80	Madam Guerri D-882	8500C
UT20014-95-80-60:96	Thein Diner D-882	80C
UT20014-95-80-47:25	Hammond's Coffee D-882	10C

There was nothing out of the ordinary, coffee, dinner, and a female companion over the past day. She searched on the second name:

Cypheridge, Daigle		
Time of Transaction	Location	Amount
UT20014-95-80-90:80	Refueling Station 342	10C
UT20014-95-80-90:70	Refueling Station 342	200,000C

It appeared as though he left D-882 for a brief moment yesterday, picked up some coffee, and probably his bounty, then returned back to the planet to spend some time with his female friend.

Lazily, she checked on the third alias transaction history:

Gonzalez, Soren		
Time of Transaction	Location	Amount
UT20014-95-81-14:15	Yawen Motel D-882	1000C
UT20014-95-81-13:02	Madam Guerri D-882	8500C

She chuckled to herself—he apparently paid the same woman twice—but then she paused, curiously. Normally, buying the company of a woman also resulted in the purchase of some drinks at the same place. But neither account had any record of those kinds of purchases. To boot, he paid her twice—meaning he was obviously plastered.

She sat back for a moment, smiling. Burk must have created a new alias that she hadn't found yet.

However, before she could start a search on transactions on the house where Burk had spent the night, she angrily turned around and smacked her dashboard to answer the video call that had coming in repeatedly since she logged onto the pirate web.

"For crying out loud, what?" she barked to the person on the other end of the video call.

"That's not very nice, now is it?" Smiling, Sage Teon was leaning into his video camera eagerly.

"Go on, what do you want?" she said, crossing her arms over her chest.

"Just to chit-chat!" he said sarcastically. "What with your charm and charisma, who wouldn't want to talk to you all day long?"

She stared back at him, silent.

"I mean, you are just a fabulous person to talk to."

She blinked at him.

He blinked back.

She blinked again.

He blinked back.

"Oh come on, Lyssa!" he said finally, sitting back. "What crawled up your ass today?"

She turned sharply to him. "Don't call me that."

"Fine, *Razia*, whatever," he said, rolling his eyes.

"It's not whatever," she snapped at him. "One of these days, Lyssa Peate is going to disappear, and all that will be left is Razia."

"Who will be the most wanted pirate in the universe," he smiled at her. "Yeah, I got it. Old habits, you know."

"Well break them," she snapped. "I don't want your crew finding out."

"Re-*lax*. They're off celebrating anyways," Sage said. "Just me on the ship today."

She opted not to inquire further, knowing exactly what he was calling about. She turned back to the bank application, comparing the three known aliases with a timeline of purchases from the bar and a different on the night before, and seeing if any of the same names popped up-

"Well, if you must ask," he interrupted.

"I didn't," she responded, trying very hard to keep her focus on the list of names she was comparing and not Sage's stupid face in the video call.

"Have you seen the news lately?" Sage asked.

"No," she snapped, scrolling through the names of people who purchased drinks at the same time. A few names she recognized, but a few she didn't, and so she began searching on each of the unknowns to see where else they—"

"*Lyssa*," Sage whined.

"Oh Leveman's freaking Vortex, yes, I saw it," she sighed, turning to

look at him. His face was pressed close to the camera again, a wide smile on his face.

"And?" he pressed.

"You broke in somewhere and you stole some stuff, what else is new?"

"No, no, no," Sage said, sitting back. "That security system was brand new, and was supposed to be one of the most impenetrable out there. I knocked it down in just under two days and took a whole bunch of diamonds."

"Uh-huh," she said, trying very hard to focus on cross-checking the names of the men at the house with their bank accounts. Most of them seemed to only have one account—that is, they had multiple transactions on the same day, spanning back weeks. She just knew that-

"Soooooooo...."

"God in Leveman's Vortex," she said, swirling around again to glare at him. "Go bother someone else!"

"I can't," he said, folding his arms over his chest. "My stupid bounty's up to eleven."

Her eyes widened and she sat back, pursing her lips into a thin line.

"I mean, not that that's anything good or anything. I mean, it's...er... What's your bounty at now?" Sage squeaked, realizing that he'd really stepped in it.

She looked at him with the meanest, iciest glare she could possibly muster.

"Well it's certainly not eleven," she said, closing all of her search windows and refusing to look at him.

"Oh come on," Sage said, trying to salvage the situation. "I'm sure it's not that bad—"

She turned back to the pirate news and typed in the name, *Razia*.

Only one profile appeared—a picture of her, two or three years younger, and the following information:

	594) (No last name listed), Razia
Wanted For	Engagement in piracy, bounty hunting
Reward	500C
Known Alias	None

Known Accomplices	Tauron Ball, Sage Teon
Pirate Web affiliation	Dissident* (probationary)

"Five hundred ninety-four," she deadpanned, exiting out of her profile. "And still on probation."

"Oh," Sage swallowed. "Dissident hasn't taken you off yet?"

"No," she snapped. Although most pirates belonged to webs, membership was tightly controlled by the leaders of the webs, the runners. Runners only wanted the best pirates in their webs, so when a new pirate or bounty hunter wanted in, they were put on probation. For bounty hunters, the runner would tell them which pirate they were allowed to hunt and capture. Once they proved their merit, the pirate was promoted to a full member of the web.

"Two years," Razia grumbled. "Two years I've been on probation."

"Well, at least you're hunting someone, right?" Sage said, in that tone of voice he used when he was trying to look at the bright side. It was quite literally the most annoying thing he ever did. Besides existing.

"You know, I realized Dalton Burk has another alias, but can I go after him? No!" she growled.

"Oh, what other alias?" Sage asked curiously.

"You know that Dissident's only doing this because I'm a girl, right?" Razia said, ignoring his question.

"Well, I mean," Sage shrugged. "They don't want girls in the pirate webs?"

"I've been in the pirate web for ten years!" she whined.

"Yeah, but you were on Tauron's crew for eight of those years," Sage said, tiredly. They had this conversation at least once a month. "Doesn't really count."

"Counts for you," she grumbled.

"If I could change Dissident's mind, you know I would have done it by now," Sage said, gently. "You gotta keep doing what he wants."

"Seven hundred," she said, finally. "The bounty he wants me to capture is the seven hundredth most wanted person in the universe. That's a seven, with two zeroes. He's worth two hundred credits."

"Ouch," Sage winced.

"That won't even pay for the hour of parking that it will cost me to go find him and take him to the bounty office," she sighed. Which was why, she thought, she was headed to the Academy to sell the planet she had just excavated.

"Look, the offer is still open," Sage said, folding his hands behind his head. "You know Dissident is always yelling at me to do more bounty hunting. I could really use someone like you on my crew—"

"UGH!" she cried, throwing her hands up. "I don't want your help!"

"Well then," Sage sighed, tired of the conversation. "I guess you'll just have to stay on probation until Dissident decides he wants a girl in his web. Which is never."

"Get sucked into Leveman's," she snapped at him.

"Bye Lyss," Sage smiled sweetly before ending the call. She was about to call him back and scream at him for hanging up on her but…

Her external pressure gauges began to beep, sensing an increase in gravity. She closed out her bounty hunting screens, displaying the stars in front of her. A small, white vortex was visible in the distance—but even from this distance, the ship was being drawn in.

She turned off her engines, continuing to move forward through momentum and the gravitational pull. She quickly pulled up a fourth application from her list—this one she had coded herself. It was a simple program, intended to perform the same calculation based on a set of variables, such as the weight of her ship, the distance and angle to the center of the vortex, and the location of other celestial bodies—even those too far for the eye to see.

She turned on her smaller engines to push her ship slightly higher, to increase the angle of entry, until the program turned green. She turned on the autopilot to continue on the trajectory, sat down, and buckled herself into her seat.

Her body began to feel heavier, like there was something pulling her into her seat. Even her eyelids felt heavy as she kept an eye on both the autopilot and the application, still showing green.

Then, as if something had reached out and grabbed her ship, she was hurdling towards the Vortex, now so large it was filling the width of her front windows. She could see comets and asteroids that were being pulled in as well, and watched as they, on a slightly different path, crumbled to pieces in the gravity. Her eyes were back on the program, and the green status.

Then, instead of a great force on top of her, the ship leaned to the right, and Lyssa went with it, nearly flying out of her chair, save the straps that kept her in place. She could see her ship speeding up, growing closer to the white center.

Then the green status blinked red.

Lyssa kicked her foot on the dashboard to jump start her engines. Suddenly, she was propelled back into her seat so hard she almost saw stars.

In fact, she did see stars. But these were outside of her ship, as she was now safely being flung in the direction of the Academy on purely the forward momentum of the vortex.

As her gravity stabilizers slowly began to re-engage (having been overpowered by the incredible force of Leveman's Vortex), she unbuckled her straps stood up, intent on continuing to work on Dalton Burk until she reached the Academy.

But Sage's words were still ringing in her ears.

Sighing, she sat down in her chair, staring out into the blackness of space with a slight pout.

It wasn't fair that Dissident treated her differently because she was a girl. It wasn't fair that Sage had everything handed to him, and she had to practically beg on bended knee. It wasn't fair that other pirates were on probation for maybe two months, and she was going on two years.

It just wasn't fair.

But even with all of that unfairness, the humiliation, and the struggle to be seen as something other than a pain in the ass, being Razia was better than being Dr. Lyssa Peate hands down.

Razia had the freedom to do whatever she wanted. She didn't take crap from anyone—and she could stand up for herself. She didn't need anyone or anyone's help. She had no damaged past—and what scars she had, she barely noticed.

Razia spent eight years with Tauron Ball—one of the most well-known pirates of the last twenty years. Tauron taught her all of the tricks to find the most difficult bounties—but even he was impressed at the way Razia could sort through the most mundane bank records to weed out aliases of the smartest pirates.

He had faith in her; he never doubted that she could be as good—or even better—than he was at bounty hunting.

After two years on her own, she never doubted Razia could be the best—but she was starting to wonder if she was ever going to get the chance to prove that to everyone else.

Or the time.

"Deep Space Exploration Vehicle Z-633, please identify yourself."

"Dammit," she sighed, looking to the ceiling.

"Dr. Lyssandra Peate, license number 9448639 requesting access to the Odysseus Station," she said back into her intercom.

"Welcome back, Dr. Peate," the intercom buzzed back. "You are clear to access dock E, number 478."

"Superrr," Razia said, getting to her feet to change into some DSE attire.

Until Razia could make some money, Dr. Lyssa Peate would have to foot the bill with yet another planet sale.

And bounty hunting, as usual, would have to wait.

CHAPTER TWO

The Planetary and System Science Academy was the official planetary discovery and classification body of the Universal Beings Union (UBU). The Academy included a school and its graduates, the latter whose labs filled all of the levels of the Odysseus station, an extra planetary ship that orbited the last moon in the capital system of the UBU, S-864.

Planetary space was at a premium in the UBU—with every new civilization added came the pressure to find a place for all of them. Corporations would sometimes buy entire systems to house their corporate headquarters and employees, even schools and universities would claim planets for their students. The military was also a big buyer of planets, using them to house and train soldiers, and—for planets with little other value—test weapons and other explosives. DSEs sometimes made millions of credits on planets; it was one of the most lucrative careers in the UBU.

For her part, Dr. Lyssa Peate was hoping this latest planet would give her enough to not have to return here for a long time.

She was now dressed in her DSE-appropriate clothing – white button-up shirt, with dull grey pants. She had pulled her long brown hair into a bun and donned a pair of black thick-rimmed glasses, and completed the look with a white lab coat.

She walked out into the small cabinet-covered room, checking her sweaty backpack for anything she would need to take with her to complete her presentation to prospectors—representatives for planet buyers. She stuffed a couple of paper receipts in her pocket and a few notes, and popped a half-eaten meal bar in her mouth.

She was still chewing on the bar when she walked out onto the dock, looking around for anyone that knew her. She ignored the two Universal Police officers who walked right by her without even a second glance. They were probably heading to the Academy's renowned hospital wing—with all of the odd injuries and lost limbs that came with planetary exploration, the Academy had developed a reputation for having top notch medical doctors.

Taking one more glance around the room, she felt confident that the coast was clear…for now.

She stepped off her ship and used her mini-computer to lock it, walking briskly to one of the seven lifts on the back end of the docks. The room itself was cavernous, big enough to hold the huge DSE ships—floating labs that held teams of DSEs and other scientists. Most DSEs worked in large teams, working for weeks on a single planet to get a good price. Recent graduates of the Academy—many light on experience and funds, were hired by more established scientists, who took full advantage of having a team to do all of the work for them. Most of these scientists, without having to focus on planet excavation, became more involved with the Academy itself, publishing papers and research topics on mundane topics like the pollination patterns of flowers on medium-sized planets with high concentrations of nitrogen in the atmosphere. But some DSEs spent their time focusing on the universe's mysteries, such as Leveman's Vortex.

Lyssa picked up the pace towards the lift.

It was these kinds of scientists that she dreaded the most. Dr. Sostas Peate, Lyssa's father, was infamous for his almost obsessive work on the vortex. He never published a paper nor gave a presentation, and his long absences from the Academy only increased his aura of mystery. By the time Lyssa became his young assistant (she only four years old at the time), he was renowned for his secret work.

When he disappeared some years ago, the focus shifted to Lyssa, now eleven, who had just shown up at the Academy as a new student. As the months ticked on, interest waned by most scientists, who assumed that Sostas was either dead or preferred not to be found. When Lyssa began disappearing on the weekends and between semesters, some began to turn their curiosity to her.

Of course, the reality was that Lyssa was spending all of her free time on a pirate ship, bounty hunting with Tauron. But letting everyone speculate otherwise was a convenient excuse and it kept most of her professors from asking too many questions when she skipped class or arrived late.

She reached the lift and began pressing the button furiously.

She graduated with her doctorate two years ago, which gave her free reign to come and go as she pleased. Still, having a cover story about continuing her father's work had unintentional consequences.

The lift door opened and Lyssa's heart dropped as she saw who was on the other side of it.

"Dr. Peate! Fancy seeing you here!"

Dr. Opal Pymus, was a middle aged scientist, his bald, round head framed by slick black hair. His thin lips were always pressed into a slimy smile whenever they met, and his small eyes, black and beady, always seemed to be trained on her.

"Hi," she snapped, stepping into the lift. Pymus was one of the few scientists who had continued the dogged investigation into Sostas' mysterious work. Sostas had become quite adept at avoiding these kinds of scientists; unfortunately, Pymus somehow had weaseled his way into becoming Lyssa's direct supervisor. Most supervisors did nothing except for ensuring that their employees adhered to Academy policies related to planet excavation and selling, but Pymus was much more hands on.

In that he never left her alone.

"I'm so surprised that you're back so soon!" Pymus sighed, pretending to make small talk as the lift rose from the docks. "I suppose you haven't been focusing too much on Leveman's Vortex, lately? We'd see you about as much as your father!"

"Yes, well," she said, struggling to come up with some kind of excuse that would get him off her back. "I need some money to buy some new satellites."

"What kind of satellites?" he responded, barely stopping to breath.

"The kind that can stand extreme gravitational pull," Lyssa responded, trying to remember if she'd used this excuse before. She had been caught before telling him the same story—he had a good memory unfortunately.

"How interesting!" Pymus cooed, tapping his chin. "And what would you be doing with these satellites."

She cursed internally; she thought that would be enough this time. She felt like snapping at him to mind his own business, but Pymus wasn't above giving her a reprimand for her attitude. And with two already this year, a third would put her in front of a disciplinary committee, who might not be above digging deeper into where she'd actually been going. Without a full-time bounty hunting gig, she wasn't quite ready to give up her steady paycheck.

So she swallowed the barb she had at the ready and responded with, "Well, I would like to see if there's an angle of entry by which an object would not destroyed."

"Oh my dear child," he laughed. "Are you trying to see the Great Creator yourself? You may want to start by visiting that lovely temple at your mother's house. That priest of hers can do wonders to ensure you're on the right path."

She smiled again; reminding herself that sitting in front of a committee would be more trouble than just keeping quiet. She was still on probation, she still needed gas money. She shouldn't shoot herself in the foot.

"And speaking of, I have not received a response to my latest message," he said, eyeing her curiously.

"Oh, well my apologies, I thought I had responded," Lyssa lied. In fact, she'd set up an automatic filter for his messages to go straight to trash.

And speaking of her mini-computer, it was buzzing with an incoming video call.

From Dissident.

"Shit," she muttered, under her breath. Her only contact with him were five minute phone calls where they discussed the next bounty she was allowed to capture. It was never a good sign when he was calling her.

Luckily, the lift doors opened, giving her an exit.

"Please stick me in the line-up for today!" Lyssa cried before darting off the elevator. She stood in the hallway, frantically looking around for anywhere she could take a private call, and ended up ducking into a stairwell.

Taking a deep breath, she pulled down her hair from the bun and took off her glasses, dreading what was going to come out of this call.

"Hi Dissident," she said, as his face came onto her mini-computer.

Dissident was a grizzled old man, with patches of scruff on his ashen face and a cigarette constantly in his mouth. She had never met him in person, not even when she was on Tauron's crew. Somehow, talking to him always made her nervous, like she was always in trouble. Mostly because she usually always was.

"Am I to hear that you're hunting Dalton Burk?" he said, his voice gravely from years of smoking and heavy drinking.

She closed her eyes and made a face. Damned Teon.

"I'm just having a little fun," she said, making a mental note to punch him in the face the next time she saw him. "I'm not actually—"

"Did I tell you," Dissident seethed, interrupting her, "that you could hunt Dalton Burk?"

Razia clenched her teeth. "No."

"Oh, then have I granted you full membership to my web?" Dissident asked, his voice low and dangerous.

She looked to the ceiling and sighed. "No."

"I'm sorry, what was that?" Dissident said.

"No, you haven't," Razia replied.

"So, then, I'm confused," Dissident said. "If I haven't given you permission to hunt Dalton Burk, and you aren't a member of my web, then WHY ARE YOU HUNTING HIM?"

Razia swallowed, trying to think of a good reason why she would be hunting him. Instead she responded with, "I'm bored."

"Oh, you're bored," Dissident laughed. "Well, have you gotten that bounty I gave you the other day?"

She sighed and shook her head.

"Are you too good for my bounties?" Dissident said. "Would you like to see if another web would take you?"

Razia shook her head again.

"That's what I thought," Dissident smiled. "Now, go get the bounty by the end of the week or *you are out of my web*," Dissident growled before the call went dark.

She sat in the empty stairwell for a moment, blood pulsing in her ears and an embarrassed blush rising to her cheeks. She hated the way he spoke to her, but there was really no getting around it at this point.

She stood up and began re-assembling her DSE attire, sadly placing her glasses back on and pulling her hair into a bun. She turned and slowly began the slow trudge up the final six flights of stairs to her lab.

After all, before she could go get the pathetic bounty, she had to make enough money to cover the cost.

***

Lyssa sat in front of the old laboratory computer, quietly working on her presentation for the afternoon. This lab belonged to Sostas; since he was never legally declared dead, it was still registered in his name. Since she still knew the entry code, she could still use it, much to the chagrin of her older brothers, who coveted this space.

The only light in the room came from the large monitor, as all of the lights in the ceiling had long since burned out. There were also tables of microscopes and weights covered in a thick layer of dust, equipment that was at least twenty years old. Very early in his career, Sostas had designed machines to analyze and process planet specimens for chemical signatures, so this lab was just used for the software required to put together the Academy-sanctioned planet excavation presentation.

She scrolled through her slides, mentally writing the story she was going to tell as she tapped through the different data points. She flip-flopped the slide about the water with the notes about the air—it had a higher concentration of oxygen than other planets, which usually fetched a higher price. And with hundreds of DSEs presenting every day, it was important to get to the good stuff up front.

Her stomach grumbled.

She frowned, looking at the presentation. She was about halfway done, and only had a few hours until she had to present. She rubbed her belly and pressed on, continuing to add more data points to the presentation.

Her stomach growled again, and this time she began to feel her blood sugar drop.

She looked at the time and realized with a scowl that it was just about the rush hour for food.

Her stomach growled more, and she started to feel nauseated.

"Fine, fine, fine," she grumbled grabbing her lab coat and heading over to the mess hall.

Of course, by the time she arrived, there was already a queue out the door. She stood in line moodily, her stomach feeling like it was going to eat itself inside-out. She listened to the idle talk in front of her and behind her, talking about recent planet findings, and comparing scientific notes.

She looked up to the front of the line and scowled. Three blonde-haired doctors were standing near the register, just about to pay and get their trays. And these three happened to be some of her older brothers – led by Dorst, her second eldest brother and main-coveter-of-her-lab.

Figures, she thought with a petulant scowl. They would be at the front of the line. She folded her arms over her chest and tried to nonchalantly hide herself behind the doctor in front of her, lest they see her.

After an eternity, she finally made it to the front of the line. She grabbed her tray and stood in the center of the food hall. By this point, her stomach and mood were in the absolute pits. The food trays were filled with foul-smelling meats and dishes, none of which she recognized. Instead, she made a beeline for the fresh fruit.

Quickly and hungrily, she began filling up her tray with as much food as she could—until she saw the price. Unlike the rest of the food priced per pound, these were priced per piece. And they weren't cheap.

She was short on credits anyways, and she didn't want to spend money on anything that wasn't related to bounty hunting. Furtively, she glanced around the cafeteria to see if anyone was watching, then slipped the fruit into her jacket pocket-

"HEY!"

She whirled around and was face to face with Dorst. He had many of her maternal bloodline features—blonde hair, a strong jaw, and a nearly constant look of disapproval.

Especially when it came to her.

"What?" she snapped, her blood sugar still dangerously low.

"I saw you sneak that fruit," he said, holding his own tray, filled with something that resembled meat. "You have to pay for that, you know?"

"Oh?" she said, grabbing another piece and taking a big bite out of it. "This one too?"

"I mean it Lyssandra," he growled. "I will—"

"What?" she laughed. "Are you gonna tell Jukin on me? Is he going to take a break from not catching pirates to come arrest me for stealing fruit?"

He glared at her.

She took another bite, feeling a rush of relief as glorious food entered her stomach.

"You know, playing nice won't change anything," he said.

"Oh, is this what you consider nice?" she asked, looking around and taking another huge bite. "Here I thought I was being an asshole—"

"This ploy for attention won't get you very far, you know," Dorst seethed. "When you decide to let us know where Father has gone to, then perhaps—perhaps—we'll decide to let you come home."

She rolled her eyes. "First of all, why would I ever want to go back there? Second, and for the last time, I don't know where he is."

"I'm sure," Dorst said. "And you aren't stealing food for him."

Her face contorted into a confused look. "This isn't for...what?" she said.

He answered by huffing off to pay for his food.

She stood for a moment, dazed by the familial encounter. It had been years since she'd returned to the family estate, affectionately (by them, anyways), known as the Manor. Mostly because, as Dorst had just made painfully clear, until she told them where Sostas had gone, she was no longer welcome as a member of the family.

Lyssa didn't much care about being a Peate for much longer—she was much more interested in becoming Razia the Bounty Hunter.

Who was slowly dying of hunger, she realized with a jolt. She hurried over to pay for the food on her tray, hoping that no one would notice the bulges in her pockets.

Or maybe she did; "fruit stealer" might add a few credits to her bounty.

***

The presentation wing of the Academy was a long hall of auditoriums where planets were presented and smaller side-rooms where the purchase occurred. Planets could only be sold in this hall by licensed DSE, and could only be purchased by licensed prospectors on behalf of their clients. Most prospectors used to be DSE, but found their true calling (and bigger paycheck) as a buyer for other organizations.

Lyssa walked into the auditorium where she was to present. As usual, the lineup was running behind, so she took a seat in the back and looked around at the prospectors in the audience. It was easy to tell which ones were hired by multi-trillion credits corporations, and which ones were representing smaller clients. One woman in the back corner looked like she had been styled by a team of designers. Lyssa hoped she wasn't interested in her planet.

The DSE up on the stage currently was droning on and on about a planet he found comprised completely of water; the only land above sea level was tiny island where an underwater mountain had breached the surface. The buyers in the audience were talking amongst themselves; the smartly-dressed woman was looking at her mini-computer annoyed, as if she had a thousand other things to be doing than sitting here listening to this pointless planet presentation.

There was sparse applause; the DSE was walking off the stage, trying to keep all of his papers in his arms. Two or three government prospectors followed him to the back room off to the side; Lyssa was sure that he wasn't going to get a good price.

There was one more DSE before Lyssa, so she had a little time to play around. She pulled out her mini-computer, drowning out the monotone from the stage, and logged into the pirate news via the secure connection on her ship. Her pirate dashboard, minimized for her mini-computer, came up on her screen.

She checked her own bounty first—she was now 600. She grumbled and sighed, looking down the latest news:

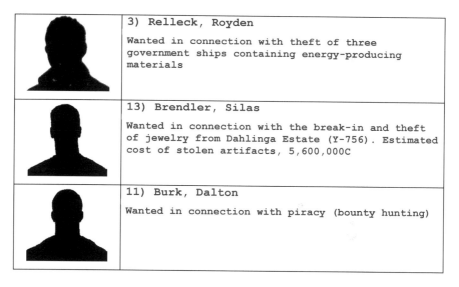

	3) Relleck, Royden Wanted in connection with theft of three government ships containing energy-producing materials
	13) Brendler, Silas Wanted in connection with the break-in and theft of jewelry from Dahlinga Estate (Y-756). Estimated cost of stolen artifacts, 5,600,000C
	11) Burk, Dalton Wanted in connection with piracy (bounty hunting)

She bit her lip.

Well, what Dissident didn't know…

She really wanted to find that fourth alias for Burk. She opened the bank transactions, still up from her last search trying to find Burk's fourth mystery alias. She closed her eyes, trying to walk back to her thought process from before.

She was looking at his three unknown aliases.

Something about one of them had given her pause.

She opened her eyes and frowned. She really needed to start writing things down. Or not answering calls from Sage Teon. Who was an asshole for telling Dissident that she was hunting Burk.

With another glance to the front of the room, she realized she was running out of time before she had to present. Quickly, she opened the profile of the first alias, scrolling through each transaction trying to pique her memory.

Davi, Zuma		
Time of Transaction	Location	Amount
UT20014-95-81-12:80	Madam Guerri D-882	8500C
UT20014-95-80-60:96	Thein Diner D-882	80C
UT20014-95-80-47:25	Hammond's Coffee D-882	10C

She paused on the prostitute charges.

That's what it was! He had paid money—twice—to the same girl, but apparently did not pay for any drinks, even though he must have been very drunk. Which meant that he was paying for his drinks with a fourth alias she hadn't found yet.

Immediately, she searched for a list of purchases on the prostitute house, filtering the results between the first purchase Burk made there and the last:

Madam Guerri		
Time of Transaction	Account	Amount
UT20014-95-81-11:50	Davi, Zuma	8500C
UT20014-95-81-12:15	Turro, Neshua	50C
UT20014-95-81-12:49	Turro, Neshua	50C
UT20014-95-81-12:49	Giersch, Cecil	8500C
UT20014-95-81-12:70	Turro, Neshua	55C
UT20014-95-81-12:85	Czar, Ezekial	50C
UT20014-95-81-12:92	Diezel, Ky	50C
UT20014-95-81-12:93	Turro, Neshua	55C
UT20014-95-81-12:99	Lulah, Rylot	8500C

Mentally, she named the pirates down the list

Zuma was Dalton Burk

Giersch was on Burk's crew

Czar was on Waslow Needler's crew

Ky was Needler

Lulah was Royden Relleck...

But Neshua Turro—she had no idea who that was.

She searched on Turro's universal bank account:

Turro, Neshua		
Time of Transaction	Location	Amount
UT20014-95-80-47:28	Hammond's Coffee D-882	25C
UT20014-95-80-90:72	Refueling Station 342	50C
UT20014-95-81-12:15	Madam Guerri D-882	50C
UT20014-95-81-12:49	Madam Guerri D-882	50C

He had been to the same coffee shop and refueling station as Burk. Not only that, but his transactions went back as far as a month ago—meaning the account was very recently created.

Which meant that Neshua Turro was really an alias of Dalton Burk.

Happy with herself and her bounty hunting instincts, she made a note of Burk's fourth unknown alias on her hit list, until she remembered that she wasn't actually allowed to hunt him.

Groaning quietly, she returned back to the bounty roster, scrolling lazily through the hundreds of profiles until she landed on seven hundred, the bounty Dissident told her to bring in.

Number seven hundred was a petty thief who apparently lived on D-882. Lyssa knew this because she could see the address of his rent payments. Not to mention his daily food and drink purchases—all at a restaurant two blocks from where he made his rent payment. He also spent a lot of money at a casino three blocks away.

"Make it a little harder, why don't you?" she sighed, slumping down lower.

Sparse applause brought her attention back into the room; it was now her turn to present. She closed out her pirate web application and shuffled up to the stage, mentally shifting from Razia the bounty hunter to Lyssa the DSE. She climbed up the stairs, blinded for a minute on the bright lights of the stage.

Her mini-computer automatically synced her presentation and it appeared in the big screen behind her. She picked up the slide advancer and looked out into the sea of blackness.

"The fifth planet in the system X-5567..."

***

Her brief presentation complete, Lyssa headed to the other end of the stage, walking through the door to the bidding room. Compared to the vast auditorium, this one was small and smelled odd. Lyssa sat down on the table in the middle of the room and waited.

Slowly, the prospectors entered the room, looking nonplussed and annoyed. Lyssa was one of the last presenters of the day, maybe there hadn't been many planets worth buying today. If that was the case, she might actually do well today.

"Well, shall we get started?" Lyssa said, not even bothering to look up. "Let's say twenty thousand."

"Twenty one," one of the government buyers said quietly.

"Twenty two."

"Twenty five."

"Eighteen."

Lyssa looked up, as did the rest of the room. The smartly-dressed woman was standing in the doorway, her blood red mouth shaped into a small line and her nose pointed at the ceiling. Up close, Lyssa was even more intimidated by her, although the men in the room seemed to sit up a little higher.

"I think the number we were at was twenty five—" Lyssa said, amazed at how small her own voice sounded.

The woman began to laugh derisively. "Twenty five thousand credits? For a planet that you barely excavated?"

"I did plenty of excavation," Lyssa countered, nervously. The other buyers, rapt with attention, began nodding and looking at their copies of her presentation.

"I will give you fifteen thousand for it," the woman said.

Lyssa blanked at her, and laughed a little bit. "You can't cut five thousand off of my original asking price..."

"Is there anyone in this room willing to pay twenty thousand for the planet?" the woman asked, looking around the room.

"Come on!" Lyssa said, looking to the last person to bid. He shrugged helplessly as the woman's lips curled into a smile.

"Ten thousand," she responded.

"I am not selling you this planet for ten thousand credits," Lyssa said,

28

wondering when she had lost control of this room. "There is plenty of data to support at least....at least thirteen."

"Fine, twelve," The woman said.

"Fine," Lyssa said, scared that this woman was going to go into the single digits.

"Excellent," the woman said, typing something into her computer. "We will deposit the funds..." She tapped a button on her mini-computer. "Now. Thank you for your business."

Lyssa suddenly realized that she had just sold a planet for eight thousand credits LESS than she had started.

"DAMMIT!" she said, nearly kicking over the table as the buyers milled out. Although she had money again, it was probably only enough for her to hunt one bounty—and even that was cutting it close.

She didn't have time to excavate another planet—she had to get the bounty in the next twenty four hours.

She buried her head in her hands and let out a tired sigh.

CHAPTER THREE

Three hours away from the capital system was D-882, a desert planet that could sustain life, but just barely. But it was near enough to a well-traveled transporter route, and so it quickly became home to a thriving metropolis for pirates. The main city was filled with bars and clubs, casinos, and other guilty pleasures, but only stretched as far as the small amount of water deep under the surface could sustain. The only other inhabited spot on the planet was on the complete opposite side of the planet—a jail intended to house the pirate population.

But, thanks to the efforts and regular payments to U-POL brass by the runners, the prison remained empty except for the poor officers assigned to maintain it.

Most of the U-POL officers worked in the giant marble and glass skyscraper that stuck out like a big, white sore thumb in the middle of the main city on D-882. It was this giant monstrosity that Razia was flying her ship around, more focused on trying to find a damn place to park her ship. Because of the limited space on the planet, parking within the inner city was at a premium. Many of the docking buildings set aside spaces for the top pirates in the galaxy, but as Razia was barely a speck on the radar, she would have to hunt for a space like everyone else.

She grumbled, realizing that she was going to have to park in the out lands—the uninhabitable part of the city that was used for landfills, dumping, and cheap parking. It would add another two hours onto her trip both ways, but at this point, she might not have any other choice.

She sped outside of the city, finally finding a docking building that she could park in. The bright lights and buildings suddenly cut off at the city's borders, replaced by giant pits of garbage and refuse. Mixed between the garbage pits were tall cylindrical buildings, docking stations. The docks functioned a bit like a puzzle, with as many small ships cramming around the big ships as the parking manager would allow. Razia's ship was on the smaller side, so she was a little more flexible on where she could park.

Finally, after what seemed like forever, she found a parking manager willing to accept her ship.

But, unfortunately, it was about fifteen hundred credits per hour.

"Damn," she muttered, looking at the clock. She had to get the bounty, and get to the bounty office, within the next six hours, or else she'd hear it from Dissident. But, he probably wouldn't kick her out...

She thought about it for a minute.

No, he would.

"Daaaamn," she said, accepting the charges to park.

She slowly navigated her ship into the parking deck, coming to a rest in the parking dock next to a gigantic ship. She hopped off the ship to check on the distance between her ship and the monstrosity next to her. She calculated the kind of blast radius this huge ship would need—and whether her ship would be in the crossfire. She had been on the business end of a big ship once, and it cost her nearly ten thousand credits to get the damaged fixed. Yet another setback she was still working through.

Nervously satisfied that her ship would be fine, she grabbed her jacket from inside and locked the ship up using her mini-computer. She paused on the dock landing to check and see if bounty number seven hundred had made any transactions in the past hour.

He hadn't.

The elevator opened and a burly man covered in hair seemed shocked to see her on the lift. She ignored him and leaned against the wall, scrolling through the bounty lists absent-mindedly.

Another floor, and again, another startled look.

Sage had slipped to number twelve, she noted with a scowl.

The elevator opened again and she leaned her head against the cool steel wall. Were they really stopping on every floor?

She could feel four sets of eyes on her and shifted her weight to another leg, trying to ignore it.

The door to the lift opened to a shuttle station. Because this docking center was so far out from the inner city, shuttles had been built to move people in and out. Unfortunately, because they were built by pirates, the system was unreliable, rickety, and took forever. She looked up at the broken down screen and rolled her eyes; the next train would be at least twenty minutes.

Sighing, she took a seat on the far end of the station, away from the curious glances and looks. Then she pulled out her mini-computer and began looking through the latest news:

	17) Conboy, Conrad Wanted in connection with transporter hijacking. Estimated cost of stolen materials: 600,000C
	2) Hardrict, Cree Wanted in connection with piracy (bounty hunting)
	1) Gongago, Olvire Captured by Cree Hardrict

Razia chuckled to herself—it wasn't often that the top bounty was captured by the second most wanted. She clicked on Hardrict's profile—he was one of Contestant's goons. Between him, and Relleck—who was now number two now that Hardrict was number one, Contestant had two of the five most wanted pirates in his web.

She sighed. If only Dissident would take her off probation, she'd knock both of them out in a heartbeat.

After an eternity of waiting, the shuttle finally came. She took a spot on the end of the shuttle, and was glad for no one else on the car. She peered out into the darkness as the shuttle traveled underground towards the downtown, lost in her own thoughts.

She caught her reflection in the window, and was suddenly reminded of that awful woman who cut her latest planet in half. That woman seemed to exude confidence in herself; and the woman who was looking back at her seemed defeated, almost ready to give up.

Razia wouldn't be so weak, she told herself, lifting her chin higher. Razia was strong, confident, and would have told that woman where to stuff her eight thousand credits.

The station she got off at was dingy and dimly lit, with one slow long escalator. The shuttle system was built far underground to protect it from the punishing sun on the surface. But that also meant that the escalators to get to the surface were extra-long, going for three stories in some cases.

Razia stepped onto the first step and allowed it to carry her. She willed herself not to look behind her to the ground that was slowly moving away from her, focusing instead on the top which was still so far away.

She unintentionally looked behind her, and her breath caught in her throat at the distance between her and the ground. She started to imagine what would happen if she suddenly lost her balance, tumbling down the escalator into a river of molten fire.

She began walking up the stairs with purpose, her hands shaking as she clawed the moving railing for dear life.

She reached the top of the station which opened up to the streets of the city, blinking with advertisements, boobs, and alcohol. The streets were lined with open doors leading into dark and dingy bars. It was hot and dry, and whatever breeze there was did nothing more than knock the dirt around. Iron tables and chairs littered the outside of the bars with ratty looking overhangs to keep the sun off. There were a few people outside, sitting around drinking, or looking at their mini-computers.

She took a left off of the main street and then another right, checking again to see if her bounty had moved.

It hadn't.

"Damn," she whispered.

Taking a left down a side street, and then another right, she walked into a nondescript bar. It was dark and dusty, but out of the sun, it was much cooler. She scanned the bar, and found a lonely patron sitting at a booth in the back.

She trotted over, a smile growing on her face.

"I thought I heard the pitter-patter of dainty feet," the man said, looking up from his tablet computer and smiling.

"Hi Harms," Razia said, slipping into the bar next to him. He was older, and his beard was starting to show curls of grey. He smiled at Razia much as a favorite uncle would.

"What brings you out this way? Not that I don't always love it when you visit me—but I assume you don't need my services today?"

Razia sighed. Harms was a pirate informant, who knew the comings and goings of all the top pirates. He wasn't affiliated with any web, as neutrality was better for business. He was the person a bounty hunter went to when bank accounts, aliases, and the pirate webs came up empty. Sometimes the amount of detailed information he knew about everything was unnerving.

"So I heard from a little birdie that someone was hunting Dalton Burk," Harms smiled at her.

"I'm not hunting him," Razia said, unable to keep the grin off of her face. "I was just...curious if he had a new alias."

"Uh huh," Harms said. "And did you find a new alias for him?"

She shrugged nonchalantly. "Maybe I did."

"What is that three?" Harms said, impressed.

"Four," Razia responded.

"He'd better hope that you never join the web," Harms laughed.

Razia started to laugh, but then dropped her head on the table.

"This is humiliating."

"I know, honey," Harms said, patting her comfortingly on the hand. "What number did he give you this time?"

"HANDS UP EVERYONE!"

Their conversation was rudely interrupted as a group of U-POL officers, no more than twenty-one or twenty-two years old, came barging into the bar, looking around. They were dressed in the finest gold-trimmed uniforms with a special patch on their breast.

Their leader, a fresh lieutenant with combed and short brown hair, a baby face, and wide eyes, was looking around intently. As the place was empty, except for Harms and Razia, he and his two compatriots came marching over, looking very much as if they wanted to arrest someone.

"We are members of the U-POL Special Forces, conducting a raid on this known pirate bar," the lieutenant announced, trying very hard to make his high voice sound lower than it was.

Harms winked at Razia, who watched them, amusedly. The U-POL Special Forces were an "elite" unit of policemen dedicated to the eradication of pirates. However, as long as a pirate belonged to one of the four webs that paid huge sums of money to U-POL brass and overseeing politicians, even the Special Forces had no power to arrest them. And although she was on probation, Razia was still covered under the agreement.

"Mr. Harms, you are clear," he said, nodding at Harms.

"Thank you Officer Opli," Harms nodded. "Do you want a drink—"

"As for your friend," the officer said, turning to Razia. "Give me your identification."

"Give me your identification....what?" Razia smirked. "I know your mother taught you some manners."

"Razia, don't be a twit," Harms said, giving her a look. "Give him your ID."

Razia rolled her eyes, as she pulled her C-card out of her pocket, making sure to give him the right one. The lieutenant's eyes lingered on the fact that she had two C-cards, but took only the one she handed to him, scanning it to check her identity.

He grimaced when he saw she belonged to a web.

"You're free to go," he sniffed.

"Since when do they let girls in the pirate webs?" The other officer leaned over the lieutenant's shoulder.

Razia snatched her card back and gave him a dirty look, "Move along now, junior."

"Watch yourself," the young lieutenant said, giving Razia one final, authoritative glance.

"Idiots," Razia sniffed, sticking her C-card back in its slot.

"Oh come on, he can't help it," Harms chuckled. "You know Jukin makes them do rounds around here to keep busy. I see that poor kid about once every two weeks."

"I guess he's got to let them do something, since he can't arrest pirates anymore," Razia smiled.

"Pirates that belong to a pirate web," Harms corrected. "And you had better watch yourself missy. You'll be in a world of trouble if Dissident ever kicks you out of the web."

Razia was brought down to reality and grimaced. "Ugh, I don't want to get this bounty."

"What number is it again?"

"Seven hundred."

Harms smiled at her. "At least that's not the last guy on the list again?"

"Close enough," she sighed, sitting back. "I just want a chance to prove how good I can be. How good I am…"

"The only way to get what you want is to keep at it," Harms smiled. "So, you should go get your bounty, like Dissident wants."

"Yeah well," Razia said, gulping down her water. "He hasn't moved in a few hours."

"Maybe he's got an alias you don't know about!" Harms said, half-joking.

Razia sighed, frustrated.

"So what else is new?"

Razia thought about her slimy boss, Pymus, and getting an awful price for her planet because of some woman who was too pretty to be a real planet bidder, and nearly getting mauled by some giant cat, but couldn't share any of that with him. Harms didn't know about her other life—Dr. Lyssa Peate and that whole other world that she lived in. And she planned to keep it that way.

She shook her head sadly.

"Well, you know I love to chat with you," Harms said gingerly, knowing he was about to offend her. "But I see another customer hanging out at the bar...and unfortunately, he's a paying customer so..."

"I get it, I get it," Razia sighed, standing up.

"Keep your chin up, kid," Harms said, as she skulked away.

***

With nothing else to do, Razia headed over to casino district. It had been a good long while since her bounty had made a purchase, and she was

35

sure he'd be active any minute now. She passed under the bright lights, still blinking in the bright desert sun, and made her way down the line of casinos.

She ducked into one doorway, feeling the cool air conditioning hit her like an icy blast. The sounds of a million slot machines filled her ears, and the cigarette smoke made her cough. Zooming in on the picture of her bounty, she studied his face. He was middle-aged, but looked much older, probably from a life of piracy. His skin was brown and leathery, and his eyes were a dull grey. The last place he'd spent money was the bar, so that was probably a good place to start asking around.

She pushed open the glass door to the bar and the jingling and song from the slot machines quieted. A few sets of eyes were watching her, especially when Razia sauntered up to the bar and sat down.

The bartender looked up from his paper, sniffed, and then continued reading.

"What's a pretty thing like you doing here all alone in a place like this?"

It was only a matter of time before they started coming out of the woodwork. She was holding out hope that once she actually made it as a respected pirate, it would stop. Razia tapped her fingers on the table and waited patiently for the bartender to come, ignoring whoever it was that was trying, pathetically, to hit on her.

"Come now, don't be like that—" She felt a cold and sweaty hand reach around her. With a sigh of frustration, and faster than the man could react, she shot out her elbow and connected with his chest, whipped her hand up to hit the bridge of his nose with the back of her hand, and brought her fist down on the base of his neck to knock him out.

She wasn't strong, but she knew the spots to hit.

The other men of the bar stared at her, mouths open. She flipped her hair behind her shoulder and sat back down, acting if nothing had happened, although inwardly, she was counting the minutes until he would wake up again.

She unhooked her mini-computer, zooming in on the picture again.

"Have you seen him?" she asked the bartender, pushing her mini-computer towards him.

"Oh yeah," he said, nodding and thumbing over to the left side of the bar. "He's been out for hours."

"...what?"

"Yeah, come over here and look," he said, leading her around to the end of the bar. She blinked, furiously, looking down at the drunken sleeping body of the bounty she was supposed to bring in. There he was, leathery skin, dull eyes and all. Mouth open, drool pouring out, on his back, a bottle in his hand.

"This the guy you're looking for?" the bartender asked. "Is he your husband or something?"

"Ridiculous," she said, pulling out some handcuffs and pulling him up. He was lying on a very odd looking purse. "What is that?" she asked the bartender.

"A purse," he sighed. "He took it from some poor dear before he came in here."

"For crying out loud…"

***

Since Razia had neither the strength of ten men nor a crew, she had fashioned herself a floating gurney with canvasses and discs that hovered a few inches off the ground on the four corners. Her bounty was still passed out cold, but she tied him up tight just in case he managed to wake up. Dragging her bounty behind her, she hurried past the U-POL building, glinting in the dying sunlight towards the bounty office—a dark, dank little building next door. This was where pirates were turned in—and bounty hunters received payment for their efforts.

Unfortunately, there was a queue of bounty hunters out the door, each with a captured pirate in tow.

Looking at the clock, she stood there trying to calculate how long each person would take, and multiply that by how many of them there were, and then subtract that from the time she had left, adding in time to run and get to her ship and turn it on and leave as soon as possible. To her utter dismay, Sage Teon was next in line to talk to the man at the window, who would take the captured pirate and pay the bounty hunter. Two of his crew members had a third man held steady between them.

Figures.

She sighed and looked at her mini-computer again. As long as she could get to the front of the line in the next hour and a half, she'd be ok with Dissident.

"Oh…wait…" she said, looking at the clock again. She'd parked over four hours ago – and at fifteen hundred credits an hour….

If she didn't get back to her ship soon, she'd really be in trouble.

She looked at the front of the line. Teon was nowhere to be found, and the line was shuffling up slowly.

"HEY!"

It was Ganon, Sage's pilot. He had dark skin and lively dark eyes, complimented by a big boisterous smile. He was one of the first pirates that Sage had hired on his crew, and his closest friend. He always seemed to be in a constant state of drunkenness, evidenced by the gregarious way he barreled over to her with his trademark smile on his face. Razia held up her hand, anticipating that he would try to throw her into an over-the-shoulder hug.

"Don't touch me," she said, dangerously.

"Ok, ok, ok!" he said, laughing so loudly that it echoed off of the walls. "Woo…you've got a bounty! Look at this, Sage!"

"Yes, that's what happens when you're a bounty hunter," Razia snapped, hoping this conversation would end quickly. The last thing she wanted was to draw attention to herself with such a pathetic bounty in hand. Sage came walking over amusedly, with his other man Nalton, a quiet, tall, man with a penchant for knives, right behind him.

"You will not believe what just happened!" Ganon continued, slapping Razia on the back. "Sage, you have to tell her!"

"I'd…rather…" Sage said, suddenly looking nervous and like he'd rather continue walking out the door. Ganon waved him off, and turned to Razia, excitedly.

"Ok so get this: After we did that museum thing, we'd noticed this guy would NOT leave us alone, right? And Sage was like, aw, he'll get tired of us, just hold off But I mean, this guy-right Nalton? I mean, this guy!"

"Very nice," Razia said, shifting uncomfortably. Ganon's loud voice echoing off the walls, and some of the other pirates ahead of her were starting to stare.

"Ganon, I really don't think—" Sage laughed, trying very hard to get his friend and crew member to get the hint.

"So, finally, we're all at Eamon's…you know what Eamon's is, right?"

"Yes," Razia snapped. It was one of many clubs that catered to the top pirates—only. As Razia had found out three weeks ago when she had been tossed out for sneaking in through a window.

"Ok, so we're at Eamon's, and Sage gets fed up with him bothering us, and we do our bit," Ganon grinned. "And, guess who it is. Guess who!"

Razia sighed.

"Dalton Freaking Burk."

"WHAT?!" Razia screamed, whirling around to face Sage, who was already in reactive mode with his hands up in fear.

"Look, I didn't want to turn him in!" Sage said, quickly before she exploded at him. "I mean, he just wouldn't leave us alone! What was I supposed to do?"

"Sage, you *knew* I wanted him!" Razia cried. "What in Leveman's—"

"I don't know why you would be, seeing as you're only…six hundred? Seven hundred?"

Both Sage and Razia's faces shifted to a mirrored look of annoyance and disgust. It was Royden Relleck, a young, handsome pirate with buzzed brown hair and high cheekbones. He had joined the pirate web only four or five years ago, but had quickly become Contestant's favorite for his brash cockiness. For the longest time, both Dissident and Contestant had the two best webs of the four major ones—each one-upping the other. Relleck considered himself the Tauron Ball of Contestant's web, and never missed an opportunity to capture Dissident's pirates, or taunt his favorite ones.

Or, in Razia's case, his most embarrassing ones.

"I know Dissident is desperate for good pirates, but I doubt he'd let a *little girl* hunt someone like Dalton Burk," he finished, smugly folding his arms over his chest.

"Well Contestant let you in, what's your excuse?" Razia retorted, before Sage could say anything. "Where's all of your boyfriends? I'm surprised you let them out of your sight. Hope you don't run into any pirate who can hit."

"Then it's a good thing I ran into you and Teon, then," Relleck shot back, sneering at her bounty. "Leveman's Vortex, I haven't even heard of that guy—is he a real pirate? Looks like he was already drunk when you got to him. Hope you didn't break a nail."

Before Razia could respond, Sage chimed in with an unhelpful, "Leave her alone, Relleck. She's still on probation."

"God in Leveman's Vortex, Teon," Razia swore through clenched teeth.

"Probation?" Relleck laughed. "You've been on probation for what....two years now? Why don't you quit embarrassing yourself already?"

Razia watched him turn and walk away, and smiled knowingly. "Hey, at least I didn't lose a couple hundred credits in five minutes at the casino last night."

Relleck stopped dead in his tracks.

"What'd you say?" he whispered, turning around.

"I said," Razia repeated, slowly. "I may be in the six hundreds, but you obviously need to work on your poker skills. And your lady skills—three times you've visited a cat house in the past week? Can't get a woman to sleep with you unless you pay them, hm?"

"How?" Relleck cut her off. "How do you know that?"

"Oh, you mean, how I know all of your aliases?" Razia said, feigning innocence. "How I've been tracking you for the past six weeks?"

Relleck's eyes narrowed.

"Because I'm a damned good bounty hunter, that's why," she said. "Now why don't you quit embarrassing yourself and get lost." She paused and chuckled. "And next time, try to make it a challenge, will ya? Leveman's, you're worse at hiding than Teon here."

Relleck glared at her wordlessly, and hotly turned around and slunk away.

"You sure shut him up," Sage grinned. "And I don't know what you're talking about, I'm good at hiding—"

Razia turned her deadly gaze to him. "Get out of my sight."

"Wait-what did I do?" Sage said, defensively.

"Take your pick," Razia growled. "First you got me in trouble with Dissident by blabbing about me hunting guys I'm not supposed to, and then you capture my bounty, then you go and tell Relleck that I'm on probation—"

"Hey, I was just trying to get Dissident off your back by telling him how good you are," Sage tried, but Razia wasn't listening.

"We're fighting, Teon," she said, looking forward and doing her best to ignore him.

"Oh, come on!"

Seeing the look on her face was enough to tell him to quit talking and start walking.

Razia stood in the line, ignoring the curious looks by the pirates around her. Relleck was awfully cocky, and he had every right to be. Still, Razia would have liked nothing more than to wipe the smug smirk off of his face.

She looked down at her bounty, who let out a loud, whiskey-soaked belch.

After an eternity, she reached the window. The man on the other side was smoking something with a purple smoke coming out of his mouth. He gave her an annoyed look as she handed him her handheld computer. He peered out the window to look down to see if it was the real person.

"I'll give you fifty for him."

"Fifty?!" Razia sputtered. "He's worth two hundred!"

"I could give you none," he glared at her.

"Fine, just give it to me," she snapped, yanking the card out of his hand. Besides she had to get back to her ship—she had just looked at the time. But if she ran back, and got lucky with a shuttle, she could make it just in time...

***

"N-no....oh....damn it!" She yelled, throwing her C-card down to the ground. She had exceeded the hour by four minutes and twenty-eight seconds, so, of course, they charged her for an entire extra hour.

She now only had less than six hundred credits in her account.

She would have to do another planet.

Now.

CHAPTER FOUR

It could never be said of Razia, or rather, Dr. Lyssa Peate, that she never learned from her mistakes. So angry that she was back on the Odysseus station AGAIN, she wouldn't budge under fift thousand credits for the planet she had so hastily excavated in two days.

That would be enough to last her for a few weeks—at least. And maybe then she could finally get some traction with Dissident.

Speaking of, she needed to call him and get her next bounty assignment from him. She was walking down the hall in the presentation wing, keeping an eye out for anyone who would bother her. She hadn't seen Pymus at all since she had arrived yesterday—he had placed her in the queue for today without so much as a response to her email.

She paused at a custodial closet, believing it to be the safest place for her to make a quick video call, and quickly slipped inside. She pulled down her hair and took off her glasses, dialing Dissident's number.

"What do you want?" he grumbled.

"I got whatshisface," she said. "So who's next?"

Dissident grunted as if the mere act of lifting his finger to scroll through the bounty roster was causing immeasurable pain. Razia waited, silently hoping that maybe he would forget the number that he had given her last time, and maybe giving her someone in the four hundreds—he'd done that before.

"Seven-thirty?" Dissident said, after a few minutes of overly dramatic sighing.

Damn, she thought. "That's pathetic."

"If you have a problem with the bounties I choose for you, then you are free to try another runner," Dissident smirked. "But I don't think—"

Razia was about to respond when the door to the custodial closet came flying open and she found herself face to face with Dr. Pymus.

"Dr. Peate!" he cheered, almost too happy for his own good. "What in Leveman's Great Vortex are you doing in here?"

"I-I—" she said, quickly turning off her phone and sticking it in her lab coat pocket. She slid her thick glasses back on and tried to look natural pulling her hair back up into a bun. "I was looking for—"

"No matter," Pymus said, obviously not caring as he reached in and pulled her out to start walking down the hall. "We have been looking everywhere for you!"

"We?" Lyssa said, looking over her shoulder. A teenage boy, about sixteen, with neatly combed sandy blonde hair, was standing behind them with an excited grin on his face. Lyssa had never seen the kid before, but he looked slightly familiar.

Pymus was smiling at her in that odd, fake way that he did. "May we walk over to your laboratory for a chat?"

"I'm actually on my way out," Lyssa said, hoping to make a quick escape, and avoid any associated annoying conversations about her father. Unfortunately, Pymus was quicker than she was, and wrapped his arm tight around her shoulder, marching her down the opposite way.

"Dr. Peate, I have excellent news!" he said, squeezing her for emphasis. Lyssa, never one for being touched in any way, was disgusted.

"Does it involve you removing your arm?" she grumbled, trying, unsuccessfully, to get away from him.

Pymus continued, unabated, "You have been allowed an opportunity that most DSEs aren't able to have until they have at least ten years of experience. But, I pulled a few strings, I made a few calls, and I called in favors from the highest levels in the Academy!"

She rolled her eyes; Pymus always liked to hear himself talk, especially when it pertained to himself.

"This experience—"

Enough was enough. "Get on with it," she snapped, untangling herself from him.

"Fine," Pymus sniffed, placing his now free hand onto the boy's shoulder. "This is your new intern, Dr. Peate."

Lyssa blinked. Of all the things that she expected to come out of his mouth, that word was not one of them. "Intern?"

"Intern!" Dr. Pymus repeated. "As you'll recall, the DSE internship semester is one of the most important periods in a young DSE's education. Learning side by side with an actual DSE well," he sighed, dramatically. "You just can't get that kind of education in a classroom."

"Uh-huh," Lyssa said, catching sight of the boy. He was wide-eyed, innocent and kept looking up to Pymus adoringly. "So what, I take him for a few days a week?"

"Oh, please, Dr. Peate!" Dr. Pymus laughed obnoxiously. "He will be with you constantly. How else is he supposed to learn?"

"Say what now?" Lyssa said, a bit of anxiety bubbling in her chest. "When you say constantly, do you mean—"

"Go on every excavation, assist on every analysis, support you on every presentation," Dr. Pymus said, enjoying the way that the color was draining from her face. "I daresay you two will become quite close."

"I'm sorry," Lyssa said, shaking her head. "I can't take on an intern right now."

"You don't have a choice," Pymus said, handing her a stack of papers in a file folder. "The Academy notified you several times of the impending internship."

She snatched it from him quickly. Maybe she should check her mail more often.

"We spoke about it last week, remember?" Pymus said, knowing full well that she had no idea what he was talking about.

"I do have some say in this," Lyssa said, flipping through the papers, each one covered in Pymus' odious, flourished scrawl. "You can't just...sign for me on this sort of thing—"

"In the event that a DSE is unable to be located, his superior may sign in his absence," Pymus quoted. "You'll find it all in the paperwork."

"This is unbelievable," she grumbled, flipping through the notes. "What in Leveman's Vortex am I supposed to do with him?!"

"What you normally do," Pymus replied, a conniving smile curling on his face.

Lyssa stopped her frantic searching of the paperwork and narrowed her eyes. How convenient that Pymus should be saddling her with an intern— and especially after the trouble he had to go through to get it approved. She was only two years out of the Academy—nowhere near enough experience to even have anything of value to teach a student.

That asshole was spying on her to get information on her father.

Pymus seemed to have sensed that his plan was discovered, as he quickly turned to the boy, "Well, take copious notes, son. They will be considered as part of your grade at the end of the semester."

"I'm sure they'll also be part of your upcoming published works on Sostas Peate," Lyssa muttered, loud enough for Pymus to hear.

He cleared his throat and nodded to Lyssa, before turning and scurrying down the hall.

Lyssa angrily watched him go and contemplated the unfairness that was her life right now. As if things couldn't get any worse for her, she now had a permanent set of prying eyes on her that was going to report every little movement she made straight back to Pymus.

For the next six months.

"So...?"

"What do you want?" Lyssa hissed, turning to walk to the docks.

He quickly closed his mouth and followed after her, keeping two or three steps behind, so as to incur her wrath.

"Whatever deal you struck with Pymus, you aren't going to get it," she snapped, not bothering to look back at him. "So don't get any expectations."

"I'm..." his voice was high and squeaky. He cleared his throat and it came out a little deeper. "I didn't have any deal with him-?"

"Oh, I'm sure Pymus is getting something out of this," Lyssa grumbled.

"I am very indebted to him for arranging this internship, but—"

"So this was your idea?" she asked, whirling on him, finally. "And why did you decide on me?!"

"You mean, you don't recognize me?" he said, his voice going high again and very timid.

"Am I supposed to?" she snapped.

"Well, yeah," he said, shrugging. "I'm your brother."

"....excuse me?"

"Your brother?" he repeated. "Vel?"

"Brother?" she said. It was no wonder she halfway recognized him—all twenty-four of the Peate siblings looked similar, except for her. "Which one are you again?"

"Vel?" he said. "I was born eighteenth?"

"Oh, little brother!" Lyssa smiled, dangerously.

"Yes!" he smiled, relieved that she recognized him.

Before he could say another word, she exploded in the middle of the hall: "YOU HAVE SIX OLDER BROTHERS, YOU IDIOT! SIX TO CHOOSE FROM! WHAT IN LEVEMAN'S ARE YOU THINKING?!"

Vel cowered, and even though he was taller than she was, he seemed to be a lot smaller. Two DSEs walking by gave them an odd look but kept walking, "S-seven…"

"What?" Lyssa hissed, dangerously.

"Beas got his degree six months ago," he swallowed. "But technically, only two, because a DSE must have ten years of experience...only Dr. Pymus made an exception for..." He trailed off, skin slowly paling with every heaving breath that Lyssa took.

Lyssa stepped back from him, licking her lips angrily and trying not to explode.

"Look, I don't know if you know this, but the rest of the family don't like me very much. So I don't know if this is some kind of teenage rebellion or what, but—"

"Dr. Peate," Vel laughed, much more maturely than a sixteen year old should have. "You are seriously overreacting. Mother was fine with allowing the internship to proceed."

"Was she really?" Lyssa said. "Because Dorst sure seemed pissed off about it last week."

Vel smiled, and Lyssa saw something behind his eyes. "I know there is some....bad blood in the family. But I hardly think that's an excuse to overlook your stunning qualifications as a DSE."

"Uh-huh," Lyssa said, seeing right through his sycophantic behavior. First of all, she was hardly the most upstanding DSE in the family— extracurricular activities or not. More importantly, there was something in her gut telling her that he was not to be trusted. The sooner she could lose him, the better she'd be.

"So, shall we get started on our first excavation?" Vel asked, happily.

Lyssa smiled devilishly. She was going to make him wish he had never even heard the name Dr. Lyssandra Peate.

"Let's go," she chuckled.

***

"And Jinjina had her....fifth child last month?" Vel prattled on, as he had since they left the Academy some three hours earlier.

Lyssa, utilizing that skill she had developed when she was in school to drown out obnoxious noises, was focused on searching on for a really terrible planet for them to excavate. Something that was filled with big creatures or massive storms—anything that would permanently scar her obnoxious little intern and make him beg anyone who would listen to get him out of the internship.

She heard him ask her a question, and momentarily stepped out of her thoughts.

"What?" she snapped.

"I asked if you could believe there were fifteen children under the age of ten in the house!" Vel said. Lyssa grimaced, annoyed that she had been pulled out of her thoughts for no reason.

She continued to sift through the planets in the star system that she had pre-claimed for herself. Some of them were gaseous planets, others inhabitable because of proximity or distance to the star. She paused on some of the moons, as those could be inhabitable from time to time, but this system was fruitless.

Vel was asking her a question again.

"Dr. Peate, you are just so focused!" he laughed. "I wondered if you were planning on coming to Mother's birthday this year."

"Uh no," Lyssa said, finally speaking.

"But why not?" Vel asked, curious. "You haven't been home in ages, I am sure she would just love to see you!"

"I think it would be better for all parties involved if I didn't," she muttered.

"Dr. Peate, you are a treasure!" Vel laughed again, and Lyssa thought momentarily about leaving him on one of these gas giants.

She tried to return her attention to the planets, but he was talking. AGAIN.

"So have you chosen a planet yet?" Vel asked. Out of the corner of her eye, she saw him with pad and pencil in hand, leaning forward to capture her every word.

"Looking," she mumbled, sliding lower into her chair.

Suddenly, her sensors began to beep, and Lyssa couldn't help the smile that grew on her face. Leveman's Vortex was a speck in the distance, but it was growing. She hadn't even considered using her greatest weapon...

"Actually, we're not going to excavate a planet," Lyssa said, nonchalantly.

"We're not?" Vel asked, confused.

"No," Lyssa said, motioning towards the rapidly approaching Vortex.

"Oh my...are we going to study Leveman's Vortex!" Vel gasped.

"That's what Pymus asked you to do, isn't it?" Lyssa said, bringing up the application to track the angle of entry. As she spoke, she carefully guided herself into the green. "Learn all the secrets of the Vortex?"

"Dr. Peate, we don't seem to be slowing down," Vel said, a hint of nervousness in his voice as the beeping from the sensors grew more frantic.

"Why would we slow down?" Lyssa said, feeling the pressure increase. "We're going in!"

"W-What?" Vel yelled, as the sensor warnings screeched. The stars were flying by so fast now that they became little white streamers, mixing in with the white debris from the outer arms of Leveman's vortex until the screen was all white.

"That's what Sostas was studying!" she said, looking back at him. "He found a way to get past the Vortex. We're going to meet him there!"

The pressure inside the ship was increasing, but Lyssa remained standing even as it pressed at her. One eye was glued on her green sensor.

"WE ARE!" Vel gasped, his eyes brimming with joy and excitement. He didn't seem to notice the increase in pressure. "I can't believe it. I'm finally going to meet my father. I don't even know what—"

"Oh no," Lyssa said nervously, her eyes still on the green. "Oh, oh no."

"What?" Vel asked, picking up on her anxiety.

"I...I..." Lyssa gasped, looking at Vel. "The...the ship is off...I miscalculated the angle...."

"W-what?!" Vel gasped, looking up at her.

"There's a formula," she stammered, her hands steady on the joystick.

"The precise angle of entry—weight of the ship, proximity to other celestial bodies. I...I miscalculated it..."

"What does that mean?!" Vel gasped.

"I don't think we're going to make it," Lyssa said, turning back to look at him with the most panicked expression she could muster.

"Then pray, dear sister, and let us hope our souls are light from a life well lived," Vel said, immediately dipping his head to prayer. "O great Divine Being, please guide our souls so that we may ascend to heaven. I have followed your lead and lived a good life. I have been kind and pious and—"

Lyssa saw the green turn to red and quickly turned on her thrusters. The force of the engines pushed her down into her chair, and she landed in a heap, laughing, even as Vel continued to pray.

She looked back at him, still chuckling as he slowly opened one eye and looked at her. The ship slowly began to stop shaking, and the stars were whirring by faster than before.

"W-what just happened?" Vel asked, terror still in his voice. "Did...were you..."

She threw him a look and turned the ship back on auto-pilot.

"Using the gravitational pull from the Vortex to slingshot us to the planet," she said simply. "Uses less fuel that way."

Vel's mouth dropped open. "That's...that sounds awfully dangerous."

"Eh," she shrugged.

"So we're not going to meet Father in Leveman's Vortex?" Vel asked, sounding disappointed.

"Well, you can go meet him there if you want, I'm sure that's where he is," she scoffed.

"Meaning he—"

"Meaning he's dead," she snapped. Then she thought for a moment. "Probably."

Vel didn't respond. Lyssa waited for a few moments before turning back to look at him. He was staring at the ground, his face a mix of disappointment, embarrassment, and anger. She watched him take a deep breath and force his face back to a smile.

"Well, Dr. Pymus did say you had a unique sense of humor," he said.

"I'm sure he did," she said, turning back to watching the stars go by and a little perturbed that she didn't rattle him more.

***

"So where should we start first?" Vel asked, holding his pen and paper at the ready. They had landed at the first excavation site on the planet—a thick, sticky jungle. Lyssa had hoped that the bugs and the temperature would get to him if Leveman's Vortex wouldn't, but so far, he seemed as chipper and happy as the moment they left the Academy.

So she turned to Plan B.

"Well the first thing we should start with is why didn't you do an air quality analysis?" Lyssa said, turning to look at him.

"W-what?" Vel asked.

"An air quality analysis," Lyssa said, melodramatically rolling her eyes. "As I sit here breathing poisonous air…"

"Well I would need a sensor for that," Vel blinked, nervously. "I can't tell the pollutant concentration without—"

"If it wasn't breathable, we would be dead by now," Lyssa cut him off, shaking her head. "You sure have a lot to learn about the dangers of being a DSE."

"Dr. Peate, you wouldn't bring me to a planet where the air wasn't breathable," Vel laughed.

"What if this was a test," Lyssa said, folding her arms across her chest. "Or I had forgotten to do the air quality calculation?"

"You didn't, though—"

"Well," she scoffed. "What if I had?"

"Then we would both be dead?" Vel tried.

"Damn straight we would be," Lyssa said, acting like she was walking back onto her ship. "You clearly are not ready for an internship. I'm going to—"

"Dr. Peate, you are so funny," Vel laughed, not the least bit concerned and ignoring the growl of frustration that emanated from his partner. "So what are we going to analyze first? I can vouch for the air…"

Lyssa swirled around, annoyed. "Start with the damned tree leaves."

"Ah!" Vel said, pulling gloves and a plastic bag from his bag. "I do love carbon analysis."

She grumbled as he began to systematically pick off leaves from different trees, carefully writing key features about each tree before placing the leaves in the bags. Lyssa, who had always used her father's sensors to analyze plants on the spot, simply rolled her eyes and began trudging through the forest.

"Are you going to pull some leaves?" Vel asked, curiously.

"You're the intern," Lyssa snapped, angrily pushing branches out of the way.

"Of course," Vel laughed, taking three steps forward and selecting another leaf. "So how much data do you normally collect at an excavation site?"

"Enough," she responded, annoyed that he was taking so long.

"But what's enough for the Academy? Planets are huge, how do you know when you've gotten a representative sample?"

"Planets are closed environments," Lyssa said. "So once you've got the basic chemical and biological composition of things, you've got enough to sell it."

"Oh," Vel stopped, staring at her. "But doesn't the Academy require a minimum of four excavation sites in order to be certified for sale?"

Lyssa sighed and kept walking, shoving leaves and branched out of her way.

"It just...doesn't seem very thorough," Vel quickly said, realizing that he might have been out of line.

"Well, that's for the buyer to worry about," Lyssa said, looking up at the sky. "If I spent all my time getting every single detail about a planet, then I'd be here for weeks."

"Isn't that what you're supposed to do?" Vel said, looking at her.

She opened her mouth, but then thought better of it. "Yes."

"But you only bring in three planets a quarter," Vel said, nonchalantly looking at a plant.

"The required minimum to stay active in the Academy, yes," Lyssa said, knowing where this conversation was going.

"So if you're only bringing in three planets a quarter, and you're not doing a full excavation...." Vel said, trailing off. "What are you doing?"

"The DSE Academy stipulates a quota of three planets per quarter to maintain good standing," Lyssa said pointedly. She didn't have to answer to him the way she had to answer to Pymus. "Therefore, I only excavate three planets per quarter."

"I see," Vel said, sounding like he was itching to ask more questions. Instead, he followed up with, "So do you think we'll find any sign of animal life?"

"Animal life usually finds you," Lyssa said.

"They taught us in our Fauna Interactivity Class that usually native species are scared by the sound of the ship," Vel said, as if quoting a book. "It's rare that you'll run into them in wild."

"Yeah, they say that to not scare you," Lyssa smirked, pushing the brush away as they ventured further into the dense forest. "The reality is, over *two hundred* DSE die every year on planets."

"That's not right," Vel said, looking at her nervously.

"Look it up," Lyssa said, continuing to walk. "Between the animal life, the dangerous terrain, and simply being all alone on a planet, millions of miles away from anyone who could help you—"

"Most DSE," Vel corrected her, not sounding the least bit scared. "Have staff and partners that go with them on planets."

Lyssa turned to look at him. "Yes, but often times, DSEs are left on an excavation site all by themselves. And by the time their teams come to retrieve them…it's too late."

"Dr. Peate," Vel shrugged her off. "I know what you're trying to do."

"You do?" Lyssa said.

"Mother does the same thing," Vel sighed, looking at her lovingly. "She worries about all of us out in the field. But I believe firmly that the Great Creator has a plan for all of us and—"

"What was that…?" Lyssa gasped eager to shut him up quickly.

"What was what?" Vel asked, looking at her confused.

"That, did you hear that?" she said, looking around.

"No, I—"

"Leveman's Vortex," she swore, looking into the darkness ahead of her. "I think we found the animal life."

"What?" Vel said, looking ahead of her. "I don't—"

"RUN, VEL!" she screamed turning to her left and bursting out on the fastest sprint she could muster.

"DR. PEATE, WAIT!" Vel called behind her.

She wasn't waiting for him, stretching her legs out as far as they would go, and pushing them to move as fast as she could. She reached down and tapped her mini-computer, without breaking eye contact with the ground in front of her.

She continued to run, listening to the rhythm of her inhale, the footfall, and exhale as she covered ground. It was some time later that she finally stopped, hitting the edge of a wide river, stopping short to catch her breath.

Looking down at her mini-computer, which was tracking her speed and distance, she nodded in approval at her time—almost six miles in forty-five minutes.

And then, just as she was feeling particularly proud of herself, she heard the telltale sounds of jogging behind her.

"Dr. Peate!" Vel said, his cheeks red from running, but that stupid, vapid smile still on his face. "You are a funny one. That was quite a jog! I normally jog at home, so I don't get a chance to do much trail running. You know there is a lovely…"

And then, just when things couldn't get any worse, she watched in horror as her mini-computer battery died.

"Kill me now," she pleaded under her breath.

***

Without her mini-computer to guide them, it was almost nightfall by the time they returned to the ship. Vel's voice was starting to sound worn and scratchy, but he continued to talk on and on and on about absolutely nothing. Lyssa had stopped even answering his questions, eager to get into a hot shower and crawl into her bed to dream about anything but the sound of his voice in her ear.

"All in all, a very productive day!" Vel said, neatly placing his bags of specimens on the silver counter. "So when are we going to start our carbon analysis? Are you of the school of thought that we should wait until returning to the Academy, or start the analysis while still on the—"

Lyssa answered him by slamming her bedroom door shut. She pressed herself against the door and closed her eyes, taking a deep, cleansing breath. It was only for six months, she kept reminding herself.

Opening her eyes, she saw that half of her bedroom had been taken over by his five suitcases, an Academy-provided air mattress and sleeping bag, and three stacks of thick books.

She took another deep breath and walked over to her bed, resisting the urge to put a hole in the air mattress. She flopped down on her small bed and pulled out the cord to charge her mini-computer.

She watched impatiently as it sprung back to life, wondering when she was going to-

The mini-computer then began blinking with notifications of missed calls from several hours ago.

From Dissident.

"Shit...." she whispered.

In an instant, she was on her feet. She burst from her room, focused on how much groveling and self-depreciation she was going to have to do, when she saw Vel, standing in front of the small refrigerator and poking through anything that looked edible.

"Dr. Peate," he smiled. "So I was looking for anything I can use to prepare us some dinner."

"We need some firewood," she said, almost without thinking. "I have some pots and pans—I can make dinner over the fire."

"That sounds lovely!" Vel said, his face lighting up. "I shall go fetch us some firewood."

"And water too," Lyssa said, remembering that the closest river was at least an hours' walk away. She walked over to her cabinets and opened them, pulling out a flashlight and a small bucket. "Here, take these."

"Yes ma'am!" Vel smiled, marching off the ship with glorious purpose.

CHAPTER FIVE

As fast as she could, Razia scampered upstairs and flew to her console, trying desperately to connect her ship to the nearest communications satellite. She tapped her foot, watching the connection slowly come online. Once it was fully connected, she typed in Dissident's number as fast as her fingers would go.

"Come on, come on, come on," she breathed, as the call went unanswered.

She tried again, and then a third time. Dissident wasn't above screening her call, but she would be damned if she was kicked out simply for not calling him back in a timely fashion.

Finally, on the fourth time, the call went through.

"I was just giving you the same pleasure of being ignored," Dissident growled dangerously. His skin was looking particularly sallow today as he sneered down at her through the video call. "Where have you been?"

"I've been...busy," Razia said, trying to keep her temper in check.

"Oh, you're busy?" Dissident said, feigning concern. "Well so am I pretending that I don't have a damned female in my web?!"

Her anger flared up, but she was in control of her mouth. "I'm sorry Dissident."

"You're sorry?" he said, her tone setting him off. "You're sorry? You know who's sorry? I'm sorry I ever let you into my web! Tauron or no Tauron, you have been nothing but a thorn in my side for years—"

Her eyes flashed, and the anger of the past week—from Pymus giving her the universe's most annoying intern to having to turn in a drunken purse-stealer and even coming face to face with her stupid brother in the cafeteria—finally bubbled over.

"Dissident, do you want to know why your web sucks?" she said, damning the consequences.

"Excuse me?" Dissident gasped, aghast.

"You're a joke," she continued, anger overpowering her fear of him.

"You spend all this time focusing on Sage Teon—who, by the way, is a terrible pirate and an even worse bounty hunter—and you don't even realize that you've got the next Tauron Ball right here—"

"You think you're half as good as Tauron was?" Dissident laughed.

"I'm better," Razia countered, angrily.

"Prove it," Dissident said. "Find Evet Delmur."

"Who?" she said, looking at him confused.

"Are you a bounty hunter or not?" Dissident sneered. "Am I not paying for your access into the intraweb?"

She gave him a look and then pulled up the bounty roster. As the first and only result came up, her heart leapt into her throat:

	250) Delmur, Evet
Wanted For	Engagement in piracy, bounty hunting, theft, grand larceny...
Reward	10,000C
Known Alias	Luka Arular, Merkaba Backus, Zowie Canales, Canet Conboy...
Known Accomplices	Gunnar Cole, Franke Eigenberg...
Web Affiliation	None

"Is this a joke?" Razia breathed. He was, by far, the highest bounty Dissident had allowed her to hunt.

"Find him," Dissident continued. "By the end of this week."

Razia looked at her calendar. That only gave her three universal days.

"And what if I do?" Razia asked.

"If you can find him, I suppose we may discuss raising the caliber of the bounties I allow you to hunt," Dissident said, sounding as if her finding Delmur was completely impossible.

"That's more like it!" Razia smiled, feeling a weight lifted off her chest. This was it, this was the break she had been waiting for.

"But if you don't find him," Dissident snapped. "You are out of my web."

"Fine," Razia said. "I'm holding you to this, Dissident."

"As am I."

The call went dark and Razia sat back, her mind running over what had just happened. Dissident had just given her a bounty actually worth something—ten thousand credits. Not only that, but he seemed pretty serious about giving her higher bounties. She wouldn't be off probation yet, but maybe if she was given a high enough bounty, one of the other runners would try to poach her.

"Dr. Peate!"

Lyssa nearly fell out of her chair as Vel came bursting into the bridge of her ship, a wide smile on his face and a bucket of water in his hand.

"How long were you standing there?" Lyssa asked, nervous that he had just overheard her talking with a known pirate runner about bounty hunting.

"Just walked in," Vel smiled. "I ran the whole way to the river."

Vel looked at her, finally, and turned his head to the side, looking at her. "Your hair is down. You look absolutely beautiful—you should wear it like that more often..."

She stared at him, still nervous that he had overheard her talking with a pirate runner.

"I found a water source much closer than the river," Vel grinned. "Will this be enough water? I can go out and start looking for firewood now—"

"You know," Lyssa said, starting to realize with a terribly guilty feeling that she was going to have to leave him here. "I think that the tree species we found earlier today—the one by that field—would make excellent firewood. I'm worried that the burning temperature of the wood in this forest won't be hot enough..."

She swallowed, hoping he would continue to believe every last lie she told him.

"Oh, you know," Vel nodded. "I think you're right. I'll head out that way—will you be okay here by yourself?"

"Yeah," Lyssa lied, feeling like the guilt was eating her alive. "I'm going to take a shower and start analysis. Just...take your time."

"Right!" Vel grinned, looking like he was pleased they were finally getting along. "I will return in an hour or so!"

Lyssa watched him jog out into the forest and tried to remind herself that she was already going to burn in Plegethon for much worse.

∗∗∗

"All right, Mr. Delmur," Razia said, cracking her knuckles. She was halfway past Leveman's Vortex, finally to a point where she could get some serious work done on her new project.

Razia analyzed Delmur's picture for a moment, trying to remember exactly what he looked like. He was middle-aged, and looked slightly neurotic with small eyes and big classes. He wouldn't be too difficult for her to take down—assuming he didn't have a crew.

She clicked on his known accomplices—usually a good indicator if the pirate had a crew or not. Happily, the first couple of names came up with pirates who hadn't been heard from in years, which meant he probably didn't have a crew.

"Let's see about these aliases," Razia said, clicking on the button to expand the list. Her eyes slowly widened as the page of aliases kept getting longer… and longer… and longer… and longer………… and longer……..

There had to be at least five hundred aliases here.

"Ooh boy," she swallowed, sitting back for a moment. Well, Dissident wasn't going to make it easy.

She brought up another window to log into the bank intranet. She typed in the first name—Luka Arular—just to see what would come up.

Arular, Luka		
Time of Transaction	Location	Amount
UT19999-25-98-09:72	Beer Taback D-882	50C
UT19999-25-95-84:28	Clover Club D-882	25C
UT19999-25-85-01:12	Berry Park D-882	50C
UT19999-25-80-12:06	Trash Bar D-882	50C

The first thing she noticed was that all of his transactions were from 15 years ago. Closing that window, she searched on the next alias:

Backus, Merkaba		
Time of Transaction	Location	Amount
UT19999-25-99-99:99	Stomehome D-882	25C
UT19999-25-96-94:72	Sunny's D-882	50C
UT19999-25-92-45:92	Huckleberry's Bar D-882	50C

Again, all from over fifteen years ago. She tried another three aliases from the middle of the list and, still, same result. Sitting back, she chewed on her thumb, deep in thought. There were a lot of aliases here; it could absolutely be possible that she just happened to find the only five that were fifteen years old.

She switched tactics for a moment, searching all records across the UBU internet for any sign of Evet Delmur to see if there was any general information about him.

Nothing.

Switching back to the bank intranet and pirate web, she looked at the list of bounties and sighed unhappily. She supposed she would have to search every single one of them.

After all, one of them had to be more recent, right?

***

Six hours, five hundred thirty-four failed alias searches, and four cups of coffee later, one thing was certain:

Razia was in serious trouble.

Not ONE alias she had come up with was more recent than fifteen years ago. And she even tried cross-checking the location of a few of them together. Nothing.

It was like the guy just up and disappeared.

With nowhere else to turn, she found herself hurrying along the dusty streets of D-882. If anyone knew where Evet Delmur was, it was going to be Harms.

She burst into his bar, red faced and sweaty, as the shuttle system was stopped for some unknown reason, and she gave up and ran the whole seven miles here. She stood in front of his table, hands on her knees, struggling to catch her breath.

"Hey, kiddo," Harms interrupted, looking to the person in front of him. "I'm kind of—"

"Emergency," she panted out, looking up at him.

Harms sighed and looked to the pirate in front of him, a rat-faced, black-haired man. "Linro, I'll call you later, okay?"

"Fine," he grumbled getting out of the booth and giving Razia a dirty look.

"Thank you," she said, slumping down into his bar.

"Here, have some water," Harms said, sliding his glass over to her. "Now what's the fire?"

56

"Dissidentgavemebountycan'tfind," Razia sputtered out.

"One more time?" Harms laughed.

"Dissident," Razia said, after she gulped down the water. "He gave me a bounty. A good one."

"Dissident actually gave you someone worth looking for?" Harms smiled. "That's amazing!"

"Yeah, he did," Razia nodded, pulling out her mini-computer. "But I can't...I can't find anything on him."

"Well that's not a reason to run in here like your hair is on fire," Harms chided her. "That was a paying customer too—"

"He gave me three days—two now," she said. "And if I don't find him, I'm out of the web."

"Dissident always threatens to throw you out," Harms said knowingly.

"Yeah, but this time I think he's serious," Razia said, trying to get him to understand. "I mean, he's never given me a bounty this high before—and he told me if I found him, he's start to give me some serious bounties."

"Wow," Harms said, looking impressed. "Who is it?"

"Evet Delmur," Razia said, looking up at Harms.

"Wait a minute, Evet Delmur?" Harms blinked, as if he recognized the name. "Dissident wanted you to bring in Evet Delmur?"

"Yeah," Razia replied, becoming more nervous by his expression. "What's the problem?"

"Nothing, except..." Harms looked as if he was trying to find the right words. "I mean he's sort of retired now. Nobody's really seen him for at least fifteen years..."

Razia's eyes nearly bugged out of her head as her worst fears were realized. "WHAT? Dissident gave me a dead bounty?!"

"He's not....dead... per say. Just not an active pirate, that's all," Harms replied, less confidently than he had sounded before. "I mean, he's still out there, somewhere."

"So if nobody's seen him, why is his bounty so high?"

"Well, when he was active, he was incredibly paranoid. So much so that he'd never been caught. He had over two hundred aliases at one point," Harms said. "Then he had a heart attack from all the stress, and decided to retire..."

"So Dissident gave me a retired, paranoid pirate?" Razia blinked, sitting back. "With a million aliases that haven't been used in fifteen years. And you can't tell me anything about him?!"

"I mean, I..." Harms said, looking indecisive. "Can't you go back and ask Dissident for another bounty?"

"I am so screwed," she whispered, dropping her head on the table. And what was worse, she put herself in this position. If she hadn't opened her big mouth…

"Maybe not," Harms said, gently. "Look, I do know that he got a job as a raw materials transporter near G-245 shortly after he retired. My guess is that he might still be doing that."

Razia lifted her head from the table to look at him. "That's it?"

"That's all I got, kiddo," Harms shrugged. Razia saw something behind his eyes that made her think he had more. But she actually didn't feel like pressing her luck—she had a planet that she could narrow down her search.

"It's enough," Razia nodded, reaching into her pocket to grab her C-card.

"No, this one's on the house," Harms shook his head. "I insist."

"Thank you," she said, unsure if she'd be able to afford Harms' high prices at this point. "I owe you one."

"Just go get him," Harms winked, watching her run away.

***

G-245, it turns out, was an uninhabitable planet with an abundance of naturally occurring raw material. Enormous mining communities were established on the surface, drilling deep into the planet's crust to extract some of the most sought-after ores. The mining communities shipped the materials to thousands of satellite hub stations, where transporters were waiting to ship the materials across the galaxy to refining stations and distributers.

Razia sat on her bridge, staring at the planet with an anxious nervousness in her chest. Even from this far away, she could see thousands of satellite stations, and little ships puttering to and from them.

It would probably take her months to hit every single one of them.

But she was down to less than two days, and she needed a miracle or to get very lucky.

"Okay, Razia," she said, talking to herself. "What would Tauron do?"

Her mind was blank.

"Seriously," she said, closing her eyes and picturing Tauron in her mind. But the only thing she could come up with was him telling her to figure it out herself.

She dropped her head to her dashboard. The cool steel felt good. But she still had no idea where to start.

She heard a beeping and for a brief moment worried that Vel, or even Dr. Pymus was calling. As luck would have it, it was neither of them.

"So I heard from a little bird that you've got a hot bounty," Sage smiled. "Find him yet?"

"No," she snapped, not looking up at him.

"Really?" Sage smirked. "Aren't you a damned good bounty hunter?

58

Isn't that what you told Relleck?"

"I'm in no mood for this," she growled.

"Oh come on," he laughed. "I'm just playing. I actually called to see if you needed any help."

"Why, because you don't think I can find him either?" she seethed.

"Well if you were having any luck finding him, I assume you'd have found him by now," Sage smiled. "As you've got less than a day to bring him in."

"Dammit," she said, burying her head in her hands. She'd completely lost track of time. The pressure in her chest was starting to build again as she turned over all of the consequences of not finding this bounty in time.

"Have you slept?" Sage said, watching her concern.

"No."

"You should probably do that at some point," he said. "You know you get cranky when you don't sleep."

"Get sucked into Leveman's Vortex," she snapped.

"Okay, okay," Sage smiled. "Just here to help. So what did Harms tell you about him?"

"He's been hanging around G-245," Lyssa muttered.

"Now, see, that's not what he told you," Sage sighed. "You never listen, do you?"

"Okay, what did he tell you then?" Lyssa said. "And why was he even talking to you about me anyways?"

"Harms said he was a transporter," Sage said. "And what do transporters do?"

She gave him a mean look.

"I'm serious," Sage said. "What do they do?"

"Transport shit."

He sighed. "You know, if you're going to have this attitude..."

She looked up at him again, expectantly.

"Look." Sage sighed again. "What kind of guy are you hunting?"

"Old guy." Razia wasn't sure what he was getting at.

"Not just old," Sage said, looking as if he was hinting at something. "Paranoid?"

"What's the other P word?"

"Pirate?" Razia said, raising her eyebrow.

"So you've got an old, paranoid pirate," Sage nodded. "Do you really think he went completely legitimate?"

"I know he's not using his real name," Razia said. "Hence my problem."

"God in Leveman's Vortex," Sage rolled his eyes. "Okay, I'm gonna make this really simple for you. Most—if not all—transporters have gotten hijacked at one point or another by pirates. It's just what makes the

59

universe expand."

"Yeah, and?"

"Do you think a former pirate would get hijacked?" Sage said. "Do you think that maybe, *just maybe*, he's got some deal worked out with the runners to keep pirates off his back?"

Razia looked up at him, her mind turning. "Are there records of on-time percentages for transporters?"

"*Yeeees*," Sage smiled, nodding at her. "Now you're getting it."

"So if I were to find maybe the top 100 with their on-time percentages—cross-check to see which ones had filed insurance claims and see if any of them hadn't."

"You're welcome."

Razia paused to glare at him. "I would have figured it out eventually."

"Yeah and by that time, you would have been coming to me, begging me to hire you on my crew," Sage said. "Which, as funny as that would be for me, I've already lived with you before, and it's not my favorite thing in the world."

Razia, searching the transporters on-time percentages, paused to give him a dirty look. "I am a fine roommate."

"You are messy, and kind of mean," Sage shrugged.

"You're just a baby, that's all," she said, pulling up transaction records of the first ten transporters.

Zephyr, Benson		
Time of Transaction	Location	Amount
UT200014-95-91-60:67	Refueling Station 8790	25,000C
UT200014-95-89-50:55	O'Pera's Diner G-294	50C
UT200014-95-84-32:56	Refueling Station 1245	25,000C
UT200014-95-80-57:16	Yankari's Diner S-6642	50C

This one on the list gave her pause. For a transporter, he didn't have that many purchases—not for gas, not for food, not even for a room to sleep in at night. While some transporters slept on their ships....something wasn't adding up.

"You said I had chicken legs!" Sage barked at her.

"You do!" Razia replied, plotting out his route on a star map. There were plenty of gaps—there was no way this guy could have made it from one gas fill up to another without refueling somewhere.

"Okay, yeah, when I was thirteen," Sage said, pouting. "But my legs are manly now!"

"Yeah, manly," Razia said, calculating the probable time that the transporter needed to stop for fuel, and identifying any refueling stations in the general vicinity based on the average rate of speed. Three stations and five transactions met her criteria.

"Well Annber said they were gorgeous," Sage muttered.

"Who?" Razia said, snapping from her thoughts.

"Girl I met at Eamon's," Sage said. "I think she's the one."

"You say that about every girl you meet," Razia said, going back to her bounty. She tried the same tactic with another gap in transaction fueling—checking any refueling stations in the area where he would have to refuel based on his current route.

And at the second refueling station, she saw an identical name.

"Found him," Razia smiled.

"No shit," Sage said, in awe of her. "You did not find him already."

Razia simply ended the call and set a course for the S-6642.

***

She sat in the diner, staring at a cold cup of coffee, and glancing at the time on her mini-computer every few seconds. Outside the window was the blackness of space, and on the other side was a dock that was mostly empty, but that had been filled with transport ships off and on for the past few hours.

Just to be sure of her hunch, she spent the entire trip over here mapping out three weeks' worth of activities and uncovering three other aliases. When added together, it painted an exact picture of a transport route going to G-245 to S-6642, a recently settled planet that was still being built up.

The diner where she was sitting was on all five alias' transaction records (at different times). Based on his total pattern and regular route timing, she could reasonably expect him to show up soon.

She looked around the diner and sighed, wondering just when he would show up. There was a rather bored looking cook behind the counter, reading a book, while the only old waitress was smoking and doing a cross-word puzzle.

By the looks of the place, it seemed as though they didn't get much business.

Her mini-computer buzzed and her heart leapt from her chest. One of the five transporter accounts had just paid for an hours' worth of parking and had begun refueling.

Any minute now.

She readied herself for action—if he ran, or if he stayed to fight. Hard to tell how he'd react to being captured after all these years.

The door opened. Razia took a deep breath and looked up, ready to meet her destiny.

He was old.

Really old.

As in, she could probably break something if she tapped him.

His back was hunched over, and his hands shook as he put his C-card back in his pocket. His hair was combed over his spotted head, and his suspenders were keeping up loose-fitting pants. He pulled off his thick glasses to wipe them in his handkerchief, and then placed them in a case in his pocket.

But it was definitely Evet Delmur.

"Hey there Fred," the waitress said, as he sidled into the seat. "The usual."

He nodded, and the waitress put a cup of coffee in front of him. "Darn kids these days, they—"

He paused when he realized Razia was staring at him.

Delmur let out a sigh and pushed himself off the stool. She watched, tense, as he sauntered over to her table.

"All right," he sighed. "What do you want?"

"Excuse me?" she said, her own voice sounding weird.

"You been pinging my accounts," he said. "Why?"

"I've been...how did you know I was pinging your accounts?"

"Honey, I own the transporter company," he sighed. "I'm not some two-bit pirate. I got alarms and alerts all over those search results."

She narrowed her eyes at him. "I thought you were retired."

"I am retired," he grunted. "So where's your boyfriend...I've got to set him straight."

"What boyfriend?" Razia asked, confused.

"The one who sent you in here to distract me while he came around back to capture me," he looked around. "I know this trick."

She blinked at him, and then slid out of the table, her temper starting to flare. "I am here to bring you in."

"So now they're sending little girls?" he chortled. "The runners have sunk to a new low."

Razia's face fell from a frown into a scowl. "Little girl?!" she hissed.

"Oh," he said, blinking. "Are you...serious?"

"Do you think I would have spent as much time on you if I wasn't?" She was beside herself with fury, and wanted to haul his laughing ass in as soon as she possibly could to wipe that grin off of his face.

"Honey, I'm retired," he said, heavily. "You run along and find yourself some other low bounty to chase after."

"No," Razia's eyes flashed dangerously. "Dissident said —"

He began to laugh.

"What's so funny?"

"Now I get it!"

"What?" Razia said, confused.

He reached into his pocket and pulled out a bag. "When you see Dissident, send him my apologies for not getting this to him sooner."

"What in Leveman's is this?" Razia said.

"Chocolates, from H-876. I fly by there on occasion and Dissident always has me bring him by some of the finest. I'm sure that's why he sent you to pick them up for him."

He tossed the bag on the table and she stared at it, dumbfounded.

"I...I'm not...I mean..."

"Because I know Dissident, and he'd rather die than let some woman in his web," Delmur laughed. "None of them runners like the idea. Just not natural."

She swallowed, praying that she could keep the redness from shame and embarrassment off her face. How could she fall for this trick? She should have known something was up when he was so eager to let her hunt someone so high...and barter with her, even.

Come to think of it, she realized with a sick feeling. He'd probably go back on his word even if she did bring him in.

"He...uh...didn't send you for anything else, did he?" Delmur said, eyeing her up and down.

"Get sucked into Leveman's and die," she growled, giving him the meanest glare she could muster.

"Ah well," he sighed. "In that case, Mabel, I will take that pie to go."

"Here you are, Fred. See you next time," the waitress said.

And with that he took his box and his coffee in a to-go cup, and walked out the door.

CHAPTER SIX

She sat on her ship, speeding back to the planet where she had left her intern, numb with shock and realization that all of her dreams had just gone up in smoke.

There was no way Dissident was going to let her stay in the web.

When she wasn't in the web, she couldn't be a bounty hunter.

If she couldn't be a bounty hunter, she would have to be Lyssa forever.

She caught her reflection in the front glass. She looked like Razia—hair down, black shirt, cargo pants. But the face was all Lyssa—defeated, miserable, and giving in.

She had been going back and forth in her mind, wondering if there was anything she could possibly do to remain in the pirate web—even so far as taking Sage up on his offer. Desperate times, and all.

Then again, who was she fooling?

She was nothing but a joke. A chocolate-fetching joke. No matter what she did, or how hard she worked, she was never going to be good enough for them.

"This is your punishment for being a lying, deceitful child."

She swallowed, forcing herself to keep it together. She couldn't think about that now.

Besides, she had bigger issues to deal with. Namely her intern, who she left all alone on a planet for over three days. She was sure the next stop was being hauled in front of a disciplinary committee.

Served her right, she supposed. If she was lucky, perhaps she would get suspended. If she wasn't so lucky...she might be looking at losing two jobs in the same week.

As she got closer to the planet, she finally gathered enough courage to make the call.

She pulled up her video call application and saw all of the calls to Sage, and to Dissident. Even a few to Harms. All of the people she no longer in her life, that she would probably never talk to again.

It was weird to think that just a few days prior, everything was going swimmingly for her. She looked at the call history, her eyes lingering on the last call, from Sage, where he had so obnoxiously helped her find Delmur.

What a waste.

Pushing those self-pitying thoughts out of her head, she began to call Vel's mini-computer.

The call rang for a while, but he didn't answer. Annoyed that he wasn't answering her call, she immediately redialed.

And then, very faintly, she heard a beeping sound.

Leaving the video call ringing, she followed the sound, to the back of the ship, down her ladder to the lower level, through to her bedroom, where Vel's bag had been neatly placed next to her bathroom.

She nervously reached into the bag and pulled out his beeping mini-computer.

Without his mini-computer, he had no way of calling for help. So for all she knew, he could be dying somewhere.

But, more importantly, without his communicator, she had no way of locating him on the big, huge, giant planet that he was currently stuck on.

"Uh oh," she whispered.

***

"Shit, shit, shit, shit," she cursed, pushing leaves and branches out of the way. "VEL!"

When she got close enough to pick up readings on the planet, she began scanning every corner of the planet her sensors could reach for any sign of large animals—roughly human-sized. Every second that ticked by without a hit, her panic grew exponentially.

"VEL!"

She'd already been kicked out of the pirate web, and she would definitely be kicked out of the Academy for killing her intern. As if her mother didn't despise her enough…

"VEL!" she screamed at the top of her lungs.

Finally, after five or six scans, she finally picked up the readings of a plausible humanoid life-form. But it was in the middle of a thick forest—and she could only land her ship in a clearing two miles away.

"VEL! ARE YOU HERE?"

And she had been out here, in the jungle, for what seemed like forever, screaming at the top of her lungs. Hoping, against hope that every branch she pushed away, every time she turned around, she would not come across a dead intern.

"VEL!" she screamed, nervousness finally seeping into her voice.

"Hello, there Dr. Peate!"

Sweet, sweet relief washed over her as she spun around—until she caught sight of him.

He was covered—head to toe—in swollen bites. Some of them were oozing white pus, and others looked just about ready to burst. His eyes were glassy, but he forced himself to smile at her.

"It appears as though you forgot to leave me some bug spray," he said, trying to sound cheerful. "I assure you, I look worse than I feel. Could I bother you for a drink of water?"

"Here," she said, tossing him a bottle on her hip. "So…um…."

He smiled at her as he gulped down the bottle.

"Did I…forget to leave you a potable water sensor?" Lyssa asked, nervously.

He continued gulping.

"I guess so," she laughed, nervously.

He finished the bottle, and, even with the bulbous swelling bites all over his body, he managed to smile at her.

"So," he said. "How did your research go?"

"R-Research?" Lyssa blinked.

"Yes, I can only assume that you went to go do some research," Vel said. "Did you find out anything interesting?"

She opened and closed her mouth, reality crashing down on her again. Delmur was gone, Razia was out of the pirate web, and all of her dreams of greatness had vanished into thin air.

"No," she spat out after a few moments.

"Well, maybe next time you'll be more successful!" Vel said, looking very much as if he wanted to scratch one of his boils. "Is there anything I can do to help?"

"I think we should just get you back to the Academy," Lyssa said, eyeing him. "To the medical wing."

"Oh, these?" Vel smiled, waving her off. "Don't worry about these. I'm sure they will go down soon."

"I think you're loopy," Lyssa shook her head, unable to wipe the concerned look off her face. "Let's get you back to the ship so you can get some rest."

"Oh, wait," Vel said, reaching into his bag and handing her a set of neatly organized bags of leaves and specimens, and other scraps of paper. "I'm not sure if this will be enough to do a presentation on, but I'm sure it will at least get us started."

She stared at him amazed. Even after leaving him with little survival gear, he still managed to gather data. And from the looks of it—he even got more readings than she normally did.

"Thanks…" She swallowed. "And hey… I'm sorry I just left you here."

"I'm sure whatever it was..." Vel smiled cheerily. "I know you're doing important work. And I understand. I'm just glad I could be helpful!"

She watched him stumbled back the way she came, towards the ship, and couldn't help but be a little impressed at how dedicated he was to Dr. Pymus.

***

They arrived at the Academy just about the time that Vel's skin started to turn green. As obnoxious as he was, and as much as she hated everything about him, somewhere deep in her soul she knew he was still her little brother. She would feel bad if he actually...died.

"Shall we...unpack first?" he said, his eyes seeming to go in and out of focus.

"I think we should head over to the medical wing now," Lyssa said, helping him to his feet.

"I hate to...impose..." he protested, as she guided him down the ladder and off the ship.

She hurried him out of the docks and into the first available lift—hoping to avoid any and all unwanted attention. She wasn't sure what her other brothers would say if they saw Vel in this state, and definitely didn't want to run into-

"Dr. Pymus!" Lyssa gasped, as the lift opened.

"Well my, my!" Pymus cheered, stepping onto the lift with them. "I had heard you'd returned from your excavation a little early."

He barely acknowledged Vel, who was leaning against the wall, pale and sweaty.

"Yes well," Lyssa gulped, wondering what sort of fall out she was going to get when Vel told him what had happened.

To her surprise, Vel popped up right and forced himself to smile at Pymus. "It's my fault, Dr. Pymus. It seems as though I walked into a swarm of nasty bugs on a planet."

"I see," Pymus said, not looking at him.

Ding

The lift opened to the medical wing, and Lyssa couldn't pull Vel off fast enough. Luckily, Pymus remained on the lift and they were safe for a few minutes longer.

"Hold on a second," Lyssa said, before they walked into the wing. "Why didn't you tell him the truth?"

"What?" Vel squinted at her.

"That I went bou...left you on the planet," Lyssa said, catching herself. "Why didn't you tell him?"

"Dr. Peate," Vel said, looking rather affronted. "We're family. Why

67

would I betray you like that?"

She stared back at him, stunned. She wondered if she should open his eyes to the kinds of betrayals she'd seen from select members of their family over the years.

Then, it occurred to her that he may simply be delirious, as he started talking to a nearby potted plant.

"Let's go, kiddo," she muttered, grabbing him and dragging him towards the medical wing.

The medical wing was a series of interconnected hallways to accommodate the wide breadth of species needing medical assistance. The first hallway they came across had several drawings of species with different amount of legs and arrows pointing to where each category should go. She pointed to the one with the one, two, or three movement-oriented appendages and they followed the arrows into a hall.

They came out of the hall where there was a long line of more halls. They walked straight forwards and picked out the arm number that applied to them (two). Following down that hallway, they took another fork at the sign marked "one sentient head," and finally came to a welcome desk.

"I'm sorry, you're in the wrong section," the tired looking woman said to a being at the front of the line. She had orange frizzy hair and two tentacles sticking out of her forehead. "You need to go back and find the hallway with the three legs and then go to the two arms, one head route."

The man grumbled and snatched his papers walking angrily back. He had some sort of white growth on his shoulder.

"Can I help you?" the woman asked.

"He...got bit by something," Lyssa said, unsure of what else to call it.

Vel handed the receptionist his C-card and she swiped it.

"Vellexore Beuregard Peate, age sixteen?"

"Vellexore?" Lyssa asked, eyebrows raised.

"It's a family name," Vel said.

"You will be seen within the hour," she said. "Have a seat over there until your name is called."

They sat down in the waiting area with other sick-looking people and things. On a scale of scratches to mortal peril, Lyssa actually put Vel in the middle. One man was looking rather gaunt, and holding a bloody rag against the stump that was his arm.

She sat back and out of habit, whipped out her mini-computer to search the pirate webs.

Then she remembered she was out of the pirate web.

She put down her mini-computer.

Looking around her, she tried to think about some other way to pass the time until Vel was called.

She opened the application again, just to see the news, she told herself.

	12) Obalone, Zolet Wanted in connection with transporter hijacking. Estimated cost of stolen materials: 750,000C
	30) Journot, Santos Wanted in connection with piracy (bounty hunting)
	5) Bernal, Arpad Captured by Santos Journot
	2) Relleck, Royden Wanted in connection with illegal sale of stolen goods

Damn Relleck, she thought. Annoyed, she flipped over to the bank application, and flipped through Relleck's different aliases. For being number two, he wasn't hiding very well—spending most of his time at skin bars on D-882.

It would be so easy, she thought. He and everyone else would be distracted by the naked females walking around that they'd never see her coming. She'd wait until he was drunk and stupid—maybe she'd pay off one of the girls to go get him alone—then capture him and get him to the bounty office before he sobered up.

"That must be some game," Vel said.

Lyssa snapped out of her planning, remembering she was sitting in the medical wing with her intern, waiting to get him checked out for bug bites.

And she was no longer a bounty hunter.

"Yeah," Lyssa said, shoving her mini-computer into her pocket. "Yeah, it's a fun game…"

"Vellexore Peate?" A nurse called.

"Here," Lyssa said, helping him up.

"Dr. Peate, I'm supposed to be the gentleman," Vel slurred, his eyes

69

going a little cross-eyed.

"Yeah, well, look at you," Lyssa said pointedly. "You can help me up all you want when your hands return to their normal size."

They followed the nurse down a long hallway with a series of doors. Lyssa could hear various moaning and screaming from some of them, and imagined all kinds of horrific injuries behind the doors. Nervously, she pulled out her mini-computer, just to check the pirate web and distract herself.

Unfortunately, she wasn't watching where she was going, and bumped right into someone. Her mini-computer fell out of her hand.

Her eyes widened slightly when a gold-trimmed arm reached down to grab her mini-computer. Especially as they followed the arm up to a lieutenant bar on the shoulders, and the stitching of the U-POL Special Forces to the face of the very same U-POL lieutenant who had accosted her at Harms' bar not last week.

She swallowed, as he smiled at her.

"My apologies," he said, handing her the mini-computer back. Lyssa's eyes drifted down to the screen, which was still displaying the pirate web, and found herself praying that he didn't look at it.

Luckily, he was too much of a gentleman to pry as he handed it to her.

"No," she said, forcing herself to stay calm as she quickly locked the screen. "I wasn't watching where I was going."

He looked at her for a moment, curiously. And for a moment, Lyssa froze, nervous that her feeble disguise was not going to work this time.

"Doctor, please keep up!"

Lyssa nodded at the U-POL officer and scampered after the nurse, faster than she probably should have.

***

"What are the U-POL doing here?" Vel asked, trying not to move on the paper covering the exam table.

Lyssa's eyes sprung to the door nervously, but then realized Vel was talking about being here at the Academy.

"They have an agreement with the Academy to use the doctors here," Lyssa said, looking up at him. "Since, you know, they're the best in the universe practically."

"I wonder if we'll see Jukin," Vel said, dreamily. "If we do, could you introduce me?"

"Why would I know Jukin?!" Lyssa snapped, still focused on the door.

"Because he's our brother?" Vel said curiously.

"Oh, yeah, right," Lyssa said. Her eyes kept drifting to the door nervously.

"I can't believe that my older brother is the captain of the U-POL Special Forces," Vel said dreamily. "He's doing such great things for the universe."

"Uh-huh," Lyssa murmured.

"He's like a celebrity at home. Mother's so proud of him, capturing pirates and trying to clean up the universe. The younger kids have never met him, but we all talk about how wonderful he is."

"He hasn't caught anyone in a few years," Lyssa said. "Or rather, anybody important."

"Oh stop being jealous," Vel chided her. "We can't all be Father's favorite child."

Lyssa thought about correcting him, but decided against it.

"Do you remember when he captured that guy?" Vel said. "That was an incredible feat."

"What?" Lyssa said, her focus finally away from the door.

"We all still talk about it at home," Vel said, smiling. "The way he was able to outsmart that pirate—"

"Tauron," Lyssa snapped, glaring at him. "His name was Tauron."

"Right, Tauron," Vel said, dismissing it. "But Jukin spent four or five years hunting this guy, and couldn't ever catch him."

"That's not—" Lyssa said before catching herself. It wouldn't do to give Vel her firsthand account of what actually happened.

"What?"

"Where in Leveman's is that doctor?" she said, louder than she meant to.

"Right here," the doctor said, walking in the door, with a tablet and instruments dangling from her pockets.

Lyssa was immediately thankful that they were no longer talking about Tauron, Jukin, or the U-POL. But now she began to worry about herself as the doctor poked and prodded at Vel's boils.

"Now, Vellexore—"

"Vel," he quickly corrected her.

"Vel, then," she said, putting a magnifier over her glasses so she could see his boils closer. "I see you forgot the bug spray."

"It's...uh...his first planet excavation," Lyssa said, watching with a slight gross satisfaction as the doctor laced the boils and rubbed a piece of test paper on top of it.

"And I take it he's your intern?" the doctor said, throwing her a quick look.

"Y-yeah," Lyssa said.

"And my sister," Vel said, giving her a look.

"Uh-huh," the doctor said, walking over to a drawer and pulling out a tube of medicine and a syringe. She took his arm and gently stuck him.

"What's that?" he said.

"This should reduce the swelling," the doctor said. "You should be fine in about an hour."

"I feel sleep..." he said, before his eyes rolled back into his head and he collapsed on the bed behind him.

"Are you sure that was just anti-inflammatory?" Lyssa said, peering behind her at her comatose intern.

"Dr. Peate, I presume?" the doctor said, looking at her tablet. "Lyssandra Peate?"

"Y-yes?" Lyssa said, starting to get concerned. "How did you know that?"

"His academic record says he's interning with you right now," she said, frowning. "Dr. Peate...this is fairly serious."

"Oh come on," Lyssa said, gesturing to Vel, who was drooling on the paper bed. "He's....he's totally fine."

"Not him," the doctor said, peering over her tablet. "My records here says that you are two years overdue for your vaccinations. In fact, you never even completed your baseline physical when you graduated the Academy."

"Say what now?" Lyssa said, already planning how much money she was going to have to give this doctor to not put her in front of the Academy for nearly killing her intern. "Well who cares about me?"

"The Academy does," the doctor said. "I'm surprised your supervisor hasn't said something to you sooner."

Lyssa considered the image of Pymus telling her to do anything and laughed.

"No, he's not a very good supervisor," Lyssa said. "So what...just a few shots and we're done?"

"No, I'm afraid it has to be a full physical," the doctor said. "Don't worry, he'll be asleep for at least the next hour."

Lyssa folded her arms in front of her chest. "I am not going to have a physical today."

"Well, if you don't, then I can suspend your membership to the Academy," the doctor said matter-of-factly. "Your choice."

"Son-of-a..." Lyssa swore, getting up and following the doctor into a separate room.

***

"There, that wasn't so bad, now was it?" the doctor said, walking out behind her.

Lyssa glared at her as she walked down the hall and rubbed her arm where she'd just received more shots than she'd probably ever gotten in her entire life. Not to mention the *invasive* examination she'd just had to undergo. She could count on one hand the number of people who had gotten that close to her personal business, and was not pleased to add some random doctor to the count.

She searched her pockets for her hair tie and realized she must have left it in the examination room. She turned around to walk back in but realized that the doors were self-locking.

"Dammit," she swore.

Well, she supposed it was high time she started wearing her hair different, as Razia the Bounty Hunter would never be seen again. Vel had mentioned that she looked-

"Vel, shit," she said, spinning around. She couldn't remember which room she had left Vel in—he was bound to be waking up soon. Stopping, she tried to retrace her steps from where she had left him.

She rounded a corner, and bumped into someone.

"We keep bumping into each other..."

It was the lieutenant again—but this time he had two other officers with him. Still irritated from her examination, she angrily brushed by them, in no mood to talk to anyone right now, least of all these stupid Special Forces idiots.

"Out of my way."

"Hey, you'd better watch yourself," the one on the left said, grabbing her arm as she passed them by. "You are speaking to three members of the U-POL's Elite Special Forces."

"Oh, you mean the twenty members who haven't gotten an inflated paycheck yet?" Lyssa snapped back. "Save yourself the embarrassment and just resign already. They always do."

The lieutenant narrowed his eyes at her, "You seem to know an awful lot about police business, ma'am."

"Oh, indeed I do," she grumbled, pushing past them. She didn't get very far, because one of them grabbed her arm again.

"I'm going to need to see some identification," he said, trying his very best to give her a stern look.

She tried not to laugh at him. "You want to see some damned identification, here's my damned identification."

With that she slapped her C-card down in his hand.

The lieutenant scanned her identification and the smiled, curiously. "That's interesting."

"Yeah, I am," she rolled her eyes. The Peate name was fairly uncommon; they probably knew that she was related to their "fearless" leader. "He's a real asshole, though, if you ask me."

"Well, Razia, this is an interesting turn of events," the lieutenant said, looking up at her.

"Yeah, I don't…" She trailed off, looking up him sharply. "What did you just call me?"

She watched in horror as the three U-POL officers raised their guns to point directly at her.

"You are under arrest for engagement in piracy," the lieutenant smiled as his compatriots raised their guns at her. "Razia."

Lyssa gaped at him for a moment unlit she saw which C-card she had given them and her heart sunk into her stomach.

To these three Special Forces officers, she was Razia, the six hundred and fifth most wanted pirate in the galaxy.

And, based on the three guns pointed directly at her head, it appeared Dissident had finally come through on his threat to kick her out of the web.

CHAPTER SEVEN

"Shit."

"Don't move a muscle," the one on the right said, holding his gun steady.

"So, about that," Razia laughed nervously. "You know, I am just so low in the bounty rankings…"

"Says here that you're an associate of Tauron Ball," the lieutenant said. "That's interesting because I thought we killed all his associates."

Razia's eyes flashed, but she wasn't distracted from trying to figure out how in Leveman's Vortex she was going to get out of this one. The hall was a long and narrow, and they'd have to really be bad marksmen to miss her. Judging on how little they actually did, she was sure they spent a lot of time at the firing range.

"Now, put your hands on your head and drop your weapons!" the second officer said, with much less conviction than the lieutenant.

"Seriously," Razia said, backing up slightly. "I can get you someone better—Sage Teon!"

"No." The lieutenant smiled. "I think you'll do just fine. It's been a while since we've hanged a pirate."

Her eyes widened slightly. "Really?! I'm like…six hundred."

"Captain Peate says that if we're to come across any pirate, no matter how small, we're to bring him in and he's to die for his crimes." The young officer on the left said, his eyes narrowing at her.

She resisted the urge to roll her eyes. That sounded like something Jukin would say.

"Well, then, why don't you go find yourself a 'him' to bring in, and leave me be..." she smiled. "I mean, nobody actually even likes—"

"Put your hands on your head," the lieutenant said, his eyes narrowing.

Just then, the door opened and a lethargic-looking Vel came stumbling out of a room. His boils had shrunken to red marks all over, but his eyes were hooded with the after-effects of the medicine.

"Who is this?" One of the U-POL officers turned their gun towards Vel.

"That's nobody," Razia stammered. "I mean, I don't even know who he is."

"I'm Vel!" he slurred. "Vel Peate!"

"Peate?" They said, looking at each other. "Are you Jukin's brother?"

"Oh Jukin!" Vel said, eyes spinning. "Yes, Jukin Peate is my....why are you pointing a gun at my s—"

Razia, with nothing else to do, grabbed Vel before he goaded the stupid U-POL officer into shooting him—or worse.

"UNHAND HIM!" They barked, turning their guns back to her.

"Say what now?" she blinked, looking at them.

"I SAID, UNHAND HIM!"

She looked down at Vel, who was starting to sober up, and the U-POL Officers, who obviously had no idea what was really going on.

To them, a dangerous pirate had just taken a hold of the brother of Jukin Peate.

She smiled at her good fortune.

"Don't move another muscle, or the kid gets it," she growled, suddenly wrapping her arm around his neck.

"L-gack!" he squawked.

"Shut up," she muttered.

"Unhand him by order of the Universal Police Special Forces!" the lieutenant demanded, his eyes narrowing and his hand tightening around the hilt of his gun.

"How about you go tell your boss that this is payback for what he did to Tauron," Razia snapped back, formulating an escape plan. If she could just get close enough to them—they wouldn't dare try to shoot her with Vel right here. "Jukin never should have messed with pirates, and now his brother's going to pay for it."

"If you harm one hair on his head, Jukin'll have your head on a platter," the lieutenant threatened.

She stepped towards them, Vel still stuck in a headlock, as if to make a break through them. Her face remained cool and calm, and very calculating, and she took another step. The U-POL officers jumped a bit, but held their guns steady. Just one more step, and she would be close enough.

Without warning, she thrust Vel to the side of her, his body smacking against the wall with a loud sound. In the brief moment that the U-POL officers were distracted, she shot out her foot to one in the stomach and let her elbow fly into the face of the other. Then she reared her fist back and punched the lieutenant in the chin, sending him backwards.

The three officers incapacitated, she turned to peel Vel off the wall and took off sprinting down the hall.

"Dr. Peate!!" Vel panted. "What is going on!?"

"Shut up and run!" she barked back.

They came to a fork in the hallway and went down the left side, and then came to another, taking another left. After a third fork, she spotted an opening door ahead. A patient was walking out with his arm in a cast, and just before the door closed behind him, Lyssa threw Vel in and jumped in after him, the door closing and locking behind them

"Dr. Peate!" Vel gasped, clutching at his chest. "What was that? Why are we running?"

"Keep quiet," she snapped, pulling her ear away from the door. "We have to stay in here for a while."

"What is going on?" Vel repeated. "Why are you wanted by the U-POL officers?"

"I'll explain later," she mumbled, searching the room for something—anything to hide her appearance. She found a makeshift hair band and was able to tie her hair up behind her head. She pulled her glasses on and adjusted them in the reflection of a shiny cabinet.

"Dr. Peate, are you listening to me?"

"Not really, no," she said, stepping back and looking around the room for something that could get them out of here. She knew that the only safe place right now was back at her ship, but people would start asking questions if Vel walked casually down the hall after he was supposedly just kidnapped.

She walked around the room, looking at each piece of equipment and sighing when it didn't seem to be able to work for her. She needed something large and hollow, or something to-

Her ears picked up on the sound of squeaking wheels outside.

She walked over to the door, opening it slightly and seeing an orderly wheeling a large garbage cart.

Five minutes later, she was wheeling said garbage cart and knocked-out orderly inside the room.

"DR. PEATE!" Vel screamed. "What in the name of all that is good in this universe are you doing?"

"Finding us a way out of here," she smiled, turning over the cart and dumping out all of the garbage. "Now get in."

"G...get in?" Vel blinked, looking at the garbage bin. "Do you know what kind of diseases and—"

"I don't care. Get in," she snapped.

"No," he said, looking up at her.

She rolled her eyes. Of all the times for him to lose his submissive nature. "Please."

"Not until you tell me why you attacked those three U-POL officers,"

Vel replied.

"If I tell you, will you promise to just get in here?" she begged, worrying about the number of minutes going by.

"Yes," he said. "You have my word."

She took a deep breath and sighed. "The U-POL are after me because I happen to spend most of my time as Razia, a bounty hunter, and I am technically wanted for engagement in piracy."

That was obviously not the answer Vel was expecting.

"*WHAT?*" he said, after processing a few moments.

"There, I told you, now get inside," she demanded, pointing at the garbage cart.

"I most certainly—"

"We had a deal," she said. "Now either you come with me now, or I will make you come with me. And believe me, if I have to make you, you will end up with a headache."

***

"I can't breathe!" Vel hissed from inside the cart. "It stinks in here."

"You'd better shut up before I roll you into a wall," Lyssa hissed back. "Or onto a ship and leave you there."

As Lyssa wove through the hallways, she passed a U-POL officer, and then another, and then several others. The more time that passed, the more they seemed to pass her. She wasn't really concerned that they would recognize her; they were too busy looking for her to notice her. Still, she took as many back hallways as she could to avoid prying eyes.

They arrived at the docks without incident, and although there were U-POL officers milling about, they lacked the gold markings of the special officers, and therefore seemed uninterested in actually looking for anyone. She could see her ship in the distance, she was home free-

"Dr. Peate!"

She closed her eyes and groaned. Almost home free.

"Oh dear, Doctor!" Pymus was rushing over to her, trying to look worried. "I have just heard about your brother! The poor child..."

"Yes, terrible," she shrugged offhandedly, inching closer to her ship.

"What a terrible, brutish thing for this pirate to do," Pymus tutted. "To think, a pirate would be so brash as to kidnap the brother of Jukin Peate! What was he thinking?"

His words triggered a memory in the back of her mind, and she felt irrationally angry.

"Her," Lyssa snapped, automatically.

"Excuse me?" Pymus did a double take.

"My brother was kidnapped by Razia, a very well-known bounty hunter," Lyssa said, smiling proudly.

"I see," Pymus nodded. "And you would know this because…?"

Lyssa backtracked a bit and looked down at the machine at her hands. "I was there, of course."

"Indeed?" Pymus sighed. "I suppose that we'll have to wait and see if they catch her."

"Don't be ridiculous," Lyssa snapped, inching closer. "She's not going to be caught anytime soon. I'm just going to pay whatever ransom she wants."

"So you're going to reward this delinquent behavior?" Pymus asked, raising his eyebrow at her.

Lyssa opened her ship and pushed the cart over to it. "You sound like Jukin, Pymus."

And with that, she pushed the cart onto the ship.

***

Lyssa sat on her chair, still in shock. They were getting as far away from the Academy and the gathering swarm of U-POL officers as they could. She was relieved that they even let her off the station—if she had waited half an hour more, she might have been stopped and her ship searched.

Her head hurting, she yanked off her glasses and pulled down her hair to rub her scalp. Her heart was still beating out of her chest from the stress and adrenaline. She kept trying to tell herself that it was over now, she could calm down.

"So a pirate?" Vel broke the silence from behind her. He sounded disgusted.

"You should probably let Mother know that you're okay," Lyssa replied, not turning around.

"Should I also let her know that her daughter is a wanted criminal?" Vel spat.

"Well I'd say it wouldn't necessarily surprise her," Lyssa joked, turning around with a half-hearted smile. "She probably thinks as much already."

Vel was not amused. "So, what? Are you trying to do whatever you can to piss off the family? Jukin becomes a police officer, you decide to become a pirate?"

Lyssa was too shocked to hear him curse to respond.

"And so, when," Vel continued, angrily. "When did you have time to become a pirate unless..."

She raised her eyebrows at him as he began to realize.

"God in Leveman's Vortex, you have been *lying* about working with Father!" Vel said, sounding like this revelation was much more traumatic than the first.

"Duh," Lyssa sighed. "I thought that was fairly obvious."

"Were you....were you.... when you left me on the planet for three days?!" Vel gaped at her.

"Okay," Lyssa said, leaning forward a little bit. "Look, I'm really sorry about that, but there was this thing—"

"I COULD HAVE DIED!" Vel screamed at her.

"You didn't seem to care if I was researching Leveman's Vortex," Lyssa accused, sitting back again.

"Continuing Father's work is important to-," Vel snapped.

"To whom?" Lyssa laughed. "Pymus?"

"Oh screw Pymus!" Vel said. "That slimy son of a bitch. He's always hanging around the Manor like he's a damn uncle or something. Everybody hates him there."

Again, Lyssa was momentarily shocked by the language. "So why are you working with him?"

"That's my business," Vel smirked, throwing her a superior look.

"Well look at you, growing a damn spine," Lyssa responded.

They continued to stare daggers at each other for a moment when the silence of the room was broken by a video call coming in.

"Who's Dissident?" Vel said, able to see the video screen from his perch behind her.

Lyssa's heart sunk into her chest. Some part of her wanted to ignore the call and avoid the embarrassment of formally being kicked out of Dissident's web. Especially in front of Vel, who was still glaring at her.

"You wouldn't want to give me some privacy with taking this call, would you?" she asked, hopefully.

"Nope," Vel responded.

She sighed and spun around, "Just do me a favor and don't say anything, okay?"

Taking a deep breath, she answered the call.

"Dissident, I can explain—"

"THERE YOU ARE!" Dissident chirped. His elation was sickening.

"Look, I'm sorry, you gave me an old man to go after, you couldn't possibly—"

"What are you talking about?" Dissident said cheerily. "You kidnapped Jukin Peate's brother, you sneaky rascal!"

The words took a moment to sink in as she stared at him. "Wait…what?"

"I couldn't believe it." Dissident shook his head. "I just couldn't believe anyone had the gall to just pluck him out of the station—a station full of scientists and all that—and take on three police officers at the same time? How in Leveman's Vortex did you think of it?"

Razia blinked, mouth open.

"I mean, sure Tauron did some crazy things in his day, but you...!" Dissident shook his head. "Contestant even said he couldn't believe it. None of his pirates have ever had the stones to stand up to Jukin Peate!"

"Wha...?" Razia said, finally able to make sounds.

She opened up the pirate news and was shocked to see her picture plastered over the intraweb:

	30) (No last name listed), Razia Wanted in connection with kidnapping of Vellexore Peate
	30) (No last name listed), Razia Wanted in connection with aggravated assault to U-POL officers
	30) (No last name listed), Razia Wanted for resisting arrest by U-POL Special Forces. Considered armed and dangerous.

Her heart skipped a beat when she saw the number next to her name. She quickly skimmed her fingers over to the bounty roster and typed in her name.

	30) (No last name listed), Razia
Wanted For	Engagement in piracy, bounty hunting, kidnapping, aggravated assault, resisting arrest
Reward	5,000,500C
Known Alias	None
Known Accomplices	Tauron Ball, Sage Teon
Pirate Web affiliation	None

"God in Leveman's Vortex," she whispered.

"I mean to tell you," Dissident said, shaking his head. "I don't know what you were thinking, but I just can't believe it. You know, not since Sage Teon has a bounty shot up that fast. I was just telling Contestant that none of his pirates are—"

"That's funny," Razia said, noticing the pirate web entry. "Because it actually doesn't look like I'm in your web anymore."

Dissident's face shifted. "Oh…well…I…"

Razia tried to swallow the smile that was growing on her face and look serious. "Looks like I'm a free agent, so to speak, doesn't it?"

"No, well, I mean…of course I will add you back…" Dissident began stuttering.

"As a full member of the pirate web?" Razia asking, sensing that this was a great opportunity and trying to not let her voice shake with excitement.

"Well that is just a little much for—"

"That's a shame then," Razia shrugged. "Guess I'll just have to go talk to Contestant—"

"Hold on, let's not be hasty!" Dissident said.

"Cause, you know, I've still got the kid. And I can do whatever it is that I want with him, probably get a nice ransom for him. I'm sure Contestant would be very interested in yet *another* one of your—"

"All right, all right, all right," Dissident said quickly. He looked like he had a bad taste in his mouth.

"All right what?" Razia pressed.

"All right, you are off probation," Dissident growled.

"Pleasure doing business with you, Dissident," Razia said, leaning forward and ending the call.

She watched her bounty for a moment, a smile growing on her face as it updated.

	30) (No last name listed), Razia
Wanted For	Engagement in piracy, bounty hunting, kidnapping, aggravated assault, resisting arrest
Reward	5,000,500C
Known Alias	None

Known Accomplices	Tauron Ball, Sage Teon
Pirate Web affiliation	Dissident

"Leveman's Vortex...." Razia said, putting her hands over her face. She sat back and tried to think, but her head was spinning. Who was she going to hunt first, and after that? Was she ever going back to the Academy again? What was she going to tell Harms?

"So...?"

Vel's voice brought Lyssa back to reality. One last thing to take care of.

"And how would *you* like to spend the weekend at home?" she smiled, setting a course for B-39837.

She heard nothing but an audible disgusted sigh, and the sound of footsteps walking to go pack his things.

***

Lyssa stood awkwardly in front of her ship, waiting for Vel to come down. Her hair was down and her attire was decidedly pirate, but there weren't any U-POL officers here at the Manor. She was fairly sure that Jukin had recruited the entire force to search for her and Vel—at least that's what he had been broadcasting over the news. The very last place they would ever look would be Jukin's own childhood home on B-39837.

She hated every inch of this planet—most especially the Manor, and would not cry a single tear if the entire planet somehow got sucked into Leveman's Vortex (which was ominously visible from almost every angle of the planet). By the hand of the Great Creator, or an incredibly lucky combination of gravitational forces, this one planet remained in the only solar system to exist near the gravitational phenomena.

It was discovered by her ancestor, a pious individual who believed the former was the case, and built an ornate Temple and even more ornate house to showcase his love for the Great Creator. Three hundred years and a thousand children later, it still stood in all of its glory—now home to the Peate clan. There was probably enough gold and silver in the house to feed several planets for years, and there were fancy parties and galas almost every weekend. This dock that she was standing in was built some century before to allow for the parties to grow bigger and larger every year.

The dock itself mirrored the Manor it its ostentatiousness. Marble columns and high arches dominated the architecture, with gold-plated chandeliers hanging from the apexes. Lyssa always found it a bit much for a simple ship dock, especially considering the number of times she saw repair crews to fix damage that a careless ship pilot had made.

She saw one such repair man deftly working on one of the marble columns, ignoring her completely. That was a fairly regular occurrence for the servants here—ignore and be ignored. She looked around the empty room and remembered how it would fill up to the brim on the weekends. Lyssa remembered once Sostas arrived at the wrong time, unable to find a spot to dock his ship at his own house. She had never seen him so angry.

Well, until she had ruined their last trip to Leveman's Vortex.

She caught herself reminiscing and stuck her hands in her jacket, annoyed. Luckily, the sound of wheels on the ramp of her ship drew her attention from thoughts of Plethegon.

"Well, it's been terrible," Lyssa smiled, sticking out her hand to shake his.

"So what am I supposed to do about my internship?" Vel asked.

"I don't know, call Pymus," Lyssa shrugged, uninterested in his problems. "Like I said, you have a selection of other brothers to choose from."

"He's not going to allow me to switch doctors," Vel sighed.

"Well, then," Lyssa said, a smile growing on her face. "Tell him I quit the Academy."

"And so what, you're just going to be a pirate now?" Vel asked, obviously not sharing in her enthusiasm. "What is it, Razia?"

"That's the long and short of it," she smiled. "I daresay this will be the last time you ever see Lyssa Peate—"

They were interrupted by the sound of a loud, blood-curdling scream.

Lyssa and Vel immediately looked to the source of the sound. A woman in her mid-fifties, wearing an exquisite blue silk gown, detailed with gold trim, that was pulling at her plump mid-section, clearly (and barely) bound by a tight corset. Her hair, dyed blonde, was curled in ringlets which were meticulously pinned atop her head, although in her rush to run into the room, strands began to fall. Her face, normally superiorly calm and with a near constant judgment of all she surveyed, was flushed red and her eyes were wide and searching.

Right behind her was another woman, twenty years younger, with the same concerned look on her face. She, too, was wearing a silk dress, but hers was cream, and simpler, and her hair seemed just slightly less meticulous, but put together none the less. A priest in black robes, and no less than five servants, each wearing a crisp white shirt and deep gold-colored jackets rounded out the group.

"Mother!" Vel said, his eyes lighting up. "I—"

"GET AWAY FROM MY SON!" The older woman, Eleonora Hedvig Serann Peate, formally known as Mrs. Dr. Sostas Peate, came barreling into the room, as loudly as a woman in her dress and station could do.

"Oh he's fine," Lyssa rolled her eyes. "You are so—"

"You vile, evil woman!" she said, turning her attention on Lyssa. "How dare you kidnap my son?"

Lyssa, about to fire back, was momentarily stunned. "What?"

"Mother, this is—" Vel started, before being yanked by the other woman, their eldest sister Sera.

"Vel, you stay with me," she said, protectively wrapping her arms around him. "Did she hurt you?"

"Sera, I'm fine," Vel insisted.

Lyssa continued to stare at Mrs. Dr. Sostas Peate dumbly as she was being threatened by a plump, ring-adorned finger pointed at her face.

"You think you can threaten my family in this manner?" she huffed, the smell of her expensive perfume familiar and terrifying at the same time. "Do you think my son Jukin will let you get away with this?"

Lyssa couldn't even think about responding, nor could she wipe the shocked look from her face. She looked to Vel, who was being coddled and caressed by Sera. The priest, named Helmsley, had been saying a prayer over him, turned to look straight at Lyssa, his icy blue eyes piercing into her.

"You, my dear, will have a lot to answer for when your soul finally reaches the Great Creator," he said superiorly. He hadn't changed since she had last seen him all of those years ago.

"What?" Lyssa responded, snapping out of her thoughts.

"I suppose an evil, morally corrupt woman such as yourself has never been to a Temple," Mrs. Dr. Sostas Peate continued, her voice full of anger and vitriol. Helmsley shook his head and looked down his nose at her.

"I have," Lyssa said dumbly.

"When you die," Helmsley whispered dramatically. "Your soul will travel to the place where it was created, the Great Leveman's Vortex. And it is there where you will pay the price for your miscreant, evil deeds!"

"You lying, deceitful child!"

Lyssa could see her Mother standing over her, with Sera and Helmsley. She was eleven, her father had just recently disappeared, and they had been screaming at her for the better part of an hour—first trying to get her to tell them where he was, and then dissolving into acerbic verbal lashes when she kept insisting she had no idea.

"You are rotten to the core, and always have been!"

She knew they were right; deep down, she knew. There was to be no escaping her fate now—she had indisputable evidence from the Great Creator himself. Their words in her ear were no comparison to the terrible fear she kept locked in her mind. The fear of falling into that damned river of fire, the ground giving way beneath her, and no one there to catch her.

Nobody was ever going to catch her again.

Her evil soul was repulsive—first her father left her, then her mother and her siblings abandoned her. Even when she had a gun against her head, begging them to save her from the terrifying pirate who had her hostage.

"Perhaps your father thinks you are worth saving."

She looked up, eyes wide and breath caught in her throat, an imaginary barrel of a gun to her head. But she wasn't on that ship, she was standing completely alone in the silent dock, accompanied only by the quiet sounds of the servant patching the walls, and a river of fire coursing in the back of her mind.

CHAPTER EIGHT

Razia stared at her reflection in the window of the drab shuttle, trying to force a smile on her face.

She was supposed to be happy, right?

She was the thirtieth most wanted pirate in the universe, she was off probation, and she was able to hunt any pirate that she pleased.

Not to mention she now had plenty of money to burn. She had made a pit stop at the Academy—she did, after all, have a fully excavated planet to sell. And, thanks in part to the shocking kidnapping of Vel Peate, she sold the planet for one hundred and fifty thousand credits to a prospector who was eager to learn the sordid details of what had really occurred.

That money was needed, as Razia had yet to be officially added to whatever list the parking managers on D-882 used to provide prime parking to the top pirates, and she was forced to park in the Outlands again. For some reason, she couldn't bring herself to even be the smallest bit annoyed by the hour and a half ride either.

She looked at her reflection in the shuttle window again and heard her mother's voice in her head.

"God in Leveman's Vortex," she whispered, looking at the ceiling of the shuttle. She had been dwelling constantly, her mind replaying over and over again. She had tried so hard to bury all of those memories, but spending just a few minutes there was enough to dredge it all back up.

She let out a loud sigh in the empty shuttle, trying to clear her head. Lyssa Peate was officially done—a ghost. From here on out she was going to be Razia, the best bounty hunter in the universe.

She forced herself to smile, hoping that the happiness would follow. The shuttle pulled into the station and she popped up, adjusting her jacket and holding her head up high as she stepped into the dim light.

***

"Well, I guess you didn't need Evet Delmur after all," Harms smiled, looking up at her as she slid into his booth.

"I still found him anyways," Razia smiled, before giving him a knowing look. "Did you know that he was still in contact with Dissident?"

"I..." Harms smiled slightly nervously. "I might have."

"Yet you still let me go after him," Razia shook her head.

"Oh, come on," Harms said, lightly batting her shoulder across the table. "You weaseled your way back into the web anyways."

"That I did," she grinned. "Figured Jukin had it coming, you know?"

"How did you break into that place undetected?" Harms asked. "That place is swarming with U-POL officers and security and—"

Razia shrugged, figuring that vagueness was better than trying to make up some ridiculous story.

"Be careful, or people will think you're a good pirate too," Harms winked. "So, Miss 'Off Probation'—which lucky gentlemen gets the honor of being your first bounty capture?"

Razia stared at him, realizing that she hadn't even looked at the pirate intraweb, let alone picked which pirate she was going to hunt first. She couldn't very well tell him that she had been moping—what did Razia have to mope about?

"Oh, well," she said, trying to buy herself some time. She opened the pirate intranet news, scrolling down the list of pirate activity to look for a name—any name that she could give Harms.

4) Stenson, Eli

Wanted in connection with hijacking of transport. Estimated cost of stolen materials: 4,100,000C

Stenson was part of Dissident's web—she couldn't capture him.

17) Teon, Sage

Wanted in connection with break in at the UBU Antiquities Museum. Estimated cost of stolen artifacts: 500,000C

She tried not to smile—it would be nice to turn in Sage and get him back for all the grief he gave her. But, unfortunately, since he was in the same web, he was off limits.

	25) Jamus, Dal
	Wanted in connection with aggravated assault on U-POL Special Forces. Two officers seriously injured.

Without even opening his profile, she spoke the first name she could find: "Dal Jamus."

Harms did a double take, nearly spitting out his drink. "Wh-What? You can't be serious."

"Why wouldn't I be?" Razia asked. If Harms thought that Dal Jamus was too tough for her, it was definitely a good choice. She put down her mini-computer, as if she had been planning this all along.

"He's...a big bounty," Harms said, leaning forward nervously.

"I know," Razia shrugged, nonchalant. "He's like, twenty-five? So what?"

"I mean, a *big* bounty."

"I can handle it," Razia said, downing the rest of her water, and starting to get excited about this guy that Harms obviously didn't think she could. "After all, this is my very first bounty off probation. I want to make sure I make an impact."

"Just make sure he doesn't make an impact out of you..." Harms muttered.

***

Razia could barely wait to begin searching for Jamus. Something about the way Harms was trying—pleading with her to change her mind, told her that once she brought this guy in, she would be flying high.

Unfortunately, she didn't have to search very hard to find literally everything there was to know about him.

	25) Jamus, Dal
Wanted For	Engagement in piracy, aggravated assault
Reward	7,505,079C
Known Alias	None

Known Accomplices	None
Pirate Web affiliation	Insurgent

He had just one bank account, which he also used to pay his rent and buy his morning coffee around the corner. She tried to find any information on the charge that he beat up a police officer, but there was no record of it.

She thought about calling Harms, but he didn't seem too happy with her when she left, so she thought better of it.

Turning back to his bank statements, she wondered why he hadn't been caught yet. New pirates were normally this sloppy—they all didn't realize the importance of having multiple aliases or trying to hide from bounty hunters. But someone this high for this long was usually a little more careful than this—or had already paid the price.

Oh well, she thought. Perhaps she was just the only one paying attention.

He frequented a bar near his place nearly every day, so that was the first place she decided to check. She walked through the door and was bathed in darkness. The smell of old alcohol and dirt permeated around her, and as her eyes adjusted to the dark bar she took stock of the place. The bar itself was against the wall, with dusty bottles lining the back, some barstools (bolted down) in front, and a crusty barkeep reading a paper in the corner.

"You lookin' for a job?" he asked her.

"Not particularly," Razia replied, continuing to look around. There were a few tables lining the wall, and a few old men scattered around. But no sign of Jamus.

She checked her mini-computer again; he hit this place every day, and he hadn't been here yet. So it was only a matter of time.

She sat down at one of the tables to wait. In the meantime, she pulled up her news to see what the rest of the pirate community was doing.

	2) Relleck, Royden
	Wanted in connection with piracy (bounty hunting)

	15) Conrad, Conboy Captured by Royden Relleck
	18) Journot, Santos Wanted in connection with piracy (bounty hunting)
	9) Bullock, Jeam Captured by Santos Journot

Santos Journot had jumped ten slots in about two weeks, she noted curiously, but there still wasn't a picture of him. He had nabbed two of the top ten pirates—

She felt a presence behind her.

Acting normally, she pretended to scroll through her mini-computer, mentally readying herself to beat the living crap out of whoever dared to cross her now.

The presence got closer and she could feel a hand reaching for her.

Without a sound, she stood up, grabbed the hand and flipped the man over her shoulder, splaying him out on the floor next to her.

"... that was uncalled for," Sage said, eyes shut, lying on the floor.

"Shouldn't sneak up on people," she grumbled, sitting back down and pulling out her computer.

"Wasn't trying to," he grunted, sitting up slowly and dusting himself off. "You're off in la-la land."

"What do you want?" she snapped, not looking up at him as he sat down next to her.

"Thought I would pop in for a drink," Sage said, motioning to the barkeep. "Water please."

"Really?" Razia narrowed her eyes at him. "Pretty odd coincidence that you happen to go to the same, out-of-the-way bar that I did. Because, you know, there are a billion places to get water—and you stopped here—"

"Pretty genius move, kidnapping your own brother," Sage said quietly, but loud enough to cause Razia to quickly forget her suspicion and look around nervously.

"Shut up!" she hissed.

"Oh relax," Sage smirked, always enjoying when she got her hackles up. "What happened anyways? I thought you hated your family."

"I do," she mumbled. "It's....a long story. Bottom line is that he was at the wrong place at the wrong time."

"Sounds to me like he was at the right place," Sage said. "I mean, you did get Dissident off your back."

"Yeah, I did," Razia grinned.

"See?" Sage nudged her. "I knew you'd figure it out eventually."

"No thanks to you," Razia said, pulling out her mini-computer to continue ignoring him.

"Oh please," Sage said, tossing her a dirty look. "Who's the one who helped you figure out how to find Evet Delmur?"

Razia glared at him, but didn't respond.

Sage continued, amused that he was finally able to shut her up. "You know, for a bounty hunter, you're pretty blind sometimes. I mean, how do you know Dal Jamus hasn't already been here and left since you've been staring at that stupid thing of yours."

She looked down at her mini-computer and then back up to him. "You know, I'm not going to take criticism from you. Besides, I know he hasn't come in because—"

She stopped, her eyes narrowing.

"How did you know I was going after Dal Jamus?" she said.

Sage was momentarily saved by a loud slam. The door was wide open, and blinding light was streaming in around a figure that took up nearly the entire doorway. The figure walked inside, and grew about six more inches as he stood tall. The door shut behind him and he came into focus.

He was, without a doubt, the biggest, burliest men Razia had ever seen. He was so tall that his head had to be scraping the ceiling. Not only that, but he had muscles so thick that he looked like he could break Razia in half with his fingers. He had a deep, brooding expression, and a thick, grizzled black beard. Three people sitting at the bar ran away when he looked in their direction so he took up the three barstools that they vacated. He banged his thick hand on the table and the bartender shakily handed him a drink the size of Razia's head, which he promptly downed in one gulp.

She started to understand why he'd been in the pirate web for so long.

"Well, Lyss, go get your bounty," Sage joked, giving her a nervous look.

Razia swallowed and tried to hide her apprehension. Sure, he was big, and muscular, and could probably knock her over with his breath, but that probably meant he was slow.

"Are you seriously considering this?" Sage said, watching the wheels turn in her head, and growing more concerned.

"Why else do you think I'm here?" she snapped.

"Lyss, I'm saying this as a friend," he said quietly. "You really should reconsider this."

"Oh, that is so typical 'you'," she snapped. "I got this. And quit calling me Lyssa—"

"OI BARMAID," Dal Jamus' voice boomed across the entire room.

Razia looked around for the barmaid, but she was the only girl in the room. It was then she realized that Jamus' beady black eyes were fixated on her, and he had a lascivious smile curled under his beard.

"Oh for crying out...I am not a barmaid!" she barked over to Jamus.

"Well then," the he grumbled, finishing his second drink. "Come on over here and I'll make you one."

Sage couldn't help but snort, Razia rolled her eyes in disgust.

Jamus didn't like that answer, so he stood up and in two steps was standing in front of their table.

Razia craned her neck slowly upwards until she reached his eyes, two black orbs staring down at her mercilessly.

"Hi."

"You do what you're told!" He swung his huge hand back, attempting to strike her, but his heavy hand was too slow for Razia. She ducked before it hit her, instead catching Sage flat on the face, sending him flying.

Razia scrambled out of the way, and climbed up onto the bar so that she was eye level with him. The rest of the patrons were quite tuned into what was going on, as it wasn't every day a woman took on someone the size of Dal Jamus.

Or anyone, for that matter.

He laughed, his voice echoing. "What? Are you some sort of bounty hunter?"

"Yeah, actually I am," she said proudly. He was taken completely unawares when Razia jumped off the bar to land a foot square in his gut. He staggered back a few feet, stumbling backwards until he fell into the table with a loud crash.

Razia jumped down to the floor, watching him stumble for a few moments, catching his breath, before stopping and growling at her.

"You....!" He roared forwards, but she ducked and reached back to throw a punch of her own into his stomach—the highest she could reach.

He started laughing.

"Mmm!" She hissed, grabbing her knuckles, which were throbbing.

Still laughing, he grabbed her by her legs, pulling her upside down. She dangled helplessly, blood rushing to her head, one foot caught in his hand and the other flailing.

"HEY! PUT HER DOWN!"

93

For a split second, Razia thought she had been knocked for a loop. Because that almost sounded like that annoying intern she had left at the Manor last week.

But that was impossible. Because she had left him at the Manor last week.

What a crazy thought, that Vel Peate would be at a pirate bar on D-882. Or that he could possibly have found her on this planet. Or that he would be here, in any capacity, and not out with Dorst or one of her other brothers on a perfectly normal planet excavation.

Because that would be impossible.

Against all of her smarter instincts, she swiveled her head, and her eyes nearly flew out of her head.

There was Vel.

And he was, in fact, standing in a pirate bar.

Eyes wide, standing in front of a man five times his size, his tiny little fists up and ready for a fight.

"What is this?" Jamus laughed, swinging Razia a little bit. "Is this your little boyfriend here to save you?"

Before Vel could respond, Razia's heel connected with Jamus' inside elbow and his arm crumple, dropping her. She landed on her hands, rolling forward, to face Vel, who looked oddly impressed with her skills.

"WHAT IN LEVEMAN'S VORTEX ARE YOU DOING HERE?!" she screamed at him.

"LOOK OUT!" Vel screamed, grabbing Razia and ducking down as a giant fist came swinging just above their heads.

"Stay out of the way," Razia growled, shoving Vel out of the line of sight. She quickly scanned the room, looking for anything that could help her. Jamus came lunging for her again, but he was slow, thanks to his gigantic size. Razia easily side stepped him, as he landed on a table.

She caught sight of a couple thick black wires hanging from the exposed rafters and got an idea.

He came thundering towards her again, and she ducked between his legs, climbing up on one of the last unbroken tables. She tested them for a second, making sure they wouldn't come out, and waited, a smirk on her face.

When he turned to come for her again, she jumped and grabbed hold of the wires, swinging back and slamming her two feet into his face with all of her might.

Her feet imprinted on his face as he went falling backwards, hitting his head on the hard bar, then on one of the bar stools before finally landing on the ground and laying still. Razia jumped down from the wires on the ceiling and stood on the table, breathing hard, waiting for him to get up. He didn't move, so she hopped to the floor, walking over to him to kick him.

Letting out a deep breath, she relished in what had just happened.

If that didn't make a statement...

"ARE YOU OUT OF YOUR MIND?" Vel screamed, running up to her. "HE COULD HAVE KILLED YOU!"

"And what in Leveman's Vortex are you doing here?!" Razia said, turning on him with her meanest, most angriest face she could muster. "AND HOW?!"

Vel looked like he was trying to summon all the brave he could muster as he stood in front of her. "I'm here to continue my internship."

"W...what?" Razia gaped, as if he was speaking in tongues.

"My internship," Vel repeated. "We still have five months left."

"I'm sorry, did you not remember when I told you that I was quitting?" she hissed in a low whisper.

"Can you get on with it then?" Vel replied, knowingly. "Because last time I checked, Lyssandra Peate was still on the roster at the System and Planetary Science Academy."

"SHUT UP!" Razia screamed, a brief moment of terror shooting through her. They were, after all, still in a pirate bar.

Luckily, thanks to the scuffle that had just occurred, the bar was completely empty.

"And until she's off, Pymus isn't letting me switch doctors," Vel finished, a smirk on his annoying little face.

"Fine," she growled, pulling out her mini-computer. "I'm calling him right now."

"Won't do you any good unless you're planning on coming clean," Vel stated, folding his arms over his chest. "And, based on what I saw, I don't think you really want to do that."

"Oh yeah?" Razia nodded at him. "And why is that?"

"You may not care if the family knows you're Lyssa Peate, but do you really want all of these pirates knowing that you're really Jukin Peate's sister?" Vel smiled. "Especially after you just got back into the pirate web?"

Razia's mouth dropped open before she could stop it.

"Yeah, I thought so," Vel smiled, knowing that he had her. "So unless you want everyone knowing not only that fact, and also that you didn't really kidnap me, you are going to let me stay here for the duration of my internship."

All she could do is stare at him, unable to believe that he had actually outsmarted her.

"What do you think this is going to be?" Razia sputtered, after a few moments. "I'm not excavating any planets."

"At this point, I honestly don't care what you do," Vel rolled his eyes.

95

"But I am not failing this course. And in order for me to not fail, I have to spend the next six months with you."

"How in Leveman's Vortex did you even find me?!" Razia screamed in frustration.

"So you can thank me for that one actually," Sage interrupted from the ground where he had been laying ever since Jamus sent him there. Blood was dripping from his nose as he poked at the bridge. "I'm fine, by the way. Thanks for asking."

"What do you mean?" Razia asked, ignoring his injury completely.

"I saw this kid yesterday," Sage sniffed, getting to his feet slowly and cupping his nose. "Wandering around a transport station near S-864. Asking if anyone knew how to get to where the pirates hang out."

Razia looked angrily to Vel, who cleared his throat sheepishly.

"Obviously, I knew who he was," Sage smiled. "So I thought I'd bring him here to you."

"Why didn't you bring him back to the Academy?" Razia growled. "I know you know where that is."

"Eh," Sage shrugged before grinning again, slyly. "I actually thought it would be funny to see the look on your face. And let me tell you, Lyss, you did not disappoint."

"You are an unbelievable asshole," Razia growled.

"So," Sage said, changing the subject happily. "We've been chatting for, what...five minutes? How much longer do you think our friend here is going to stay asleep?"

At that very second, Jamus snorted in his sleep, causing Razia to jump about ten feet.

Sage laughed, amused at her reaction and desperate attempts to hide it. "Which begs the question of how in Leveman's Vortex are you going to drag this giant guy to the bounty office?"

Razia stared at him, suddenly realizing that she had literally no plan for bringing him to the bounty office.

"Didn't quite think this one through, did you?" Sage chuckled, smugly. "Maybe next time you should actually think about the bounty you're going to hunt before you just pick it."

"Shut up," Razia said, turning to this newest problem.

"Have fun with that..." Sage said, patting her on the back. "I'm off to go see a doctor and make sure my nose isn't broken."

Annoyed, Razia watched as he sauntered out the door.

She looked over to Vel, who promptly walked over to the only table and chair in the room that wasn't broken. "Unless you're taking me to excavate a planet, I'm sure I don't care."

Which left Razia, all one hundred and twenty pounds of her, trying to figure out how to move twenty tons of dead weight halfway across the city to the bounty office.

***

An hour and a half later, a sweaty and exhausted Razia and a knocked out, snoring, drooling Dal Jamus sprawled out on the floating canvas (which was barely a few inches off the ground from his weight) were nearly to the bounty office. Vel was simply walking beside her, his focus on the book he was reading and nothing else, and occasionally throwing a smart remark about how much trouble she appeared to be having.

"For someone who seems to do this a lot, you appear to be woefully unprepared," Vel observed, looking up at giant U-POL building looming over them. "So what's that building?"

"U-POL office," Razia huffed. "And the....reason... why...we have to...go in...the back way."

"Why's that?" Vel asked.

Razia threw down the canvas ropes, her breath heavy. "Because, *idiot*, they already thought I kidnapped you once, and I'd rather not try to run from the whole group of them when I'm trying to haul in a five hundred pound bounty."

Vel smirked. "Fair point."

"Now," Razia said, tossing her hair behind her back. "If you see any of those idiots, just do me a favor and hide, okay?"

"Where are you going?" Vel asked.

"Inside," Razia said plainly, walking through the small bounty office door. And, as luck would have it, there was only one person at the window.

She closed her eyes, feeling like maybe, just maybe, her luck was turning around, and she was maybe finally going to see the light at the end of the tunnel. She walked outside and, giving Vel a smart look, turned to pull her bounty into the office.

And then he got stuck.

Razia tugged at him, nervously. But he was good and wedged in there.

"Hey lady, I go on break in five minutes!" the attendant called, amused.

"Just, give me a second," Razia pleaded, turning to pull Jamus will all of her might.

"Four and a half minutes..."

She threw him a dirty look and jumped over Jamus, trying to shove him in from the outside.

"Three minutes."

"You'd better hurry up," Vel commented from a bench outside of the bounty office. "Sounds like he's about to close."

"GET SUCKED!" she screamed, coming back into the office and

97

pulling directly on the canvas. Digging her heels in, she pulled, and pulled, and pulled, and pulled.

"Two minutes."

"GAH!" she screamed, pulling as hard as she could. With a loud POP, Jamus came flying into the bounty office on the gurney, stopping about halfway across the room. Razia scrambled to her feet, and pulled him the rest of the way.

"There," Razia smiled, satisfied. "Turning in Dal Jamus."

"Uh huh," he said, typing into his computer. Razia watched him furrow his brow, type in something else, then rub his chin thoughtfully

"What?" Razia asked, wiping the sweat off of her brow.

"Looks like most of this bounty was a fake," he said, chewing on the cigarette and not looking at her.

"What do you mean, fake?" Razia blinked, about to lose it.

"Somebody put up some money on him to put him in the top twenty temporarily," he said. "The number's there, but the money ain't gonna be paid."

"The runners wouldn't approve that!" Razia cried.

"Honey, who do you think put the money on him?" he smiled, knowingly. "Looks like this guy beat up some U-POL officers. Leveman's, I'd give him some money for doing that."

"So how much money are you going to give me?" Razia asked, trying to remain calm.

"Looks like before the bounty," the guy said, typing a few numbers into his computer. "Five thousand?"

Razia closed her eyes, for if she looked at this man another second, she would reach through the window and ring his neck.

"Whoops," he said, sitting back. "Looks like I'm on my break. I'll finish your transaction when I get back."

And just like that, the window slammed in her face.

Stunned and exhausted, she slid down to the floor to sit, her head in her hands. Every part of her body was sore, and all she wanted to do was crawl into bed and go to sleep.

Just then, Jamus let out a loud, whiskey-filled belch and Razia saw his eyes open.

"Wh..." he muttered.

"Perfect," she sighed.

CHAPTER NINE

She winced as she moved her sore shoulders, adjusting the heat pack to the spot that had just barked at her. Subduing Jamus once was enough for anyone—twice was insane. Although he was much easier to deal handle with bound hands and feet. It was more trouble to get him back on the floating canvas as the man at the window so happily pointed out that she needed to figure out how to get him into a holding cell-

But enough about that, she thought, drinking more of her coffee to try and shake the exhaustion that had settled behind her eyes. She was still in her pajamas, wrapped in her comforter, sitting on her bed, looking at her mini-computer. Her ship was in orbit around D-882, as she wanted to stay close to the pirate mecca, but didn't want to rack up expensive parking bills. Thanks to her friend Dal Jamus and his stupid fake bounty, she still had only a few thousand credits in her Razia account. So if she ran out of money... she would be forced to excavate a planet.

And she wanted to prolong that effort as long as possible.

He cleared his throat, breaking the silence of the room, and she tossed him a dirty look. He was ignoring her as much as she was ignoring him, reading yet another book in the corner of her room that he had re-claimed. Her already small bedroom was even more cramped with his air mattress, bags of clothes and personal items, and his stacks of books.

Just his presence made her want to scream.

Giving him one final, evil look, she turned back to her mini-computer, currently displaying the pirate intraweb news.

15) Fried, Max
Wanted in connection with piracy (bounty hunting)

	14) Enoch, Costa Captured by Max Fried
	60) Sloan, Flynn Wanted in connection with transporter hijacking. Estimated cost of stolen materials: 2,500,000C

She turned to the search, and found Jamus' bounty profile:

(silhouette image)	N/A) Jamus, Dal
Wanted For	N/A
Reward	N/A
Known Alias	None
Known Accomplices	None
Pirate Web affiliation	Insurgent

He had been zeroed out—customary when a pirate had been turned in—but there was no accompanying story in the pirate news. Annoyed, she wondered if maybe nobody had written one because *she* was the one who turned him in.

She went to sip her coffee, realizing with a scowl that she had run out in her mug. She moved to get up, but the dull ache in her muscles and back was too much. She tossed another look to him.

"Go fill up my coffee."

Vel lifted his eyes from his book and laughed. "No."

"You're an intern," Razia said, pulling the covers tighter around herself. "Isn't that what interns do?"

"Yes, and you're supposed to be teaching me how to be a Deep Space Explorer," Vel smiled, his voice dripping with sarcasm. "You can have your coffee when you take me to a planet."

"Asshole," Razia grumbled, drinking the last dredges of her cup.

He didn't respond, continuing to purposely read.

She turned back to her mini-computer and refreshed her bounty again to see if any change occurred.

	30) (No last name listed), Razia
Wanted For	Engagement in piracy, bounty hunting, kidnapping, aggravated assault, resisting arrest
Reward	5,000,500C
Known Alias	None
Known Accomplices	Tauron Ball, Sage Teon
Pirate Web affiliation	Dissident

She refreshed the page two more times out of boredom and frustration, but still, no change. Annoyed, she switched to her video call application and dialed Dissident's number.

"And why are you calling me?" Dissident drawled. "I thought we understood each other that you are off probation."

"Just interested to see if you've heard," Razia shrugged, trying to sound nonchalant. "You know, how I single-handedly took down Dal Jamus."

"And?"

Razia blinked at him. "And I'd say that's pretty impressive."

"Call me when you're the top bounty in the universe. Otherwise, I don't care," Dissident grunted, before ending the call.

Razia frowned and sat back, simmering for a moment.

"Didn't sound like he was too impressed."

"Get sucked," Razia grumbled.

"For someone who doesn't believe in the Great Creator, you use that phrase a lot," Vel said, pointedly.

"I never said I didn't believe in Him," Razia retorted.

"Sure don't act like you're scared of that river of fire," Vel responded, turning the page.

Razia shifted, unconsciously wrapping her comforter tighter around herself. "Whatever. Why are you even talking to me?"

"Who is that guy anyways?" Vel said, closing the book and looking up at her. "And why do you care what he thinks?"

"He's my runner," Razia replied, stubbornly avoiding sharing any other explanation with him.

"That's helpful," Vel rolled his eyes.

"He runs the pirate web," Razia said, again withholding any other detail.

"Which is what?" Vel asked.

"Ugh," she grumbled, finally deciding that an explanation would be less trouble. "Look, pirates belong to big unions, called webs, which are run by guys like Dissident, who serve as the boss and take care of admin stuff, like paying off the U-POL so we don't get arrested."

"So how come you nearly got arrested then?" Vel asked, pointedly.

"Because," Razia glared at him for bringing up such a sensitive subject. "I was briefly kicked out. But I'm back in."

"Why were you nearly kicked out?" Vel asked, sounding more curious than spiteful.

"Dissident is an asshole," Razia grumbled.

"Is he the only guy?" Vel asked. "Runner?"

"No, there's four," Razia said. "Contestant, Insurgent, Protestant, and Dissident."

"So why don't you go work for them?" Vel replied, returning to the book.

"Because," Razia mumbled. "Nobody else will take me."

"Maybe if you weren't so mean—" Vel chuckled.

"There aren't many girl pirates," Razia snapped. "Or any…other than me."

"So why in Leveman's Vortex did you decide to become a pirate?" Vel asked, closing his book finally.

"Better than the alternative," Razia replied, sounding a lot more bitter than she meant to. She saw Vel's eyes drift up to look at her. They hadn't spoken about the incident at the Manor; neither one of them wanting to bring it up to talk about it.

"So um…what kind of pirate stuff do you do?" Vel asked, clearing his throat and trying to change the subject. "Other than kidnapping your own brother?"

"I'm a bounty hunter," Razia nodded. "Usually just hunt and capture pirates."

"I don't get it," Vel said. "You would think that the U-POL would like it when pirates are captured?"

"It's considered part of the game, so it was outlawed," Razia explained. "Most pirates do some kind of bounty hunting anyways."

"Game?" Vel asked.

"The runners pay a lot of money to the U-POL," Razia said, leaning back into her pillows. "So that whenever a pirate is captured, they only spend a night in jail. And their bounty—which may be worth millions and millions of credits—is zeroed out. Which means that pirate—who may have been the fifth most wanted pirate in the universe—is no longer even on the list."

"So?" Vel shrugged.

"So, obviously, runners want to see guys in the other webs get captured," Razia said. "And they don't want their guys to get captured. Pirates go to great lengths—multiple identities and bank accounts—just to hide from each other and not get caught."

"I still don't get why it's a game?" Vel replied.

"The runners are very proud of the pirates they have in their web," Razia said. "They want the best pirates, the best bounty hunters, and to have the highest bounties—and to not have any of their own get caught by another web's pirate. It's a constant competition between the four of them."

"And the general population suffers," Vel sighed.

"Oh come on," Razia rolled her eyes. "Pirates usually only hit transporters, or really rich people with loads of insurance. And besides, the stolen stuff usually finds its way back eventually."

"So how do you hunt a pirate?" Vel asked. "It's a big universe."

"Bank accounts, mostly," Razia said. "And the occasional tip from the pirate informant."

"How can you track someone from their bank account?" Vel said.

"Most people don't have breakfast, lunch, and dinner handed to them on a silver platter, nor are chauffeured around in a fancy shuttle," Razia smirked, tossing him a look.

"Meaning what?"

"Meaning most people buy stuff at least once a day," Razia replied. "More if they're drinking—which pirates usually are. Add in gas and ship docking fees, occasional prostitute—"

"Gross," Vel said, making a face.

"Thanks to the Universal Bank, and to the money the runners pay monthly so I can have access to any bank account I chose, I can pretty much find anyone in the known universe by their money trail," Razia said proudly.

"Anyone?" Vel said, looking up at her curiously

"Anyone," Razia replied, finally pulling the comforter off of her and slowly standing to stretch her sore muscles. She had lazed around long enough.

"Where are you going?" Vel asked, watching her walk out of the bedroom.

"What do you think? Idiot...."

***

With Jamus not amounting to very much she needed to pick her next bounty carefully. Since it was probably foolhardy to hunt the top pirates in the universe, she opted for the tenth most wanted—Zolet Obalone. She considered him a prime target—recently put into the top ten because of a major transport hijacking, he was young, and most likely stupid.

	10) Obalone, Zolet
Wanted For	Engagement in piracy, grand theft larceny,
Reward	20,451,124C
Known Alias	None
Known Accomplices	Brody Marleu
Pirate Web affiliation	Protestant

He was probably going to slip up eventually. The trick would be for her to be ready before anyone else. Unfortunately, his information was rather sparse, nothing except one accomplice, whom she had never heard of before.

"This is boring," Vel said, piercing the silence of the ship.

Razia completely lost her train of thought and sighed, annoyed. She could have sworn he was more annoying now than when they were excavating. "I'm sorry. Why don't I drop you off on a planet again?"

"Or how about you tell me what you're doing?" Vel smiled. "Maybe I can help you."

"Yeah right," Razia rolled her eyes. "I don't need help."

She turned her attention back to the screen but for the life of her could not remember where she had been so rudely interrupted.

"Does it normally take you this long to find a pirate?" Vel asked, piercing the silence again.

"God in Leveman's Vortex," Razia growled. "Please shut up. It is really hard to concentrate with you yapping."

She didn't hear a response, and so she turned back to trying to remember what it was that she had been—

Suddenly, Vel was right beside her. "So what am I looking at here?"

"You are looking at backing up before I eject you from this ship," Razia growled. Accomplices! That was what she was thinking about. She reached over to tap her dashboard when she ran into Vel, who was still standing next to her.

"Move," she snapped.

"Move what?" Vel replied, sweetly.

Razia didn't respond, but roughly elbowed him in the chest as she pushed her way to the cluster of screens showing accounts in the pirate intraweb.

"Now what are you doing?" Vel asked, unabated.

Razia sighed, annoyed. "I'm trying to see if this one accomplice this guy has listed is actually another pirate."

Vel processed slowly what she had said, but it still didn't make sense. "Of course he's a pirate—"

"I mean a well-known pirate," Razia snapped, frustrated that she had to explain her thoughts with someone else. "It's strange that he only has one accomplice."

"Why?" Vel asked.

Razia took a deep breath and glared at him. "Are you going to ask questions the whole time you're here?"

"Yes," Vel replied, smiling.

"Fantastic," she sighed. "So normally, pirates have accomplices—usually their crews, sometimes friends, sometimes other pirates who helped them pull off jobs. With a pirate like him, I have a feeling he was on a crew of a more well-known pirate to learn and gain some recognition."

"Kind of like a DSE straight out of the Academy?" Vel asked.

"No, not like..." Razia rolled her eyes. "Fine, kind of like that."

"So you think this guy is a new pirate?" Vel said. "What makes you say that?"

"Well, for starters, he's brand new to the web," Razia said. "He just got off probation about two weeks ago, and he just made his first big hijacking two days later. Then some of the top guys got caught, and he was bumped up to the top ten."

"And how do you know this?" Vel said, looking at the screen. "I don't see any of this information—"

Razia pulled up the pirate intraweb and searched for Obalone. Three news stories came up, all dated within the past month:

	12) Obalone, Zolet Wanted in connection with theft of priceless heirloom antiques from B-654. Est. cost of stolen goods 750,000C
	50) Obalone, Zolet Granted full member in Protestor pirate web
	144) Obalone, Zolet Wanted in connection with hijacking of transport. Estimated cost of stolen materials: 5,000C

Vel looked over to Razia, slightly impressed. "How did you remember all of that?"

"Just do," Razia said, closing that out and going back to her search on Obalone's lone accomplice, just to see what would come up. As usual, it was mostly drinks and food from various bars around D-882. Some transactions were recent, but they were infrequent.

"Dead end?" Vel asked.

"Not quite," Razia said, deep in thought. "You see right here," she pointed to the first few transactions. "These are a few days apart."

"So what does that mean?"

"Like I said, most people buy food at least every day," Razia replied. "So if he's not buying his food on this alias—"

"Then he's got another one?" Vel offered.

"Yup," Razia said, bringing up a new window and searching on the bar where he was drinking most recently.

"Why would a pirate not use his real name as an accomplice?" Vel asked.

"Sometimes—especially with newer pirates—established guys don't want to put their name behind an unknown. If they end up getting captured or screw up," Razia explained. "My guess is that whoever this guy is cared just enough to put a name down, just not his own."

"So how are you going to figure out who the accomplice is? And how is that going to help you find this Obalone guy?" Vel asked.

"If I can figure out who the accomplice is," she said, pulling up the bar transaction history where his accomplice last purchased a drink. "And if it's a big pirate, then by process of elimination I can figure out what the connection is between this guy and Obalone."

"What if it's not a big guy" Vel asked.

Razia paused. "Then I try something else."

"Sounds incredibly tedious and boring," Vel sighed.

"No, it's a puzzle," she smiled, her eyes scanning the bar transaction history.

Cliff Bell's		
Time of Transaction	Account	Amount
UT20014-95-95-47:50	Marleu, Brody	20C
UT20014-95-95-47:41	Beckett, Edward	20C
UT20014-95-95-47:36	Linus, Kent	20C
UT20014-95-95-47:27	Beckett, Edward	20C
UT20014-95-95-47:25	Fascinelli, Koa	20C

"Hello there Silas Brendler," she grinned, her eyes pausing on the last name on the list.

"Who?" Vel blinked.

"See that guy right there," Razia said, pointing to his name. "That's one of Silas Brendler's secret aliases."

"How do you know that?" Vel asked.

"Because I've been hunting him for a few months," Razia said, bringing her hit list, displaying all of the pirates she had discovered already.

Hit List	
Relleck	Kodah Mottola, Owen King, James Nolte, Alfie O'Hara
Burk	Zuma Davi, Daigle Cypheridge, Soren Gonzalez, Neshua Turro
Lee	Bawley King, Jesse Opal, Oliver David, Boo Jameson
Brendler	Koa Fascinelli, Ellington Nixon
Needler	Jackson Money, Jack Oscar, Aleph Miller

"You've found all of these guys?" Vel wondered, sounding impressed,

"Well, up until recently I wasn't allowed to hunt any of them," she noted, darkly. "And I'm not sure if any of these names are still secret. But I know," she pointed to Brendler's name. "That is Silas Brendler."

"Meaning that this Obalone guy was on Brendler's crew?" Vel asked

She nodded, the wheels turning in her head. "Most likely, but I still have to cross-check the names when the transactions occurred with other places Brendler's been, just to make sure they match up. Then I need to dig into Brendler's back history of transactions to a time when Obalone may have been on his crew—different name, of course—and then see if there was any time when a new name started showing up and...oh, I bet he's still using his original name as his alias—"

Vel's eyes widened as she continued rambling on, her fingers dancing over the dashboard.

***

As it turns out, Obalone, otherwise known as Kent Linus, had been on Brendler's crew for about five years before he struck out on his own. Based on his transaction history, Razia was fairly sure that he believed no one knew his secret. Except her, of course.

Obalone had paid for a few nights a hotel near the casino district on D-882, so that was where Razia headed first. She skipped a little bit, a small smile growing on her face. Obalone probably thought that he was completely safe, otherwise he wouldn't be staying at the same hotel for multiple nights. She played out in her mind how she was going to corner him—sneaking in through his balcony was absolutely out, and she wasn't too good at picking a lock-

"So what's the plan?" Vel asked, breaking the silence. "How are we gonna find this Obalone guy?"

"I thought I said to keep out of sight," Razia growled. He insisted on coming with her, and she was in no mood to convince him otherwise, eager to go find her bounty as soon as possible. She was sure she wasn't the only person looking for him; others were probably hot on his trail, too.

"I'm telling you, nobody remembers me," Vel said, sticking his hands in his pockets. "I was at that transport station for hours and nobody even gave me a second look."

"Except Sage Teon," Razia mumbled.

"Well, I happen to think he's keenly interested in everything about you," Vel smirked. "He's the one who told me to bring the whole Jukin's sister thing. Told me it would shut you up real fast."

Razia stopped in her tracks, her face contorting into an angry scowl. She muttered an obscenity under her breath and kept walking.

"How does he know so much about you?" Vel continued, amused.

"We've known each other a long time," Razia said, continuing to walk. "Besides you, he's the only other person who knows about me."

"Why's that?" Vel asked.

Razia stopped in her tracks, turning on her heel to face the other way. Obalone had just bought a drink at a bar across town.

"Because he was there when Razia was created," she said, turning to march the other way.

"Where are we going now?" Vel asked.

"Obalone's on the move," Razia said, breaking out into a slight jog.

Vel sighed and followed her, but not before spending a few moments eyeing a dark haired pirate with a buzz cut who had been staring at them since the moment they stopped.

***

"So it seems like," Vel huffed, wiping sweat off his brow. "This bounty hunting thing is a lot of walking around."

"Yep," Razia said, eyes glued to her computer.

Linus, Kent		
Time of Transaction	Location	Amount
UT20014-95-95-47:35	Foran's Grand Pub D-882	20C
UT20014-95-95-47:25	Foran's Grand Pub D-882	20C
UT20014-95-95-47:01	Light Up Lounge D-882	20C
UT20014-95-95-38:37	Light Up Lounge D-882	30C
UT20014-95-95-32:20	Bronx Bar D-882	25C

Obalone was moving around now—hopping from bar to bar to bar. She had checked at least five of them so far, but just always missed him. "If you're tired, go back to the ship."

"I run five miles a day," Vel snapped back at her.

"On a treadmill," Razia countered. "I run fifteen miles on planets regularly."

"I also run at home," Vel snapped. "It's just really hot here."

"That would be because it's a desert planet," Razia said, refreshing his transaction list again. He hadn't purchased anything in the last half hour, which meant she had no idea where he was.

"Why are we stopping?" Vel said.

"I need to think," Razia said, closing her eyes and resting her chin on her hand.

If she was Obalone, and she was being hunted, where would she go?

To a planet to lie low for a few days and make some money, the voice in her head said. Now it was starting to sound like Vel.

"Shut up, Vel," she muttered without opening her eyes.

"I didn't say anything!" he huffed.

She chewed on her thumb and furrowed her brow, struggling to quiet the different thoughts in her head. She needed to think like a pirate—without any kind of safety net.

Except he did—he was on Brendler's crew until very recently. So would he go back to Brendler if he thought he was in danger of being captured? The better question is would Brendler take him back?

She opened her eyes and looked around. Obalone was just here half an hour ago, so he couldn't have gotten far. He had no ship to speak of—and he was tipsy if not drunk at this point, having been to five different bars in the past four hours.

But obviously not drunk enough to make a purchase.

"So are we just going to stand here all day?" Vel drawled. "If so, I need to get my sunscreen—"

"I bet he created a new alias," Razia said suddenly. "Or maybe, he's had the alias all along..."

She opened the bank application and opened the transaction history of the bar in front of her.

Foran's Grand Pub		
Time of Transaction	Account	Amount
UT20014-95-95-47:35	Linus, Kent	20C
UT20014-95-95-47:30	Dumont, Thomas	20C
UT20014-95-95-47:26	Noell, Tyson	20C
UT20014-95-95-47:26	Baldwin, Vance	20C
UT20014-95-95-47:25	Linus, Kent	20C

Methodologically, she searched the transaction history of every one of the men who purchased a drink, moving swiftly to the next one when the purchases didn't pique her interest. Finally, with the fourth name, she seemed to strike gold.

Baldwin, Vance		
Time of Transaction	Location	Amount
UT20014-95-95-47:30	Foran's Grand Pub D-882	20C
UT20014-95-94-48:10	Light Up Lounge D-882	20C
UT20014-95-93-48:45	Bronx Bar D-882	30C

"Got him," Razia grinned, as the two accounts synced up almost perfectly. Either Obalone had a close friend who had been spending a lot of time with him over the past few weeks, or he had a second alias.

"Good, I was starting to melt," Vel sighed, getting up from the bench he had settled himself into.

"That little clever..." Razia chuckled, ignoring Vel's complaints as she scrolled through her new find's history. "He's been double booking hotels..."

"What?" Vel said, peering over her shoulder to look at her computer.

"He'll rent out a room, and then not show up," Razia said. "Throws people off his scent, makes them think he's not as smart as he lets on."

"Fooled you," Vel pointed out.

"Temporarily," Razia scowled, looking up as the transaction history refreshed and a new purchase—about three blocks away—showed up. "But it looks like he's just around the corner."

"So now what?" Vel said.

"Go back to the ship," Razia said, crossing the street. She rolled her eyes when Vel ignored her and kept walking beside her. She had no time to argue with him; she could see the bar where Obalone had last made his purchase. She was just about in the front door when someone stepped in front of her, blocking her entry.

"Well, what do we have here?" Relleck smiled. He was standing in the middle of the doorway, hands in his pockets, looking quite pleased with himself.

"Out of my way, Relleck, I'm busy," she scowled, trying to step around him.

"Can't be that busy," Relleck smiled, moving to block her. He nodded to Vel, who was looking at him curiously. "Who's your friend?"

"Nobody," Razia snapped, stepping back and giving him a look. "Move."

"Ooh," Relleck laughed. "So is this your new boyfriend or something? You'd better be careful, I bet Teon is the jealous type. Although I would love to see the two of them in a fight—pay money for it, in fact."

"Get out of my way, Relleck," Razia growled, knowing that the pleasure of capturing Obalone would far outweigh any taunts that Relleck could toss her way.

"Get out of your way, what?" Relleck replied, sweetly.

"Please, you son of a bitch," Razia responded, with the same level of sweetness.

"As you wish, m'lady," Relleck said, bowing extravagantly as he moved out of the way to let her pass. Razia angrily stormed by him and into the bar...

...and to her utter horror and surprise, there was already a gaggle of pirates in the bar, signs of a struggle, and Zolet Obalone, bound and gagged, in the center.

"Oh, good job guys!" Relleck cheered, roughly bumping into Razia as he passed her. "I trust he wasn't too much trouble..."

"HEY!" Razia screamed, shocked. "That's my bounty!"

"Oh?" Relleck said, turning nonchalantly to look at the young man in his captivity. "Because it looks like I'm the one who captured him. Looks like my luck is finally changing, after all..."

Razia's mouth dropped and all she could do was sputter. "You...you..."

"Thanks for the assist though," Relleck smirked, walking over to her. "It was a pleasure following you all day. I have to say, it is absolutely breathtaking to watch you work."

Razia's eyes narrowed at him. "You weren't—"

"And by work, I meant watching your ass run all over town," Relleck said, tossing a look back to his crew, who laughed and began looking at her up and down. "Quite breathtaking."

"Get sucked into Leveman's," Razia retorted.

"Oh, I'd like to get sucked, but not there," he said, licking his lips. "You gotta quit looking so pissed off all the time though. You got a pretty face, you shouldn't frown so much. You'll get wrinkles."

Far from smiling, Razia contorted her face into the meanest, nastiest glare she could muster.

"Well if you're not going to be pretty for me, then get lost," Relleck said, turning to walk back to the bar to join his crew, who were giving him high fives and staring at her as if her clothes were going to fall off at any moment.

Enraged, she turned around to leave with some shred of her dignity intact.

"There it is!" Relleck called, to the cheers and whistles of his crew. "Walk slow, baby, so we can watch you go."

Razia stormed out of the bar, enraged.

"What happened?" Vel said, running after her. "Did you get the bounty? I saw that guy earlier today—who is he?"

She stopped to turn back and look in the bar.

"My next bounty."

CHAPTER TEN

Unfortunately for Razia, Relleck's profile was already updated with his new capture:

	1) Relleck, Royden	
Wanted For	Engagement in piracy, grand theft larceny, bounty hunting, illegal sale of stolen goods	
Reward	50,874,900C	
Known Alias	Cash Hermann, Emil Hexum, Vita Uzamo, Rylot Lulah…	
Known Accomplices	Mos Leitch, Pied Kingslee, Speck Mohr, Momoa Moriss…	
Pirate Web affiliation	Contestant	

"I don't understand," Vel asked. "What's the big deal about a pirate being number one?"

"It changes things," Razia mumbled, chewing on her thumb. "It's no longer about the game—catching others, getting a higher bounty. Once you're number one, it becomes an exercise in keeping your ass out of jail."

"I mean, he's bound to get caught eventually, right?" Vel said.

"Yeah, but now it's a lot harder to capture him," Razia frowned. "There are two types of pirates when they get to the top. Some go into hiding—create a bunch of new aliases and just disappear until their number goes down."

"I thought everyone wanted to be number one?" Vel asked.

"Some don't," Razia said. "It's a lot of pressure to constantly be on your toes."

"And what about the second type of pirate?"

"Relleck is not the kind of person to hide out," Razia sighed. "In fact..."
She opened up his real alias—Royden Relleck—and gave Vel a look.

Relleck, Royden		
Time of Transaction	Location	Amount
UT20014-95-96-55:25	Nemo's Bar D-882	50C
UT20014-95-96-50:30	Direct Payment Seven Hawn	80,000C
UT20014-95-96-48:31	Direct Payment Dan Beckham	80,000C
UT20014-95-96-45:50	The Old Elwood D-882	50C
UT20014-95-96-45:47	The Old Elwood D-882	50C

"He's not even trying to hide?" Vel said. "Seems a bit brash."

"Yeah, but look at this guy," Razia said, searching for one of the men Relleck had very recently paid. His bounty was somewhere in the 400's, but he looked about the same size as Dal Jamus.

"He's got six of these guys from the looks of it," Razia said, looking earlier in the transaction history. "Now it's just a waiting game—until he runs out of money or his bounty goes down."

"How long could that take?"

"Weeks? Years?" Razia sighed, closing out his profile.

"So what's that mean for you?"

"Means I need to go find someone else to hunt until that happens," Razia pouted. She really wanted to take down Relleck. But she was gonna hear it soon if she didn't capture a good pirate quick. She hadn't turned anyone in since Jamus—over a week ago.

"Don't sound too excited by it," Vel said.

"Meh," she sighed, opening up the intraweb to see if anyone piqued her interest. "I want to hunt someone who's going to be worth my time. My bounty needs to go up."

"How does that happen exactly?"

"For pirates, when they hijack or steal something, the person they stole from, or their insurance company puts up some cash towards the capture of the pirate. The thinking is, the higher the bounty, the higher chance that pirate is going to get caught. For bounty hunters, normally pirates toss in some credits if a bounty hunter is hunting a bunch of their pirates, or if there's someone they really respect."

"How did your bounty get so high?" Vel asked, looking at her curiously. "Did you ever look?"

"I assume most of it comes from pirates who were happy that I stuck it to Jukin," she shrugged.

"But did you ever look?"

"I can't—the bounty office numbers and transactions are off-limits," she replied. She began scrolling through the pirate intraweb.

	15) Journot, Santos Wanted in connection with piracy (bounty hunting)
	4) Stenson, Eli Captured by Santos Journot
	14) Needler, Waslow Wanted in connection with hijacking of raw materials from G-284. Estimated cost of stolen goods 400,000C.

"Needler is back, hm?" Razia smirked, pulling up her list of old bounty research.

"Who?" Vel asked.

	14) Needler, Waslow
Wanted For	Engagement in piracy, bounty hunting
Reward	15,022,589C
Known Alias	Diezel Ky, Kingslee Dreavyn, Kuli Emet, Imre Ever...

116

Known Accomplices	Ezekiel Czar, Finlee Arthur, Hartan Joseph, Jai Blue...
Pirate Web affiliation	Insurgent

"Waslow Needler," Razia said. "He was on my list of possible bounties to capture when I was on probation, but he got captured. Looks like he's made his way back into the top twenty."

She clicked on her hit list application:

Hit List	
Relleck	Kodah Mottola, Owen King, James Nolte, Alfie O'Hara
Burk	Zuma Davi, Daigle Cypheridge, Soren Gonzalez, Neshua Turro
Lee	Bawley King, Jesse Opal, Oliver David, Boo Jameson
Brendler	Koa Fascinelli, Ellington Nixon, Brody Marleu
Needler	Jackson Money, Jack Oscar, Aleph Miller

She clicked on each one, immediately linking to that alias' Universal Bank profile page.

"Any good?" Vel asked as she swiftly went through them.

"Active," she nodded, her lips still pursed. "But he's got another one, too. There's too many gaps."

"So who is this guy?" Vel asked, as she closed all the windows.

"He's Insurgent's top bounty hunter," Razia noted. "Pretty decent one, at that."

"So if he's a bounty hunter, why do you want to capture him?" Vel asked. "Isn't there some kind of bounty hunter code?"

"The only loyalty I have is to Dissident, unfortunately," Razia sighed. "Bounty hunters are considered pirates like anyone else – fair game to hunt and capture. I mean, technically, someone out there should be hunting me too."

"So how does that work, anyways?" Vel asked. "Do you pay for everything with Lyssa or just certain things?"

"Parking, gas, anything that could give away my ship's location—or mine—gets paid with Lyssa," Razia explained. "Anything where someone could find a date and time stamp and place me, that I pay with Razia."

She paused to smile, "Well, until I establish myself as bounty hunter, that is."

"Then what?"

"Then I just create a bunch of new aliases and try to stay hidden," Razia said. "Like all the other pirates."

"If I were you, I would use your DSE as long as I could," Vel observed. "Seems like it's the perfect cover."

"Except I actually have to be Lyssa Peate in order for that charade to work," Razia replied, more heated than she expected. "And that's kind of the point." She stood, heading towards the door.

"Where are you going?" Vel asked, curiously.

"I have a hunch that every pirate and bounty hunter this side of Leveman's Vortex is standing by and waiting for Relleck to slip up," she said, slipping her mini-computer into her pocket. "So I'm just going to go to where Relleck is and I will probably find Needler."

"Ah, well," Vel said, forcing himself to yawn. "If you don't mind, I think I'm going to let you take care of this one by yourself."

"Why?" Razia snapped, turning to look at him sharply. Vel hadn't been more than five feet from her since they had been re-united at Dal Jamus' bar. And now he was just going to...go to sleep?

"All of this bounty hunting is exhausting," he said, following her down the ladder to the lower level of her ship. "Besides, I have to read some books for school."

"You don't have to write your paper for another five months," Razia said, eyeing him curiously as he walked back to the bedroom.

"Good luck!" Vel smiled, before closing the door behind him.

***

Razia didn't trust Vel as far as she could throw him, but she also realized that there was very little trouble he could get into locked away on her ship. Still, she couldn't help but ponder what he might be up to as she sat on the shuttle from the out lands.

However, she forgot all about him when she walked into the bar where Relleck was making purchases. It was filled to the brim with pirates and bounty hunters. They were huddled around tables, crammed against the bar, sprawling out from doors and peering in through windows. Every eye in the joint was focused on a table in the center of the room, where Relleck was surrounded by four gorgeous women, and six big, burly men daring anyone in the room to come any closer.

He looked drunk, either from excitement, booze, or the women, and oblivious to the thousands of eyes staring at him. He obviously thought he was invincible—and he was, for now. But he wouldn't always be.

Razia folded her arms across her chest, forcing herself to focus on the task at hand. She scanned the room, pausing on each face to compare it with who she was looking for. Somewhere in this gaggle was-

"Sage?" she blinked, her eyes connecting with a familiar face across the room. His face lit up when he recognized her, and before she could react, he was happily walking over to her.

"What are you doing here?" he grinned, lightly nudging her.

"I could ask you the same thing," she said, curiously. "Not really your scene..."

"I need a bounty," he sighed, not sounding enthused at the idea at all.

"What?" Razia said, not believing her ears. "You don't bounty hunt."

"Well, I'm tired of Dissident bitching at me," Sage said. "Sage, when are you going to go bring in a good bounty." he said, mocking Dissident's hoarse voice. "When I'm damn good and ready, that's when."

"He never calls me to bitch about me not bringing in a bounty," Razia pouted.

"So I figured," Sage said, ignoring her comment and turning to look at the room in front of them. "With half of the pirate population here staking out Relleck, I could just take my pick."

"Guess we had the same idea," Razia nodded.

"And who are you hunting?" Sage asked.

She gave him a look. "Like I'm going to tell you."

"Oh come on." He nudged her. "I don't want you...what is it...*fighting* with me?"

She rolled her eyes and pursed her lips.

"What are the parameters of this 'fighting' situation anyways," Sage teased. "Does it mean you aren't talking to me, or does it mean you're just going to be mad at me, and what constitutes—"

"I'm after Needler," she said, just wanting him to shut up.

"Good, I'm totally going after Needler," Sage cackled, nudging her again.

"You're an ass," Razia said, but couldn't help but smile at him.

"Where's your bro?" Sage said, looking around. "Thought he was practically glued to your side."

"Finally able to shake him," Razia said, thinking back to his odd behavior. "Said all this piracy was wearing him out."

"That is just adorable," Sage cooed. "Your kid brother, following in your piracy footsteps. I wonder what your big brother would say..."

"Oh yeah," Razia said, turning to punch Sage hard in the shoulder.

"Ow!" Sage said, rubbing his shoulder. "What was that for?"

"Telling him how to blackmail me!" Razia growled, turning back to face the front.

"All right, so I can't capture Needler," Sage laughed. "Who, by the way,

is right over there."

Razia immediately forgot about murdering Sage when she followed his gaze and saw Needler sitting in the corner. She huffed—she swore she checked out all of those guys.

"So that leaves me," he sighed. "Who here is a big enough bounty to get Dissident off my back?"

"Relleck," she offered.

"Har har har," Sage laughed. "I'm not stupid."

"Well, Needler looks to be hanging out with Conboy Conrad over there," Razia said, quickly scrolling through the bounties to check and see how high Conrad was in the list. "I mean, he's not as high as Needler, but he's still one of Insurgent's top guys. Surprised he's back here, Relleck captured him a few weeks ago."

"How do you remember these things?" Sage said, gawking at her.

"I pay attention," Razia snapped.

"Eh," Sage shrugged, looking at his bounty profile. "I guess he'll do." He grinned at her. "C'mon, let's go."

"What, now?" she said.

"Yeah, like we used to do for Tauron, remember?" Sage said. "You and me against some guys twice our size and age?"

"As I recall that didn't end well for both of us," Razia laughed. "Many times."

"Well, now we're older and bigger," Sage said, before looking her up and down. "Well, some of us are bigger."

She paused for a moment.

"All right, fine," she shrugged, following him.

***

Razia stepped off of the lift, happily looking at her Universal Bank account—for the first time looking at the total amount, versus the transaction history.

Fifteen million credits.

It felt good to finally have some cash in her account. She gleefully trotted up to her ship, wondering, breathlessly, if it was finally time for her to create a new alias.

Perhaps, she thought, grinning madly, it was time to finally become Razia.

She started climbing up the ladder on her ship, a call to Harms on her mind asking him if he could put her in touch with Dissident's guy at the Universal Bank. Her happy thoughts stopped when she saw the faint light of her dashboard on the otherwise dark floor. Slowly she pulled herself up, carefully peering into the open cabin to see who or what was on her screen.

To her surprise, it was Vel, intently staring at something on the dashboard. He was absorbed with what was on the screen. As her eyes focused on the bright dashboard, she realized he was looking at bank records.

Wait a minute, she thought to herself. Why was he looking at bank records?

And that's when she saw the man he was looking at was most assuredly not a pirate.

"What in Leveman's Vortex do you think you're doing?" she growled, her voice low and dangerous, turning on the lights.

"Shit!" Vel cursed, quickly closing all of the windows and turning around nervously. "I didn't...uh...I was doing some research for my paper—"

"Right, because looking up Sostas Peate's bank records will help you with your carbon analysis," she said, humorlessly.

"Fine," Vel said, folding his arms over his chest. "I wanted to see if he was still...still making transactions."

"I get it," she laughed, her arms folded across her chest. "That's why you've been so interested in bounty hunting, huh? Is that why you decided to come back? So you can dig for more dirt for Pymus?"

"You know, I'm curious," Vel said, folding his arms in the same manner and returning her icy glare. "Have you ever looked for him?"

"Excuse me?" Lyssa said, shocked.

"You look for people for a living—and are pretty damned good at it too. Have you ever tried to look for him?"

"Why do I need to look when I know the answer?" she growled. "He *left*. And he doesn't want to be found by me, or by you, or by anybody. So I suggest you drop it."

"What are you so afraid of?" Vel barked.

"I'm not afraid of anything," she glared, her lip curling in anger. "But you will be if you don't quit running your mouth."

"Oh yeah, and why's that?"

"Because If I *ever* catch you touching my dashboard again, I will leave you on a planet again," she snarled, right in his face. "And this time, I'll make it a real dangerous one and I might not come back."

"Whatever," he rolled his eyes and stormed off the bridge.

She sat down, the fight replaying over and over again in her head. To try and drown it out, she decided to look at her bounty to see if it had been raised a little bit.

	32) (No last name listed), Razia
Wanted For	Engagement in piracy, bounty hunting, kidnapping, aggravated assault, resisting arrest
Reward	5,000,500C
Known Alias	None
Known Accomplices	Tauron Ball, Sage Teon
Pirate Web affiliation	Dissident

Not even a single credit—and she'd even dropped two slots.

She kicked her console in frustration, and sat back, rubbing her temples. She didn't understand what was going on—Needler was worth over fifteen million credits, he was one of Insurgent's best bounty hunters. That should have gotten the attention of *somebody* who wanted to put some more money towards her bounty.

Well, she thought, trying to temper her frustration, perhaps it hadn't been updated yet.

She turned to the intraweb to see if the capture had been reported. To her annoyance, there were two brand new items:

	15) Teon, Sage Wanted in connection with piracy (bounty hunting)
	30) Conrad, Conboy Captured by Sage Teon

Angrily, she closed out of the list. She and Sage had turned in their bounties at the exact same time—how come his had already been updated AND his bounty had jumped two slots? Conrad was worth half of what

Needler was!

Her immediate reaction was to open her video call application and start typing in Dissident's number, but then she thought better of it. Last time she spoke to him out of anger, she ended up hunting a retired pirate halfway across the galaxy.

The best thing to do would be to capture another bounty, and hope that soon she would start showing up in the intraweb.

She opened up her hit list of pirates, and took a little pleasure in deleting Needler off of her roster; it was bad form to capture the same pirate over and over again.

The others on her list were mildly interesting—Brendler, Burk, Lee. But her eyes kept drifting up to Relleck's name. Her ego getting the better of her, she clicked on one of the four aliases she had uncovered for him—just to see what would come up.

King, Owen		
Time of Transaction	Location	Amount
UT20014-95-97-12:89	Park Chili Diner D-882	50C
UT20014-95-97-10:78	Centaur Motel D-882	15,000C
UT20014-95-96-10:60	Centaur Bar D-882	20C
UT20014-95-96-08:45	Bosco Cafe D-882	50C
UT20014-95-93-55:87	Cobo Joe's D-882	50C

Interestingly, he was actually using this alias—in fact, he had just purchased some food in the past five minutes. Even more curious was the location—a bar in the outskirts of the city.

Why would Relleck use a secret alias in front of all of those bounty hunters, she thought. Even with his goons, he wasn't going to be the most wanted pirate forever—and good aliases were hard to come by.

She found herself itching to put her coat back on and go see what was going on.

***

Reckless excitement coursed through her as she swiftly walked along the dark city streets. Relleck had purchased three more drinks on his secret aliases, which meant that he was definitely hiding somewhere. She came up to the bar where he was supposedly making purchases, and quickly ducked out of the way.

He was sitting in plain sight with a beer in hand, looking dejectedly at the half-drunk bottle.

She looked about herself, expecting to see goons stationed at every corner. But she was completely alone on the street.

Slowly, he rose to his feet and pulled on his jacket drunkenly. He obviously had had a few, as he stumbled onto the street, oblivious to where he was. She slipped off after him, keeping her distance. As far as she could tell, Relleck was completely alone.

Perhaps he'd just gotten too fed up with being the top pirate in the universe and just wanted someone to catch him?

In that case, Razia would be more than happy to relieve him of that heavy burden.

She continued to walk behind him, keeping in the shadows and staying just as far behind him to not raise his suspicions. But from the way he was stumbling and leaning about, she probably could have been right behind him and he wouldn't have realized it.

She saw her opportunity when he turned and tripped into an alley way. Picking up her pace, she jogged after him, knowing that he was going to be trapped with no escape. A smile on her face, she appeared in the alley way to see Relleck standing there, looking quite sober, his arms folded across his chest and a satisfied smile on his face.

That is, Relleck and two of his largest goons.

"Uh oh," Razia breathed, twisting on her foot to dash away. Before she could take two steps, she felt two sets of hands clamp down on her arms and toss her backwards, roughly hitting the brick wall of the building. Dazed, she felt thick hands wrap around her arms and lift her upright to face Relleck.

"Well, well, well," he said, neatly cuffing his shirt one sleeve at a time. "I have to say, I have been trying to get your attention for a couple of weeks now."

The world was slowly coming back into focus for Razia as she tried to figure out how she was going to get herself out of this mess.

"I'm hurt that you haven't been hunting me, Razia," Relleck sighed dramatically. "And here I thought that you and I had a connection? A special bond."

"Your definition of bond is a little warped," Razia muttered, struggling to break free. The burly men had a vice grip on her arms.

"You know, as a general rule, I don't really beat up on the lesser pirates," he began, walking up to her. "And I really don't feel right hitting a girl."

"Wonderful," Razia snapped, trying to keep her face emotionless, knowing exactly what was coming next. "So what are we doing here?"

Without warning, he whirled around and punched her hard in the stomach. She winced, but did not cry out, clenching her teeth hard together. She wasn't going to give him the satisfaction.

"Is this the only way you can ask a girl out, Relleck?" Razia gasped, her voice labored from the ache in her stomach. "Besides paying her, of course."

"You have spunk," Relleck chuckled, walking up to her. "I like that in my women."

He hit her again – this time in the face. She tasted blood in her mouth.

"And you know, if I wasn't getting paid to—"

"Why don't you pick on someone your own size?"

Furiously, Razia looked past Relleck to see Sage standing in the alleyway.

"Well, well, Razia, looks like your boyfriend has to come in and save you again!" Relleck laughed. "I should have known that wherever Razia is, Sage Teon isn't too far behind."

Sage didn't rise to his taunts. "Let her go, Relleck."

"And what are you going to do about it?" Relleck taunted.

Sage cleared his throat. Out of nowhere, his crew of seven appeared behind him. In the corner, Razia saw Vel appear, standing mostly behind Ganon, but ready to fight.

She scowled. That little shit must have called Sage.

Relleck and Sage stared at each other for a minute, until Relleck sniffed and grabbed his jacket from one of his goons.

"C'mon guys."

The two goons released Razia and she wiped the blood off of her lip, trying not to look as if she was in as much pain as she actually was.

"You got lucky, Razia," Relleck said, turning to look at her as he walked away.

Once they were around the corner, Sage dropped his icy glare and swooped over to Razia. "Are you ok?" he asked, reaching out a hand to her.

She batted it away angrily. "I'm fine."

"You really aren't, you're bleeding," Sage said, reaching out again. "Let me take you back to my ship and clean you—"

"*I DON'T WANT YOUR HELP!*" Razia snapped, feeling infuriatingly ashamed. Her words echoed in the alley.

"Really?" Sage blinked, a hint of anger in his voice. "Because from where I was standing, Relleck was about to beat the crap out of you. Would you like me to call him back and tell him to continue? It's a damn good thing Vel told me what you were up to—"

Razia turned her ire to Vel, who tried very much not to wither under it.

"As much as you'd like to think otherwise, you are not invincible," Sage continued softer, obviously trying to temper his anger. "And you cannot take on three people at once. Especially when two of them are twice your size."

"I wasn't trying—"

"Lyss, he's the number one bounty in the universe," Sage said, throwing up his hands. "You know he's not going to go anywhere without his crew? What were you thinking?"

"I don't need a lecture from *you*," Razia snapped. "And don't call me that."

"You know, sometimes I wonder," Sage continued, his voice rising again. "Because you seem to have forgotten everything Tauron taught you about how to be a good pirate. I mean, the number one rule – don't get into a fight you can't win!"

Razia continued to stare daggers at him.

Sage stared back, with the same level of animosity.

His crew and Vel waited with baited breath, wondering who would be the first to blink.

Finally, Sage threw up his hands, letting out a loud cry of frustration.

"You are the most stubborn, the most...you drive me insane," he exclaimed. "Let's go, guys."

Razia watched as Sage and his crew walked away. Once they were out of sight, she sighed and leaned against the wall, clutching her aching stomach.

"Your search results, and Sage called and..." Vel started before Razia turned to glare daggers at him.

"We're fighting."

CHAPTER ELEVEN

"YEEEOOOW, that is a shiner!" Harms said, leaning in close to the camera. "Relleck really got you good, didn't he?"

"How bad is it?" Razia asked, poking at her sore cheek, which had turned a blotchy purple.

"I dunno, honey, you might want to go see a doctor," Harms said, peering down at her.

"Not that," Razia sighed, throwing her hand down. "My...my reputation."

"Oh...well," Harms hedged. "You did get beat up."

She made a face.

"Aaaand Sage did come to save you—"

"HE DID NOT!" Razia barked, sitting up.

"I have heard it from two of the three people that were there, and I hardly consider you an impartial party," Harms winked. "Hey, at least Relleck didn't turn you in, huh? Then you'd be right back to where you started with Dissident."

"He hasn't..." She swallowed nervously. "He hasn't said anything ...has he?"

"Well...." Harms trailed off. "I mean, he wasn't happy, of course. To be honest, he's not been too pleased with Sage recently—he wants him to focus more on bounty hunting, so he sort of blamed you for distracting him—"

"I have nothing to do with what Teon does with his time," Razia huffed. "And I did not ask him to show up."

"You don't have to," Harms smiled. "You know Tauron made him promise to take care of you."

Razia deflated, wondering what Tauron would have done if he was still alive. Begrudgingly, she knew it was probably something very similar to what Sage had said, and she started to feel even stupider for putting herself in such a position. If only Vel hadn't thrown her off her game.

"Oh buck up, kiddo," Harms said. "We all make mistakes. You just gotta

127

lay low for a little while—"

"I can't lay low!" Razia exclaimed, sitting up. "Are you kidding me? I have to get back out there, I have to find someone really good to—"

"Take a week," Harms repeated. "Let the story die down. People have short memories. And it'll give those bruises some time to heal—ego included."

Razia said back and frowned.

"Quit pouting," Harms chuckled. "Just a week. You'll be back in the game in no time. And next time—find a bounty that plays to your strengths, okay?"

The call went dark, but Razia didn't move for a few moments, the corners of her mouth still downturned and her bottom lip still protruding. She knew what she needed to do, but she really, really didn't want to.

After a few minutes, and with great anguish, she pushed herself to stand and started charting a course to the farthest reaches of the known universe.

***

"I can't believe we're actually excavating a planet," Vel grinned, taking a deep breath in the green forest air.

Lyssa ignored him, her eyes focused on lacing up her running shoes. She was still angry with him for being a party to Sage's unwelcome intrusion, and was even angrier that she was actually excavating a planet with him. He was acting like nothing was amiss, happily cheering when he realized where they were going, and having one-sided conversations with her.

Her mini-computer buzzed at her hip, and that familiar anxious dread filled her chest. She unhooked it slowly, nervously hoping it wasn't Dissident calling her or sending her a message. She was sure it was only a matter of time before he called to berate her—or worse.

The message, thankfully, was just a marketing message.

She stood up and adjusted her running shorts over the other, painful bruise on her stomach, and pulled her hair up into a ponytail. She stretched her arms over her head, and felt the tension from the last few days in her shoulders. She bent down to touch her toes, her hamstrings tight from too much sitting and not enough stretching.

Between her legs, she saw Vel walk off of the ship wearing shorts and running shoes.

"Uh, no," Lyssa said, snapping upright.

"Oh good, you're talking to me again," Vel smirked, stretching his legs.

Instead of responding, she turned on her heel and sprinted out into the jungle. She was running fast—faster than she normally did—and after a few moments started to feel a stitch in her side and the bruise on her stomach. Eager to break free from Vel, she pushed through it, until finally she could keep the pace no longer.

She coughed a bit, leaning over and trying to catch her breath.

To her dismay, she heard footfalls behind her.

"Really, you have to quit doing that," Vel rolled his eyes, coming into the clearing and handing her his bottle. "You know I run faster than you do anyways."

"Go away," Lyssa growled, not taking the bottle.

"No," Vel replied, shrugging and taking a swig.

"AARGH," Lyssa said, standing upright and starting to jog. The pain in her bruise was barking at her again, so she had to stop.

"What's wrong?" Vel asked.

"Nothing," she mumbled, trying to focus all her angry energy into getting as far away from Vel as she could. Vel, however, was having other thoughts, as he easily jogged beside her, his eyes focused on the uneven ground ahead, but his attention on her.

"You should slow down, there's no way you can keep this pace," Vel said, sounding only slightly winded.

"I'm not talking to you," Lyssa spat.

"Sage actually called looking for you," Vel said, matter-of-factly. "And I just saw who you had been searching—the transaction records, and I told him."

"Stupid Teon," Lyssa grumbled. "He's always ruins everything."

"How is saving your ass ruining everything?" Vel asked, confused as they leapt over a fallen tree. "I would think you would be thanking him—"

"They already don't respect me," Lyssa said, her brows furrowed. "I don't need to think I can't fight my own fights."

"Well, don't get into fights you can't win then," Vel said, looking over to her for a second before turning back to watch where he was running. "Isn't that was Sage was trying to say?"

"Sage is a moron," Lyssa snapped.

"Are you really trying to tell me that you would rather get beat up than have somebody come help you?" Vel said pointedly.

"Comes with the territory," she insisted, stubbornly.

"Why would anyone want to be a pirate?" Vel asked, looking to the sky through the tree leaves. "All you do is get beat up. Or beat other people up."

"It's not all about that," Lyssa said, the euphoria from running starting to loosen her attitude. "It's the thrill of the chase, finding someone who can't be found. That other stuff—the physical stuff—is just secondary."

"So why did you go after someone like Relleck?" Vel asked, pointedly. "Even I knew he was always going to have those big guys with him, and I'm not even a bounty hunter!"

"Because I thought he got lazy," Lyssa said, after a few moments.

"Or you got cocky," Vel retorted. "And you wanted to get him back for taking your bounty last week."

Lyssa snorted, but didn't respond, breathing evenly as they continued to run side-by-side.

"I bet," Vel continued, looking at her. "I bet that he knew you knew that alias, and he was trying to get you to bite."

"How would he..." Lyssa said, before trailing off. She did actually tell him that she knew that alias. Before the whole U-POL incident, when she saw him at the bounty office, and he'd pissed her off. She'd all but broadcast that she was onto him.

"That's your problem," Vel said, continuing in the absence of her retort. "You're too easy to read."

"I am not easy to read!" Lyssa barked back at him.

Vel gave her a knowing look.

"Whatever," she rolled her eyes.

"Look, I watch you go through these bank accounts," Vel said, looking forward again. "You're incredible. I don't know how you keep all those minute details straight in your head—who's got what alias and how much they're worth and what they last stole. And I definitely don't know half of what goes on in that brain of yours."

"So?" Lyssa snapped, uncomfortable with the praise.

"So, you should play to that," Vel replied. "Go after the guys who come out of nowhere and can't be found. Nobody else is going to spend four days pouring through a transaction history."

"Instead of what, then?" Lyssa raised her eyebrow.

"Instead of going after guys like Dal Jamus," Vel smiled. "Unless you want to hire an actual crew, like Sage."

"I do not like how close you two are getting," Lyssa frowned. "It's like you're ganging up on me or something."

"Right, because your little brother and your closest friend are plotting to destroy you," Vel chuckled, elbowing her. "By preventing you from getting captured and saving your ass when you're an idiot."

She didn't respond, but the smallest smile appeared in the corner of her mouth.

***

The next morning, Lyssa awoke sore but refreshed. She looked over to Vel, who was still sleeping on the floor. She gently walked over to the light and flipped it on, rudely awakening him.

"Time to get up, intern," she announced, loudly. "We have a planet to excavate."

"Uuugh," he moaned, looking up at her. "Why are you awake right now?"

"Let's go!" she barked, walking out of her bedroom. She came back in with a box of gear and started dropping things on top of him.

"Ow, what..." He yawned as heavy things continued to fall on him. "Why are you so happy today?"

"Get up!" she cheered, taking the now empty box back to the cabinets.

"Great Creator in Leveman's Vortex," Vel gaped, looking at the machines sprawled about him. "Are you actually teaching me how to be a DSE?"

"Not if you don't move your ass and get dressed," she smiled sweetly, before disappearing again.

They set out in the forest they had run in the evening before, the early morning sunlight streaming through the thick canopy above. Their feet crunched on the decaying leaves underfoot, and the occasional breeze rustled the tree leaves. Every so often, Lyssa would stop and break off a twig or a leaf and stuff it in one of the machines around her hip, looking at her mini-computer.

"So...what are you doing?" Vel asked, after a few minutes.

"Excavating," Lyssa replied, walking to the next tree.

"Ah," Vel noted. "How?"

"What?" Lyssa said, looking back at him. "I'm doing carbon analysis. Don't you know anything?"

"Yeah, that normally involves taking samples of the leaves back to a laboratory and using a series of complex and time-consuming chemical experiments to determine the pH balance, the composition of plant cell walls, and testing for known toxins," Vel smiled. "And I don't think that stuffing them into a machine is—"

"The pH balance is 6.7, the cell wall is a polysaccharide-based, and it is safe to touch by...." Lyssa scrunched up her nose as she thought. "92% of all known life in the universe."

"And how did you find that out?" Vel asked, folding his arms over his chest.

"This." Lyssa unhooked the sensor from her belt and tossing it to him. "Carbon analyzer."

"W-what?" Vel blinked, looking at the analyzer and back to her.

"Carbon analyzer," Lyssa repeated, as if it wasn't a big deal. "Scans and analyzes the carbon material for chemical signatures."

"Wait," Vel said, looking down at the machine and back to her. "So...a machine that basically does three hours' worth of DSE analysis and documentation in—"

"Five seconds," Lyssa said, showing him the screen on her mini-computer. "Cuts the excavation time from a week to two days. I also have a water analyzer, and one to test animal life, but I rarely use that one—"

"Hold on a second," Vel said, still stuck on the carbon analyzer. "So you're telling me that you have a machine that can basically revolutionize the entire process of planet excavation—not to mention the entire science of Deep Space Exploration..."

She looked at him, unimpressed.

"And why haven't you sold these and made a billion credits yet?" Vel continued. "Forget being a pirate, forget being a DSE—if you sold these designs, you wouldn't have to work another day in your life!"

"Not my design," Lyssa shrugged, as if that was an appropriate answer.

"Well whose design was it?!" Vel blinked. "And why didn't they—" He trailed off, looking down at the carbon analyzer and then back to Lyssa.

She raised her eyebrows at him, then turned to continue walking.

"Wait a second," Vel said, his mind still processing. "These are Father's?"

"Well, he designed them," Lyssa said, walking ahead of him. "All of his stuff went with him when he....left. Except his journals, he left those in the lab at the Manor." She paused to pull off a leaf from an odd looking vine and handed it to him.

"Journals?" Vel asked, curiously, taking the leaf from her and sticking it in the analyzer.

"Yeah," Lyssa said, continuing to walk. "Mostly scribbles, but a few of them had the designs in them."

"Why didn't he patent these?" Vel asked, his voice noticeably subdued.

"Oh, he just built these so I could do his excavations for him," Lyssa smiled. "He thought it woefully beneath him to spend even a moment doing a planet excavation. But he needed to stay in the Academy to get access to the library for his research, so he had to excavate at least three or four planets a quarter. So he'd send me off with these things strapped around my waist for a few hours."

"You?" Vel said, doing the math in his head. "But you couldn't have been more than—"

"Four? Five?" Lyssa nodded, staring intently at a leaf she had just pulled.

"That's terrible," Vel said.

"Sometimes he forgot about me," Lyssa smirked, trying to find humor in the situation. "I remember once, I was wandering around for two days before I found him again." She laughed, looking to Vel amusedly. "He didn't even realized I'd been gone. Barked at me for being so messy and tracking too much dirt onto the ship."

"So he'd just let you wander around on planets while he did...what?" Vel asked slowly.

Lyssa was saved from answering him, as they had come to the edge of the forest. Or rather, they came to the edge of a rather steep cliff. The valley was covered in lush trees for as far as the eye could see, cut in two by a deep blue river that flowed all the way to the horizon.

She looked down at the valley below, and felt her heartbeat in her chest. In her mind's eye, she saw the ground crumbling beneath her feet, a river of fire—and she could almost smell sulfur...

Instinctively, she reached out to the nearest tree.

"I don't think we brought repelling equipment, did we?" Vel asked, peering over the edge unafraid. "There's a river down there...don't see the source of the water though. We should probably test it to see if it's potable."

"I'm okay up here," Lyssa whispered, her arms tightening around the tree.

"I think it would be—" Vel said, stopping short when he saw her, white as a sheet, clinging to the tree. "What's wrong?"

"Nothing's wrong," she lied.

"Are you...are you scared of heights?" Vel asked, a small smile appearing on his face.

"Don't be ridiculous," she snapped, her voice shaking slightly.

"You sure look scared of something," Vel said, standing and grinning. "That or you really like that tree."

She looked at herself and realized she was, in fact, holding onto the tree for dear life. She forced herself to let go and try to look unfazed.

It obviously didn't work, as Vel began laughing at her, gleefully.

"I can't believe it," Vel shook his head. "The great and powerful Dr. Lyssandra Peate—Razia—is afraid of heights."

"I am not afraid of heights," she insisted.

"Prove it," Vel said, clearly enjoying this way too much. "Come over here and look over this ledge."

"Fine," she said, not moving.

"Well?" Vel grinned.

"I'm coming," she nodded, slowly letting go of the tree, and taking two small steps towards the ledge.

"Come on!" Vel teased. "Don't make me-*make you*!"

He lunged at her, and she let out the most uncharacteristically girlish squeal of terror, running back towards the thick forest, as fast as her legs could carry her.

Vel found her, holding onto a thick tree with both arms, white as a sheet and shaking slightly. He began laughing as he trotted up to her—so amused to see her finally lose her cool at something so simple.

"THAT'S NOT FUNNY!" she screamed at him.

"Not afraid of heights, hm?" He smiled.

"I'm not," she insisted, hugging the tree tighter. "I don't like falling."

"I just can't get over this," Vel said. "You, of all people, afraid of—"

Then, the ground shook slightly.

"REALLY?" Lyssa screamed, giving him a dirty look.

"I didn't do that," Vel swallowed, looking at her with wide eyes.

The ground shook again, this time with more intensity.

"Har har," she mumbled, still holding onto the tree. "You got me, I'm af—"

The ground shook again, so violently that Vel fell to his knees.

"Earthquake?" Vel asked, looking up at her.

Before she could answer, another violent tremor shook the ground and a crack appeared in the rocky ground—right between them.

They looked at each other for a moment, unsure of what to do next.

Without warning, the world shook again and the crack turned into a gap.

"Lyssa....?"

The ground shook—but only on his side of the gap, which was now so wide, it was no longer a gap but a huge crevasse between them.

Vel looked up at Lyssa, his fear finally matching hers, and moved to jump across the deep split in the ground to meet her, but he was thrown from his feet as the ground moved.

But only on his side.

In fact, the ground on his side continued to shake, but not violently. Vel was moving side to side, as if the ground was swaying. And he was getting farther away from her.

"LYSSA!" he squeaked.

Lyssa got to her feet to try and get to him, but then she was knocked to her knees by another shake. A few feet behind her, another crack appeared, which then turned into a gap, and then she, too, was moving away from the ground behind her.

Slowly, she pulled herself across the dusty ground to look down the ledge at the ground below.

To her shock and surprise, there were two protrusions jutting out from the bottom of the cliff, almost walking in the river below, sloshing the water as each "leg" moved forward. She looked forward to Vel, who was now at least twenty feet away, and saw the same movement.

"I THINK THIS ROCK IS ALIVE!" Lyssa screamed to him, actually quite curious about this new discovery.

"I DON'T CARE!" Vel yelled back to her, clinging to a tree. "HOW DO WE GET OFF!"

"Just hang tight!" she called back, reaching down for her mini-computer.

It wasn't there.

Panicking, she looked around and didn't see it anywhere. Her utility belt was gone too.

"Dammit," she muttered, realizing that it must have come off when Vel was trying to throw her off the cliff. Scowling, she thought about how much she was going to yell at him for horsing around earlier. But now she had a big problem—she couldn't call the ship to her.

With no mini-computer to call the ship, and no utility belt, she only had one option.

"WHAT ARE YOU DOING?" Vel called out to her as she stood and went to the other edge. She swayed for a moment, almost losing her balance behind her.

She paused for a moment, timing each time the ground pitched forward, so she could use the momentum.

Then, with a quiet prayer, she took off flying.

She landed with thump half on the cliff, grasping for anything to hold on to, as she felt herself slipping off the cliff.

Vel sprang into action and grabbed her by the shirt, yanking her upwards. She lay on her back for a moment, heart beating out of her chest.

"You are insane!" Vel said, falling over with each sway. "What were you thinking!?"

"Need my stuff," Lyssa panted, her body still flooded with fear and adrenaline. "Where's my stuff."

"What stuff?" Vel asked.

"Mini-computer," she swallowed, pushing herself upright.

"I don't know, you don't have it?" Vel said, looking around. And then his face dropped.

"What?" she said, nervously.

"It's over there."

Lyssa followed his gaze and realized that there was a third moving rock creature. Which was currently carrying her utility belt and mini-computer.

"Uh..." Lyssa grimaced, pushing herself to stand.

"Leave it," Vel said. "You don't need it."

"And how do you think we're going to get back to the ship?!" Lyssa gaped at him.

"And how do you expect to get over there?" Vel retorted.

"Same way I got over here," Lyssa said, dusting herself off nervously.

"No, Lyssa—WAIT!" Vel said, as she took off running.

With another death-defying leap, she flew over the gap, landing on the ledge. This time, her foot connected with a grip and she was able to hoist herself onto the cliff side.

Her utility belt and mini-computer were laying near the ledge, perfectly intact. She quickly fired up her mini-computer and called for her ship, scanning the sky for the familiar glint of silver.

She heard the sound of engines firing to life nearby and watched her ship rise from the forest. With another gentle swipe on her mini-computer, she steered the ship over to where Vel was teetering.

She realized with a jolt that she couldn't land the ship on the small strip of land on top of the creature. Not only that, but she couldn't get the ship close enough for Vel to grab on; the force from her ships engines kept knocking him down.

"VEL!" she called to him, still on the creature behind them. "You're gonna have to jump on!"

"WHAT?!" he said, eyes wide. "WHY?"

"I CAN'T LAND IT!"

"I don't think I can make it!" he called back to her, looking at the distance between him and the ship.

"Yes, you can!" she called out to him. "Just get a running start!"

He looked at her nervously.

"YOU HAVE TO DO THIS NOW!" Lyssa screamed, struggling to keep her ship steady. "You can do this, I promise you can!"

He nodded, carefully coming to his feet, trying to balance between the swaying of the rock creature and the power from the ship's engines. He slowly walked backwards, aiming to get a running start.

Lyssa's heart leapt into her chest as he almost lost his balance and teetered backwards, but was able to steady himself.

"ANY DAY NOW, VEL!" she barked.

She stopped breathing as he took off running, pushing off the ground and flying towards the open hatch of her ship.

"Oh Great Creator in Leveman's Vortex," she whispered.

His one hand connected with the edge of the lowered hatch.

She gulped as he hung for a moment, dangling above the valley hundreds of feet below. With a mighty heave, he threw his other hand onto the hatch and forcefully pulled himself up.

Lyssa sighed, relieved as he sat down safely on the lowered hatch door and waved at her.

Her relief was short lived, as she realized she was next. Not only that, but she couldn't jump and hold the ship steady at the same time. She looked ahead of her, trying to calculate how fast the rock creature was moving and where she would have to place her ship to be able to make the jump. Her mind was fuzzy from fear and nerves, and she couldn't concentrate.

She looked to Vel, who was watching her intently.

With a gentle movement of her finger, she maneuvered the ship in front of her rock creature—and waited, readying herself to make one final leap of faith when the time was right.

She watched the gap shorten, and waited for her instincts to kick-in.

"Now!" she screamed, taking off running and flying across the open gap, her heart beating madly in her chest as she flew across the gap.

Her fingers connected with cool metal, and she felt Vel's hands wrap around hers.

"I got ya!" he smiled.

But her hands were slippery from sweat, and she slowly watched herself slip out of his hands, a chill running up her spine as she began to fall.

The wind was rushing in her ears, and she knew what was coming next.

Then her whole body jerked upwards.

For a brief moment, she wondered if she had hit the water and her soul was headed to Leveman's Vortex for her final punishment.

Then she registered the trusty emergency cord, magnetically connected to her utility belt, slowly reeling her in.

Her whole body went lax, and in her relief, she began to laugh.

She reached the open hatch and Vel pulled her onto the ship roughly, immediately pulling her into a full body embrace.

"I'm fine, I'm fine," Lyssa said, her heart still beating out of her chest.

"What in LEVEMAN'S VORTEX IS WRONG WITH YOU!" Vel screamed, his face inches from hers. "DON'T DO THAT AGAIN!"

Lyssa was too shocked to fight him as he embraced her again. She could feel his heart thumping wildly in his chest and found herself gently patting him on the back to calm him down.

"I'm okay, I promise," she whispered.

"What is this thing?" he said, looking down at the cord still attached to her waist.

"Emergency cord," Lyssa said, unhooking it and letting it roll back to under the ship. "There's a sensor in my mini-computer that senses when it's losing altitude. Immediately tells the ship to release this cord that attaches to my utility belt."

Vel blinked at her, unable to form words.

"I told you," Lyssa smirked, starting to feel like her old self. "I don't like to fall."

CHAPTER TWELVE

"It's so nice to eat something other than meal bars," Vel sighed, digging into his sandwich. It was lunchtime at the Academy when they had arrived, and, after an hour in line, they settled into a desolate corner of the cafeteria to enjoy their non-dehydrated food.

"What, do you think this is the Manor?" Lyssa said, in-between bites. "Which, let me be clear, that food is just terrible—"

"How would you know?" Vel gave her a look. "You haven't eaten there in ten years."

"And I never will again," Lyssa smiled back.

"Whatever," Vel rolled his eyes, before widening them in fear.

"What?" Lyssa said, before following his gaze. Dr. Pymus, his hair slicked back, his mouth pursed, and his eyes sweeping the cafeteria, was standing in the doorway. Without so much as another word, Lyssa quickly ducked under the table.

To her surprise, Vel joined her moments later.

Lyssa looked at Vel, who returned her look. The sight of him under the table was too much, and she began laughing at him.

"What?" he said, laughing with her.

"I can't believe I'm hiding from my own boss," Lyssa chuckled. "With you, of all people."

"I don't want to deal with him either," Vel muttered. "He's going to want an update on the internship!"

"So do what I always do," Lyssa shrugged. "Lie."

"What am I supposed to tell him to make him believe me?" Vel responded. "If I tell him we were researching Leveman's Vortex, he'll want to know specifics."

"You could always tell him you've been bounty hunting," Lyssa grinned.

"Because I'd love to get arrested by Jukin," Vel responded. "Remember, I'm not actually in a pirate web."

"Do you think it's safe yet?" Lyssa said, trying to look for him. As the words left her mouth, a pair of black pants and shined shoes appeared in front of them.

"I know you're under there, Lyssandra."

"Wait a minute," Lyssa said, poking her head up. "Dorst?"

Indeed, it was their second eldest brother, and not the obnoxious Dr. Pymus, who was standing in front of them, arms folded, mouth turned down in a frown, and eyes boring a hole into the two of them.

"What do you want?" Lyssa snapped, pulling herself to sit upright. Vel quickly joined her, although he was most definitely happier about seeing Dorst than Lyssa was.

"What were you doing under there?" Dorst asked, eyeing Vel up and down as he adjusted his shirt from crouching under the table.

"Oh, I dropped a pen and we were looking for it," Vel smiled.

"I'm sure," Dorst said, looking daggers at Lyssa. She simply returned the animosity with a saccharine smile.

"What can I do for you, Dorst?" Vel asked, taking a huge bite of his sandwich.

"I heard you had returned to the Academy and I wanted to check on my little brother," Dorst said, purposefully ignoring Lyssa, who had started to chow down on her own food. "Making sure you were still in one piece."

"Don't worry, Lyssa's only almost killed me....twice now," Vel smirked, giving Lyssa a look.

"That's not funny, Vel," Dorst snapped. "You know just as well as I do that Mother was not happy about you returning to this internship. Especially after the last...incident."

"Which incident was that, Dorst?" Lyssa asked, taking a huge bite of her fruit.

"When you let a pirate kidnap him," Dorst responded angrily. "Why in Leveman's Great Vortex would you leave him alone like that? He's only sixteen—"

"Yeah, and I was eleven," Lyssa shot back without thinking.

"What?" Vel and Dorst said in unison.

Lyssa looked down, feeling a little embarrassed blush on her cheek. "He's fine, obviously."

"What do you mean, you were eleven?" Vel pressed.

"Vel, I also wanted to stop by and make sure you were attending Mother's birthday celebrations," Dorst sniffed, blatantly ignoring Lyssa's outburst. "She is very much looking forward to seeing you again since you haven't been home in a few weeks."

"Lyssa can drop me off," Vel said, waving him off, before turning to look at her amusedly. "I might even get her to stay."

"HAH!" Lyssa barked, giving him a look. "Next family celebration I'm going to is her funeral."

Dorst gaped at her, as if she had just uttered something blasphemous, "How *dare* you—"

"Oh she's just being a twit," Vel said, waving Dorst off. "Ignore her."

Dorst looked between the two of them—Vel ignoring Lyssa's outburst like it was nothing new, and Lyssa not the slightest bit annoyed that she hadn't gotten a rise out of him.

"Uh huh," Dorst cleared his throat. "Well, please remember that this is a serious…internship. I hope that you are spending your time wisely."

"Oh, don't worry," Lyssa chuckled, tossing a sly look to Vel. "He's learning LOADS."

Dorst finally looked at her, and his eyes focused immediately to the yellowing blotch on her cheek from where her bruised eye was healing. "Do you have a black eye, Lyssandra?"

"It's a scratch," she said, before adding under her breath, "Took you long enough to notice."

"Well, please keep in touch, Vel," Dorst said, trying very much not to care. "We are looking forward to seeing you at Mother's celebrations in the coming weeks."

Lyssa watched him walk away and pulled out her mini-computer dramatically, nodding approvingly.

"What?" Vel asked.

"That was the longest conversation I've had with him without him bringing up Sostas," she grinned, meanly. "I'm impressed!"

"So you want to tell me what you meant by that whole 'eleven' comment?" Vel asked, eyebrows raised.

"Nothing," Lyssa muttered.

"Because it sounded to me like you were kidnapped by a pirate or something," he continued, unfazed. "Which would actually answer my question about how—"

"Okay, I'm done here," Lyssa said, standing up with her tray and walking away.

"Lyssa," Vel called, getting up to follow her. He got about three steps before he was stopped.

"Have a moment, Vel?" Dr. Pymus smiled, wrapping his arm around the nervous young man before he could respond.

***

Lyssa stared at the old computer screen, her eyes darting over the text and tables in her presentation. She was working on the section about water quality, and realized that she didn't have nearly enough information to make a good recommendation.

Rubbing her chin thoughtfully, she looked around the empty laboratory, as if to check and see if invisible people were watching her type in false data into the presentation. It wasn't the first time she'd lied on a planet presentation; but DSEs often made mistakes with analysis, so she hadn't been caught yet.

She heard a quick rap at the glass laboratory door, looking up to see Vel waving at her.

Annoyed to be pulled from her thoughts, she pushed herself away from the table and opened the door for him.

"Where've you been?" she asked, grumpily.

"I didn't know you had a lab," Vel said, looking around. "Doesn't look like it's been used in a while…"

"It's not mine," Lyssa said, checking the data on her analysis and what she had typed into the presentation.

"Another paternal hand-me-down," Vel smirked.

"Yup," Lyssa nodded. "Dorst wants this lab, though. He's gotta share with Hasidus and Kasan," she said, referring to their third and fourth eldest brothers. "They had to pool their money to afford that tiny closet they have now."

"You should really give them this lab," Vel chided. "You know you don't use it."

"Using it right now," Lyssa insisted stubbornly.

"You're using it to put together a presentation which you can do on any machine in the universe," Vel replied. "Besides, it might help you mend some fences between them."

"I don't want to mend any fences," Lyssa grumbled. "Besides, they should be trying to mend fences with me first."

"Tell me about when you were kidnapped," Vel asked, quietly. "What happened?"

Lyssa sighed and sat back, chewing on her lip for a moment with a frown.

"Please?" Vel pressed.

"When I was eleven, just…three months after I had started at the Academy, Tauron kidnapped me off of an Academy field trip."

"Why?" Vel asked.

"He was trying to get a rise out of Jukin," Lyssa replied, looking down at her hands. "Jukin had recently purchased his commission as Captain of the U-POL Special Forces. The unit had existed before him, but it was always stocked with the laziest, the most inept police. Jukin was singularly focused on whipping it into shape, hiring new recruits who shared his vision for a universe without piracy," Lyssa explained. "He was immune to bribes, to threats against his own life. So Tauron thought he could be persuaded if one of his precious sisters was in danger." She paused, chuckling darkly.

"Problem was, Tauron chose the wrong sister."

Vel was watching her closely, but said nothing.

"Put a gun to my head," Lyssa continued with a steady voice "Told Jukin that if he didn't quit targeting pirates that he was going to blow my brains out."

"What did Jukin say?" Vel asked, almost afraid to know.

"Be my guest," Lyssa whispered. The memory was vivid.

Vel's mouth dropped in shock and his brow furrowed. "He didn't…"

"So then Tauron called Mother," Lyssa continued numbly. "I mean, he figured that if he couldn't get what he wanted out of Jukin, maybe he could at least get a good ransom for me, or maybe Mother could have convinced Jukin to stand down, but…"

Vel hadn't taken his eyes off of her.

"Well, I guess you can figure out how well that one went," she said, smiling.

"Obviously not the way she reacted when I was kidnapped," Vel whispered.

"Actually, there were some striking parallels," Lyssa chuckled. "Mostly about Mother saying I was a terrible person. Soul is going to be damned to Plegethon, all that."

"That's not fair," Vel shook his head. "They had no right to treat you that way."

"I'm used to it by now," Lyssa shrugged, looking down at her hands distractedly.

"So…is that why you wanted to become a pirate?" Vel asked after a few silent moments.

"Tauron was completely and utterly against the idea," Lyssa chuckled. "Not only was I just an eleven year old girl, but I was the sister of the Captain of the Special Forces. He thought it was too dangerous—both for him and for me. But," she smiled. "I kept coming back again and again. Took transporter ships to D-882 and sat at Harms' bar for hours—sometimes days—waiting for him to show up. After about six months, he finally relented—on one condition."

"What's that?" Vel asked.

"He said I had to continue my studies," Lyssa said, looking around the lab. "I could come stay on his ship on the weekends and during semester breaks, but I had to stay in school." She chuckled again. "He made me do the most menial of tasks—laundry, cleaning the ship, cooking for the crew—anything to get me to not show up the next weekend. I didn't care though, anything to get away from the Academy.

"How did you get into bounty hunting?" Vel asked.

"When they weren't making me do menial stuff, I'd sit and watch

Tauron look for guys. It didn't take him very long to realize I was pretty good at it," Lyssa smiled. "I found some of the most difficult pirates for him—unfindable guys, really. Sometimes we'd work on them together, sometimes I would do them all by myself. Sometimes I could find the guys in an hour—sometimes I'd been pouring over my mini-computer for three weeks in the back of class."

"Professors didn't stop you?" Vel asked.

"They all thought I was working on Leveman's Vortex," Lyssa smirked. "Let me skip class sometimes too. Tauron didn't like it when I did that, though."

"I find it incredibly ironic that a pirate was the reason you finished your degree," Vel laughed, shaking his head.

"He said he would make me a full member of the web when I got my degree," Lyssa said, her smile fading slightly. "Unfortunately....Jukin got a hold of him first."

She swallowed the lump in her throat.

"I think he'd be proud of you," Vel said, placing a hand on her shoulder.

"Yeah, whatever," Lyssa said, brushing his hand off of her shoulder. "I have a stupid presentation to give in an hour, and I'm not even halfway done. So quit yapping and go sit over there."

Vel sighed, but left her alone to stare at the screen. Although it was a few minutes before she began typing again.

***

"The rock creatures do not appear sentient," Lyssa droned on, flipping through her presentation to the sparse audience. "They appear to migrate regularly—unable to determine the frequency."

She saw someone yawn in the audience and sighed. Big, giant moving rocks did not equal a highly priced planet. To make matters worse, she saw that smartly-dressed woman show up halfway through her presentation.

"In summary, A-2244245 has a plethora of key features—potable water with a small concentration of minerals, regular temperature regulation, and a sizable non-liquid surface—that make this planet an excellent purchase."

She looked around the room and saw minimal interest.

Annoyed, she pulled her mini-computer and walked off the stage. Vel, who was seated in the front row, popped up and followed her into the small buyer's room.

"So that's a planet selling presentation?" Vel observed, sitting down in one of the empty chairs across from her.

"Welcome to your future," Lyssa smiled, looking at her Lyssa Peate bank account. She really could have used some money this trip; but based on interest, it didn't look like she was going to get even five thousand credits for this planet.

"I don't remember testing the water for minerals," Vel said, raising his eyebrow at her.

She smirked and put her finger to her mouth slyly as the door opened and a few prospectors filed into the room. Vel got up and moved to the back as more prospectors came in—more than Lyssa expected, to be honest.

And then, to her chagrin, the smartly-dressed woman who weaseled her out of thousands of credits walked into the room, this time wearing a killer black dress and bright white pearls, but heels that clacked loudly against the tile floor. She had her mini-computer pressed to her ear as she stood next to Vel, obviously annoyed that she was here.

Lyssa quickly sent a message to Vel's mini-computer.

That bitch underbid on my planet—8k!

She watched him jump as his mini-computer buzzed with the incoming message. He read it, then looked between Lyssa and the woman standing next to him. She watched him type back into his mini-computer.

I got this.

Lyssa, confused at his meaning, nonetheless realized she was wasting time and stood up, tapping on the table to get everyone's attention.

"So let's start the bidding at-."

"Fifteen," the woman in the back said, putting her hand over the speaker of her mini-computer, then returning to her call.

"I was gonna say twenty-five," Lyssa grumbled, angrily. Vel looked to the woman and to Lyssa, and motioned for her to fight back.

"Yeah, twenty five thousand credits," Lyssa repeated, louder.

"Ten," the woman said, over her phone.

"Thirty."

Lyssa gaped at Vel, who had just bid thirty thousand credits on a planet.

"Excuse me?" The woman said, looking over to look at him. "This planet is not worth thirty thousand—"

"I'll be the judge of that," Vel said, clearing his throat. "The offer stands—thirty thousand credits."

The prospectors began buzzing amongst themselves, looking at their paperwork and tablets as they looked around at this new prospector in the back.

"Thirty-one!" Another said nervously, as if he was still unsure why he was paying so much money for this planet.

"Forty," Vel said, smiling as Lyssa's eyes bugged out of her head.

"This is ridiculous," the woman said, putting her mini-computer away and putting her perfectly manicured hand on her hip. "This planet isn't even worth the amount of money they're paying me to stand here—"

"Forty-five!" another prospector said, from across the room.

"Fifty!" another piped up.

"Fifty-five!"

"Seventy-five!"

"One hundred thousand credits," Vel said, his voice clear but his eyes amusedly watching Lyssa.

"I am not—" the woman said, exuding her power and influence as she turned to face Vel straight on.

"Look, if you don't want to bid, get out of the room," Vel said, returning her ferocity with his own. "Frankly, I think one hundred thousand is an incredible underbid for such a useful planet—"

"Two hundred thousand!" one prospector said.

There was silence in the room as every eye turned to look at Lyssa, dumbfounded that this planet had just gotten a bid for so much money. She jumped, realizing that she had to actually close the deal on this planet.

"Sold!" she said, laughing a little bit. She sat back, amazed at how much money she had just made, as the prospectors filed out of the room.

All except for one.

The smartly-dressed woman waited until all of the other prospectors were out of the room and the door was closed before she turned to smile sharply at Lyssa.

"That was an interesting trick," she said, walking slowly up to them. "Having your intern drive up the price of a perfectly pathetic—and barely excavated planet."

Behind her, Vel's eyes widened.

"I needed to make back the eight grand you swindled me out of last month," Lyssa responded, returning her glare.

"I like you. You have spunk," she said, placing a business card on the table. "If you ever want to get out of this dirty business of excavating planets and make some real money, give me a call."

Speechless, Lyssa watched her saunter out of the room, the clack-clack of her heels echoing even after she had closed the door behind her.

"Tell me this," Lyssa said, turning to Vel. "What were you gonna do if no one else had bought the planet?" Lyssa asked.

"Ask Mother to give me an advance on my allowance?" Vel said, smiling.

"Oh well," Lyssa began, before stopping short. "Hang on, what allowance?"

***

"Can we please buy something other than meal bars?" Vel asked, standing next to Lyssa on the ship. With so much money in her account,

Lyssa was stocking up on enough food and supplies to last her for a few weeks.

"What's wrong with meal bars?" Lyssa asked, adding another box to the request list, along with another box of toiletries and case of water.

Vel whined behind her.

"Oh quit being such a damned child," Lyssa said, adding a few frozen meals to the mix. "There. Happy?"

"Oh, not the mushroom—" Vel sighed, stopping when Lyssa turned to give him a look. "Yes, very happy."

"Now go downstairs and wait for them to deliver the goods," Lyssa barked, sending the order. "Should be here soon. Stick it in the cabinets down there."

"Why do I gotta wait for it?" Vel grumbled, climbing down the stairs.

"Because you're the intern," Lyssa responded to him from above.

"Glad to see you've finally embraced the internship, Dr. Peate!"

Lyssa groaned audibly, and poked her head down the ladder to the bottom level of her ship. Pymus was standing at the bottom, looking up at her jovially.

"What do you want, Pymus?" Lyssa called, not willing to come down.

"That's *Dr.* Pymus, dear," he said sweetly. "I haven't checked in with the two of you in a while and I wanted to make sure there was adequate progress being made."

Lyssa looked down at him and smiled. "Loads of progress. Ask Dorst."

"Oh yes, I had a chat with your dear brother!" She could hear him opening her cabinets and groaned again, quickly sliding down the ladder to the lower level of her ship. She found him, nose deep in one of her cabinets, and Vel, helplessly and nervously looking between her and Pymus.

"Can I help you with something?" Lyssa said, rudely shutting the cabinet door in Pymus' face.

"Yes, I'd like to see the first draft of your report on the internship," Pymus said, gently rubbing his goatee to make sure she hadn't given him an inadvertent trim.

"What report?" Lyssa asked, plainly.

"Dear, dear, dear," Pymus laughed, using his immaculately shined shoe to open one of the lower cabinets. "You have obligations as well with this internship. Lessons learned! Detailed reports from the planets you've been excavating."

"Yeah," Lyssa smiled, using her hip to close the cabinet door he was opening. "Otherwise known as all of my research on Leveman's Vortex."

"My dear, watch that tone," Pymus tutted, with a small warning in his voice. "Otherwise, I will be forced to write another disciplinary note. And I believe this is three of them—I will have no other choice but to put you in front of the committee—"

"Go ahead," Lyssa dared him, feeling rather in control since her victory over that woman prospector. "Because I would like to see what the committee thinks about why you put a sixteen year old intern with a doctor barely two years out of the Academy."

"This internship was—" Pymus laughed.

"Probably paid for with a lot of money," Lyssa finished for him, feeling very much like Razia standing up against Dal Jamus. "And I would wager to guess that not everyone knew about or even signed off on this internship."

"My dear, you are making serious accusations," Pymus smiled, his eyes boring into her.

"Oh, I'm just getting started," Lyssa smiled back, stepping towards him threateningly. "Because not only will the committee be very interested to know how you actually got approval on this poorly thought out internship, but they will also be interested to know why you've been so interested in me these past few years."

"I'm your supervisor—" He laughed, but she could tell that she had cornered him.

"Supervisor, yeah," Lyssa continued, taking another step towards him. "A supervisor who is constantly trying to steal not only my intellectual property, but that of my father's, and has used an internship—some poor kid's education!—to further your intent to, and I'm going out on a limb here, publish our work under your name."

Pymus cleared his throat, but said nothing.

"So," Lyssa smiled. "Shall we go down that road? Or are you going to leave me alone?"

To her surprise, Pymus simply smiled at her. "My apologies, Dr. Peate. Until next time."

And with that, he sauntered off her ship.

"'Wait—" Vel said, looking nervously at the doctor's retreating back.

"Don't worry about it," Lyssa smirked, watching him leave. "Goodbye and good riddance."

CHAPTER THIRTEEN

"I want to get Santos Journot," Razia said, sliding into Harms' booth. She was flying high—telling off Pymus, getting two hundred thousand credits for a planet. She was feeling invincible, and she was ready to kick some major ass.

"Hello to you too," Harms smiled. "Congratulations, by the way."

"Congratulations for what?" Razia said, confused.

"I don't know what you did, but your bounty just went up another five million," Harms said.

"It did?" she grinned, confused. "How? I didn't do anything?"

"Well whatever it was, you're now in the top twenty," Harms said, flipping his tablet around and showing it to her.

	19) (No last name listed), Razia
Wanted For	Engagement in piracy, bounty hunting, kidnapping, aggravated assault, resisting arrest
Reward	10,000,500C
Known Alias	None
Known Accomplices	Tauron Ball, Sage Teon
Pirate Web affiliation	Dissident

"I'm surprised you haven't been paying more attention to your own bounty," Harms said, turning his tablet back to him.

"I've been too busy looking for Santos Journot," Razia lied, sitting back.

"You and everyone else in the universe," Harms said. "He's been picking off the top pirates for weeks now. Nobody knows anything about him..."

"So what can you tell me about him?" Razia smiled, knowingly.

Harms looked back at her expectantly.

"Oh, sorry," Razia said, whipping out her Razia C-card and handing it to Harms. "Never actually had to pay you before."

"Oh...you sure you want to use this one?" Harms asked, curiously, watching the transaction on his tablet. "No other C-cards that you have in there?"

Razia smiled. She was sure that the majority of Harms' information came from the payment receipts of pirates that came to visit him.

"Can't fool you, I guess," Harms shook his head. "You may want to let Sage know. You know, as a friend."

"If he's too stupid to figure out that he shouldn't use his secret alias C-card when talking to you," Razia sniffed. "Or that you're in the business of selling people out, then he deserves to be caught."

"You're still mad at him for saving you, aren't you?" Harms teased, grinning.

Razia gaped. "He didn't *save* me!"

"Sure he didn't," Harms winked. "He didn't swoop in, tell Relleck to leave you alone, carry you off into—"

"So Journot."

Harms chuckled and pulled up his own file of Journot. "The reason why nobody knows anything about him is that he doesn't actually do his own dirty work. Somehow, he finds all of the secret alias information for all the top pirates, then hires some low-level goon to go out and get them and turn them into the bounty office."

"What about those guys, any info?" Razia asked, chewing on her thumb curiously.

"Nope, they are all hired and given their marching orders electronically," Harms said.

Razia furrowed her brow. "Why would anyone want to do that?"

"You know, one of these days, you're going to be a top pirate, and you'll be wishing for the days when you could saunter through D-882 without being bothered...." Harms said, cocking his head to the side. "That little secret alias you have can't stay secret for long."

"What secret alias?" Razia smiled, pleased.

"I see every type of transaction here," Harms said, bringing up the file he had on Razia. "Except for parking receipts. Now I know you don't just appear on planets by magic. And don't even get me started on where you've been for the past week. Not a single transaction."

She shrugged, smiling. "I guess you'll just have to wonder."

***

Razia rubbed her bleary eyes and sat back, feeling the beginnings of a migraine. She had been staring at the same search results for an hour—the list of the last four pirates captured by Santos Journot:

	10) Sloan, Flynn Captured by Santos Journot
	9) Bullock, Jeam Captured by Santos Journot
	5) Bernal, Arpad Captured by Santos Journot
	4) Stenson, Eli Captured by Santos Journot

"Any luck?" Vel asked, walking in and handing her a cup of coffee.

"No," she said, holding the cup between her hands and looking at the mess of windows and data splayed across her screen. "Not even one transaction. Not an alias, not an accomplice, nothing."

	2) Journot, Santos
Wanted For	Engagement in piracy, bounty hunting
Reward	49,054,652C
Known Alias	None

Known Accomplices	None
Pirate Web affiliation	Insurgent

"Did you look and see about the pirates he's captured recently?" Vel offered. "Any commonalities?"

"Nothing—except they were all in the top ten most wanted," she said. "There's not even a pattern with where they were caught," she said, turning around and opening the notes she took from Harms when she met with him. "A couple in D-882 and the rest scattered throughout various planets. He even found Jeam Bullock on vacation in A-326."

"That's interesting, isn't it?" Vel said. "You'd think he'd be more careful about using a known bank account on vacation."

"That's the thing," she said, cupping the warm mug between her hands again. "He had no idea it was coming. Bullock's getting up there in age, so he likes to take his vacations. He had this one alias just to be used at his vacation house. I looked it up once it became public."

She brought up his bank records for his account. All of them showed transactions on A-326.

"Did he get sloppy?" Vel asked. "Maybe someone stole his C-cards?"

"Maybe," Razia said, chewing on her thumb.

"Did you try comparing their purchase history?" Vel asked.

"Yeah," she said, bringing up a star map with a bunch of multi-colored pins on different stars. "The only commonality between all of the bounties was that they all spent time at Eamon's."

"What's that?" Vel asked.

"It's an exclusive bar for only the top pirates," she explained. "So it wouldn't be unusual for all of them—as top pirates—to go there, though. There's crazy security there, and most of the pirates were caught weeks after they went there…"

"But maybe that's the point," Vel suggested. "If he's really that good, wouldn't he try to cover his tracks? If I was trying to pick off pirates, I'd definitely hit a bar where they all congregate. Maybe he somehow stole their aliases there?"

She paused for a moment, thinking about what he just said. Eamon's had been billing itself as a place for top pirates for months, even going so far as to hire huge bouncers to prevent anyone other than the top 50 pirates in the door. She'd spend nights watching pirate after pirate stumble out, usually on the arm of some woman. They would be prime targets for anyone in that state.

"What are you doing?" Vel asked, as she began plotting a course.

"Heading to Eamon's," she said.

"So...I'm right?" Vel asked.

She turned to give him a dubious look. "No."

"But it was my idea?"

"No it wasn't," she snapped.

***

She peered across the street and narrowed her eyes. The two Dal Jamus-sized bouncers were standing outside, denying entry to a slew of pirates who were milling around.

"So why don't you just go in?" Vel asked, leaning over beside her. "You're a top pirate, right?"

"I may be banned from the place," Razia muttered.

"What?" Vel said, gaping at her.

"I snuck in through a window once," she said, trying to change the subject.

"Why?" Vel asked.

"Because," she said, turning to look back at him. "What can I do to make you stay here?"

"Why do I have to stay here?" Vel frowned.

"Because it's going to be a lot easier for me to sneak in without having a tagalong," Razia snapped. "So just...hang out here, will ya? I won't be that long."

"Fine," Vel pouted.

Razia jogged past the entrance, careful to avoid the gaze of the bouncers. She quickly turned the corner, strolling through the alleyway, counting the number of doors until she reached the one that lead into the back kitchen of the bar.

Just as she was about to open the door, it swung inwards and she froze. But not because she'd been caught, but because a pair of steely blue eyes were staring into hers, framed by a strong jawline and black, curly hair.

"H-hi," she said lamely.

"The entrance is around the corner," he said, half smiling in such a way that it made her blush. She dumbly moved out of the way as he walked out into the alleyway.

"I...um..." she stammered like a moron.

"Wait, I remember you," he said, placing the garbage, which she just realized he was holding, in the bin. "You snuck in here a few weeks ago, didn't you?"

She frowned, slightly. "I also happen to be a pirate in the top twenty."

"Oh yeah," he said. "You kidnapped Jukin Peate's brother, right?"

"Yeah," she said, happy that somebody still remembered. Especially

152

someone with such beautiful blue eyes.

"So, why don't you just go in the front door?" he asked, folding his arms over his chest. "Since you are in the top twenty."

"Oh, your bouncers don't like me very much," she said. "Probably since I—"

"Snuck in?" he offered, chuckling. "C'mon, you can come in this way. I won't tell anyone."

"Really?" she asked, her own voice sounding weird.

"On one condition," he said, his hand on the door knob. "You'll have a drink with me when my shift's over," he smiled.

She blinked at him, as if he was speaking a different language. "What?"

"Have a drink?" he repeated. "With me?"

Her cheeks turned five shades of purple. "Really? Why?"

"Why do you think?" he laughed. "I want to get to know the only woman pirate."

She blushed again, thankful for the darkness. "Okay," she responded, dumbly.

"My name's VJ, by the way," he said.

"Razia," she said and then blushed. "I mean, I think you knew that but..."

She forced herself to shut up before she made an even bigger fool out of herself.

"Nice to meet you Razia," he said, smiling back at her and opening the door for her. "So meet me upstairs? About half an hour?"

"Sure..." she said, wishing to get away from him as soon as possible so she didn't embarrass herself further. She demurely walked past him into the kitchen, tossing one final look back at him before slipping into the bar.

She was immediately brought from her elated reverie as the loud pounding of music and smell of sweat and booze hit her in full force. Grumpily putting her hands over her ears, it took her a moment to acclimate.

The room was crammed with people—mostly men dressed in dress shirts, milling around eyeing the women walking around in short shorts and tank tops. Razia didn't recognize any of them; she figured they must be crew members of pirates.

That was when she caught a familiar face and couldn't duck in time.

"HEY!" Ganon came barreling over. Before she could tell him otherwise, he swept her up in a big bear hug, lifting her three feet off of the floor.

"GET OFF!" she screamed over the thumping music.

"What are you doing here!?" Ganon asked, his voice barely audible over the music.

"Nothing!" she yelled back, trying to get away.

"C'mon!" he said, grabbing her hand and yanking her forward, either not hearing or ignoring her protests.

To her annoyance, she found herself facing a table with Sage and his entire crew sharing a pitcher of beer (or at least they were, Sage didn't have anything in front of him).

"Hey!" Sage said, his eyes lighting up when he caught sight of her. "I wondered when we were going to see you."

"What?" Razia said, barely hearing what he said.

"I said, I wondered when I was going to see you!" he tried again.

She pointed to her ear, shrugging and shaking her head. Sage pointed behind her.

She turned and to her horror, she saw Vel carrying three more sudsy pitchers of beer.

"WHAT IN LEVEMAN'S VORTEX ARE YOU DOING HERE?" she screamed at him.

"What?" he said. "Can't hear you!"

She watched, her blood pressure rising as he sat down in an obviously open spot, sliding the pitchers down the bar. Her eyes swept from Vel to land squarely on Sage, who rolled his eyes.

"Relax," he said, standing up from his seat to walk over.

"Relax?" she spat, her face livid. "RELAX? WHY IS HE HERE!?"

"Because he was wandering around the bar entrance like a lost puppy," Sage yelled in her ear so she could hear him. "So he's now on my crew."

"He is *not*—"

"As far as they know," Sage said, motioning to the rest of the room, who were decidedly not paying any attention to them. "Don't worry. It's fine."

She looked between Sage and Vel, who was wiping a thick mustache of beer foam off of his lip.

"C'mon, have a beer," Sage said, yanking a seat from another table. She looked at it for a moment before sitting down and taking the beer that Vel handed to her.

"Not a word to Mother," Razia said, leaning over the table to him.

"Right, let me just go home and tell her that I went and had a beer at a pirate bar," Vel retorted, rolling his eyes.

"Oh he's fine," Sage said, slapping him on the back. "You were drinking much younger than he is."

She nearly choked on her beer.

"Say what now?" Vel smiled, looking between Sage and Razia's red face.

"You remember that time you broke into Tauron's liquor cabinet?" Sage said, clearly enjoying this stroll down memory lane. "And you drank his entire bottle of top shelf whiskey?"

Vel took another sip of his beer and looked between them—Sage chuckling evilly and Razia trying to look mad between coughs.

"I've never seen that much come out of such a small person," Sage said. "What were we, thirteen?"

"You were too chicken to have any," Razia said, the beer starting to loosen her mood slightly. She eyed his lack of drink and smirked, "Still are."

"So, Vel, let me introduce you to my crew," Sage said, abruptly changing the subject. "That down there is Ganon, he's my pilot. Keal is my mechanic and Sobal is computer guy, Nalton, Paren, Jorwen—they're my body guys—keep all of those obnoxious bounty hunters off of my back."

They waved one by one and then continued their conversations, ignoring the three of them.

"Why don't you have a crew?" Vel asked Razia.

"She doesn't like people," Sage winked. Vel snorted into his beer.

"I just don't like you, Teon," she shot back.

"That hurts me." He leaned back into the seat. "After all, I let you sit at my table."

"Your table?" she asked skeptically.

"Yes, actually, you're not a regular customer, but this table is reserved for me and my guests. So you'd better be nice to me," Sage nodded.

"Right," she said doubtfully, looking around. Immediately, she caught sight of at least five top pirates sitting at different tables surrounded by their crews and being tended to by at least one (if not two) of the short-wearing waitresses.

She caught eyes with VJ, standing behind the bar. He smiled at her and she looked away quickly, blushing beet red.

"What's with you?" Sage asked.

"It's hot in here," she lied, trying to look normal.

Sage raised his eyebrows, obviously not buying it.

She sighed and sulked down a little lower. "I have a date."

Sage laughed, "It must be loud in here. Because I thought you said that you had a date—"

"I do," she said, annoyed that he didn't believe her.

"What?!" Sage said, he and Vel sharing the same disapprovingly shocked look.

"With who?" Vel demanded to know.

She stole a look over to the bar, and saw VJ wink at her.

"Him?" Sage said, frowning. "Why him?"

"He asked me," Razia replied, snootily.

"But he's a bartender?" Vel said disapprovingly. "What do you know about him?"

"First of all, it's none of either of your business," she snapped, helping herself to another beer. "And second of all...it's none of your business!"

"Damn well is my business!" Vel spat.

She looked back to the bar and noticed VJ had disappeared, and a rather attractive blonde woman was in his place at the bar. She was winking and flirting with the assortment of pirates assembled at the bar.

In fact, there seemed to be more women now, waitresses walking around in their skimpy shorts and tank tops handing drinks to pirates who probably didn't need any more. Razia started to feel self-conscious in her tank top and baggy pants as they breezed by her.

"I'm outta here," she said, standing up suddenly.

"Be careful," Vel said, grabbing her hand.

"Really?" Razia said, shaking it off and giving him a look. She was keenly aware that both he and Sage were watching her as she made her way to the other end of the room.

She found the staircase to the upstairs and slowly ascended the stairs, butterflies growing in her stomach. She hadn't been on a date in ... ever— she was too busy bounty hunting or excavating planets to really focus on dating.

Up ahead, a skimpy short-wearing waitress was locked in an embrace with a man. As she passed them, she recognized the man as Relleck. However, he was too engulfed in his partner to even notice she was there.

For a brief moment, she considered taking him down then and there...but then a pair of blue eyes entered her mind.

Relleck got a pass tonight.

She came to the top of the staircase and pushed open the door. The room was dimly lit, with plush chairs and couches littering the room. There was a window on the front of the room that looked over the rest of the club.

"You made it," VJ was standing behind a much smaller bar. He was pouring two drinks out of a martini shaker. "I'm glad."

"I thought you were off work," Razia said, shutting the door behind her. Once the door was closed, the music quieted to a dull roar.

"I am, this one's on me," he said, walking over and handing her a drink.

"Cheers," she said, clinking her glass gently against his. She took one sip and nearly spit it out—it burned as it went down.

"Too strong?" he said, as they sat down on one of the plush couches. "I thought you were a steely-eyed pirate woman?"

"I am," she coughed. Even one sip was enough to make her head a little fuzzy. "But not that steely."

He was looking at her intently, and the butterflies returned.

"So, how'd you get into piracy?" he asked, propping his elbow on top of the couch to look at her.

"Tauron Ball," she said, leaning into the couch. "I was on his crew."

"Really?" he said, looking impressed and extending his arm down the couch. "So you must be pretty good, huh?"

She shrugged, and took a small sip of her drink again.

"I've thought about getting into piracy," he said, gently toying with a strand of her hair. It gave her chills. "I don't think I'm smart enough though."

"Mm?" she said, focusing more on the way his face was getting closer and closer to hers.

And the way his other hand was sliding down near her back pocket where she kept her C-cards.

"What do you think you're doing," she said, his face nearly inches from hers.

"I'm..." he said, looking at her oddly. "I'm just trying to have a good time."

"Right after you pulled my C-card, huh?" she said, yanking his hand away from her back pocket. "God in Leveman's Vortex," Razia said, slowly. "You were trying to...to get my aliases, weren't you?"

The wheels continued to turn in her head and she grew more horrified. "You....all of those women down there...you've been the one stealing their alias information, haven't you?"

She smiled. "Santos Journot."

He froze, eyes wide and hands still on her hips.

And then, without warning, he shoved her roughly back, ran to the door and slammed it shut.

She was on her feet in a second, running to the door and finding it locked. She struggled against the knob for a moment before turning around and looking for an alternative way out.

The window caught her eye.

She grabbed the nearest barstool and sent it flying through the window, shattering the glass, the thumping sound of the bar below coming in through the gaping hole. She peered out of the open window and gulped.

There was only one way down.

Closing her eyes, she took three deep breaths—it was only ten feet down—she was going to be fine. Then she kicked off the ground, running for the open window.

She landed in a heap on the bar, smashing some drinks and getting the attention of everyone in the room. With the exception of one person, currently pushing his way through a thick crowd of drunk pirates.

He was nearing the door; she'd have to get there faster than him.

She jumped on the closest table and wobbled as it fell over under her weight. But she was able to use the momentum to land on the next table, then the next, then the next, ignoring the screams from the girls covered in fruity drinks. She made it to the door just as Journot slipped through it.

She turned on her heel and sprinted after him, bursting through the doors and missing the thick arms of the bouncers by just inches as they reached for her to stop her. She saw Journot running down the street as fast as his nice shoes could carry him.

She bolted after him, years of running through forests showing their benefit. She caught him to him in no time, knocking him over and grabbing both of his wrists before he could wriggle away.

"C'mon, Razia," he pleaded as she slid handcuffs on him. "Just let me go, will ya? You found me out, I can't get any more pirate information!"

"Sorry," Razia said, un-apologetically, tossing her floating canvas to the ground and unceremoniously kicking him onto it.

"UNHAND MY SON!"

Razia looked up to see an older, short gentleman with grey curls and dark wrinkled skin huffing and puffing towards her. As he came into the light, Razia did a double-take.

"Wait a second... you're a Runner!" she gasped. "You're... Insurgent... aren't you?"

The old man stood agape at her. Suddenly, her bounty capture became that much juicier and she began to cackle.

"Let me get this straight, Insurgent has been bank-rolling his own bounty shakedown?" she said, with one foot on VJ's stomach, proudly claiming her prize as he struggled underneath her.

The old man stammered, trying to think of a good retort.

"Oooh," Razia laughed. "Dissident is going to be pissed when he finds out what you've been doing...!"

Insurgent cursed and spat at the ground. "You see, Junior? I'm done supporting your half-cooked cockamamie schemes! Now I'm going to have to hear it from the other runners!"

"Aw, c'mon Pop! Get me outta here!"

"I'll see you when you get out of jail tomorrow," he said, turning around and walking away.

"Ouch," Razia said, picking up the ropes to her floating canvas. "Well, to the bounty office with you. I am so looking forward to this headline."

After a few minutes of silence, VJ piped up again.

"So, Razia, this may be a bad time to ask, but when I get out tomorrow, do you want to go get a drink sometime? I promise I won't try to uncover your aliases—"

Razia gave him one look before kicking him unconscious.

CHAPTER FOURTEEN

"How dare you embarrass me!" Dissident seethed.

"Dissident, I—" Razia stammered, shocked. She had barely gotten back to her ship after turning in Santos Journot before Dissident was calling her. But, instead of the warm praise that she expected after hunting and capturing one of the most elusive pirate in the universe—especially a bounty hunter that had been unfairly targeting and capturing his top pirates—Dissident opened fire the moment she accepted the call.

"You have made me the laughing stock of the webs!" he continued, his grizzled face flushed with anger and spit flying from his mouth. "First by making Sage Teon bail you out of a stupid mistake, now this? Capturing the son of one of the runners?"

"Dissident, he was unfairly targeting your pirates!" Razia sputtered, trying to break into his angry tirade to talk reason with him. "And Sage—"

"I don't care if he captured ME and handed my ass to Jukin Peate himself!" Dissident said. "Such a mistake taking you off probation—"

Razia's heart caught in her throat. "You can't—"

"You screw up one more time," Dissident threatened. "You do anything that makes me or this web look bad, and I will kick you out faster than you can say Santos Journot!"

And with that, he angrily ended the call, leaving his words to ring in her ear.

"Well that's gratitude for you..." Vel offered, lightly from the doorway.

"Shut up, Vel," Razia murmured, standing up and brushing past him.

"Hey, come on..." Vel said, following her. "He was the second most wanted—"

"And you see the thanks I got," Razia replied.

"Why is that so important?" Vel asked, watching her face curiously. "Getting this guy's approval of you."

"Because it is," she whispered.

"It's important to Razia," Vel countered.

"What's your point?" she snapped.

"My point is that you've spent all this time trying to not be Lyssa Peate, and I think I finally understand why," Vel said gently. "I know it still hurts that they left you on that pirate ship."

She was silent, regretting ever telling him that.

"So maybe instead of running from it, you should try to make peace with it," Vel said, wincing as if she was going to explode at him.

"Peace?" she laughed, as it if was the most ridiculous thing she had ever heard of. "As in, make peace with *them?*"

"Look, why don't you come home with me?" Vel tried. "It's Mother's birthday."

"That place is not home," she snapped.

"Give it one more chance," Vel smiled. "Give them one more chance."

"They already made it painfully clear how they felt about me," Lyssa said, looking down.

"Well, how about this: if you come home with me," Vel tried. "I will spend the rest of my internship with Dorst."

"What?" Lyssa looked up at him sharply. "Why would you do that?"

"Well, partially because I'd like to learn something during this internship," Vel smiled. "And…I think it would be good for you to come to terms with what happened. You've been carrying around a lot of hurt for a long time, and I think…I think facing it head on would be good for you."

Razia turned this over in her mind, opting to focus more on his offer than his pleasantries. "And you think that switching to Dorst is enough to get me to play nice with these idiots?"

"Well yeah," Vel smiled. "Haven't you wanted to be rid of me for weeks?"

Razia looked forward, unsure of how she actually felt.

"Of course," she nodded, after a few moments. "Yeah, of course I want to be rid of you."

"So, what do you think?" Vel smiled. "Weekend at Mother's in exchange for your freedom?"

"Deal," Razia said, wondering why the thought of being without her intern was more depressing than the upcoming weekend.

***

Lyssa never thought she would return to the Manor—let alone twice in a month. This time, however, she was decidedly Lyssa—her hair pulled back into a bun, thick glasses on her face. She didn't want to take any chances that she'd be…recognized again.

Dread took hold as her ship descended onto the planet. She could see the Manor, brilliant yellow paint and long gravel pathways, as they approached the docking station. Per the Serann tradition, the bloodline that founded B-39837 all of those years ago, all of the children of Sostas and Eleanora Peate still technically lived in the house—even after they had been married and started having children of their own, or graduated from the Academy. The elder sisters—having children in the double digits now—began to take over whole sections, and, in some cases, floors, for their own. The brothers still maintained their own quarters, although most of them only came home on the weekends or special events.

So, of course, Lyssa was sure that they would all be here for their Mother's birthday.

The dread turned into all-out panic as she landed her ship in the fancy ship dock, her mind replaying what had occurred here just a short month ago. For a moment, she almost wished that they would recognize her as Razia again, giving her an excuse to escape quickly. As her ship's engines powered down, she resisted the urge to fire them back up and blast out of here as fast as her ship could carry her.

"I am really excited that you're doing this," Vel grinned, as she joined him on the lower level of her ship, bag slung over his shoulder. "We're going to have such a fun weekend!"

"Hooray..." she said, half-heartedly, following him off the hatch into the busy dock.

When she had been here a few weeks ago, the dock was completely empty. But today, it was filled with big ships, smaller shuttles coming and going, and people—tons of people. Lyssa recognized none of them—they were probably aunts, uncles, and cousins who would be spending the weekend at one of the many guest houses that dotted the countryside. They were all wearing the traditional Serann garb—long, full dresses with layers of petticoats for the ladies and waistcoats for the gentlemen. Several porters were unloading huge trunks, getting direction from stuffy-looking servants, who were checking on clipboards wildly.

"Pretty busy," Lyssa said, looking around. "So where—" she trailed off when she realized Vel had disappeared. She suddenly felt very exposed and nervous, standing in a room full of people who she didn't know on a planet full of people that hated her.

She saw the porter carrying a load of bags out a sliding glass door and quickly followed him, hoping to run into Vel wherever he had run off to.

She found herself in the Manor's ballroom, which was buzzing with activity. The hall itself was a cavernous space, with a huge staircase, intricately carved and designed. The walls of the room were covered in dark, expensive wood, with huge paintings of the most important Serann ancestors—including Jora Serann himself, the ancestor who discovered and settled the planet. The floor was covered in the finest tile, which was being cleaned and buffed by a set of servants, crouched over and working furiously.

There were servants all over, Lyssa realized, carrying fine china and exquisite gold decorations. They paid her little attention, focusing only on the task at hand, with the same nervous worry on their faces.

She spotted a tuft of blonde hair ducking through one of two giant open doors behind the staircase. Quickly, she dodged and stepped around servants to follow him.

She took one step inside the room and immediately regretted her decision.

The dining hall was filled with people milling about a long table that spanned from one end to the other. The end closest to Lyssa was filled with young children, screaming and chasing each other (followed closely by nannies that were also screaming and chasing them). The further up the table, the older the children, some seated already, some standing around chatting. The boys were dressed in the Academy uniform, the girls in the same long dresses that the people in the shuttle station were wearing.

At the head of the table was one large, empty chair.

Lyssa felt the dread in her chest again, turning to leave again. That was when the doors shut in her face.

She pushed on them, but they were too heavy for her to move.

She turned around, feeling much like a rat in a trap, as the children scampered to their seats quickly. The sound of scraping chairs quieted down and Lyssa became acutely aware of her heartbeat pounding in her chest.

BAM.

Mrs. Dr. Sostas Peate appeared in the doorway from the kitchen. She was wearing an exquisite gown of white with a red beaded design, bulging at the stomach and bosom area. Her blonde hair formed perfectly and stiffly over her head and the makeup on her face had settled into her wrinkles around her eyes and lips to make the lines more visible. Her eyes swept over the room, looking for a child that was moving.

And then, as if like a laser, they focused on Lyssa, pressed flat against the back doors.

For a moment, Lyssa wondered if her own mother wouldn't recognize her again.

"WHAT IN LEVEMAN'S GREAT VORTEX ARE YOU DOING HERE?!"

No, that special level of hatred was reserved only for Lyssandra Peate.

"Hi...?" she grinned, waving slowly. Every single eye in the room— from the tiniest child seated at the end of the table, to Sera, the eldest sister, was focused on her.

Mrs. Dr. Sostas Peate was now the color of her red beads on her dress.

Lyssa noted that they matched quite nicely. Her huge bosom was heaving up and down and her huge fists were clenched in a ball. She seemed ready to pop out of her fancy dress.

"The *nerve* of you to show up here again!" Mrs. Dr. Sostas Peate breathed. "AND ON MY BIRTHDAY!"

"Surprise?" Lyssa smiled. She pulled herself off of the door, and slowly walked up the table, looking for a seat that she could quickly slide into to perhaps not draw any more attention to herself. Unfortunately, every seat at the table was taken—even Vel, that little bastard, had managed to sneak his way in and find his seat.

"Doesn't seem to be a spot for me," Lyssa said, trying to smile nicely.

"Shouldn't that be a hint?" she heard one of her siblings mutter. The ones that heard began to giggle meanly.

"Oh wait," she smiled, feeling her claws come out. "There's a seat for me."

And without another word, she marched up to the head of the table, loudly pulled out the seat normally reserved for Jukin (who was absent), and promptly sat down in it.

An audible gasp came up from the table.

"You-you-you can't sit there!" Sera hissed.

"Try and move me," Lyssa smiled, almost hoping that she could beat the crap out of someone.

A servant appeared, nervously, next to Mrs. Dr. Sostas Peate. "M-Madam, the first course shall get cold if—"

"Fine, fine," she snapped, sitting down in her chair. Two servants pushed her chair in with a loud scrape.

"Yes, yes, let's eat," Lyssa said, picking up her napkin and placing it in her lap nicely.

"Get sucked into Leveman's!" Sera growled at her.

"My, that's a bit intense for you, isn't it, Sera? Don't you have to go pray at your alter for that one?" Lyssa said, raising her eyebrow as her soup was placed in front of her.

"I doubt you've even seen the inside of a temple since you left here," Sera snapped back.

"Of course she hasn't," Dorst, who was sitting to Lyssa's left. "Barely at the Academy."

"And here I thought you pretended I didn't exist," Lyssa sighed, looking over to him. "Except when vaguely threatening me about taking on interns. Thanks for not doing anything while Pymus shoved that stupid kid on me."

Dorst winced.

"Dorst, I thought you said that you had intervened on your brother's behalf?" Mrs. Dr. Sostas Peate said, her beady eyes trained on Dorst, who was trying not to whither under her stare. "Especially after the whole...kidnapping incident."

"Yeah, Dorst," Lyssa piled on. "I obviously can't be trusted."

"Apparently, Dr. Pymus believes very strongly that Vel can learn a lot from her," Dorst said, shrinking slightly under his mother's intense focus.

"Yeah, more like he's trying to spy on Sostas," Lyssa snapped, pouring salt into her soup to try and make it palatable.

The mention of his name caused everyone in earshot to stiffen.

"And how is your father?" Mrs. Dr. Sostas Peate said, her voice steely and steady.

"And it begins," Lyssa sighed, taking out her mini-computer dramatically. "That only took, what, two minutes?"

"Well?" Dorst asked, annoyed.

"I don't know, I haven't seen him in ten years," Lyssa said, rolling her eyes.

Mrs. Dr. Sostas Peate sniffed but said nothing.

"One of these days, when it's your time to be judged by the Great Creator," Sera said superiorly. "You will have to answer for all of your lies."

"Oh, trust me," Lyssa smiled. "I'll have a lot more to answer for than lying to you idiots."

***

"What are you wearing?"

"At least it's not a giant tent."

"You've gained weight."

"Skinnier than you."

"Have you found a husband yet?"

"Have you heard of this thing called birth control?"

"Okay, okay," Vel said, nearly dragging Lyssa away from the throng of people in a post-dinner feeding frenzy. Once they were safely out of earshot, he turned to her disappointedly. "I thought you said you were going to be civil?"

"Yeah well, that would also require them to be civil to me," Lyssa replied. "Which, I don't know if you saw, but they weren't."

"They're just in shock," Vel said, waving her off. "And it'll take some time for them to come around. But you should be nice first."

She feigned hurt. "You mean that wasn't being nice?"

He rolled his eyes as they walked up the grand staircase to the bedrooms that comprised the second, third, fourth, and fifth floors of the Manor. Children were running around the second floor, pausing momentarily to stare at her and Vel as they passed.

"Where are we going?" Lyssa asked.

164

"Your room," Vel said, stopping on the third floor.

"Ah, yeah, actually, I think I'm going to just sleep on my ship," Lyssa said, wriggling out of his arm. "More comfortable and less...deadly there."

"Nonsense," Vel said. "You have a perfectly fine room here, and you're going to sleep here."

"Is that part of the deal?" Lyssa said. "And how long exactly do I have to stay here?"

"Until the party is over," Vel said, leading her onto the third floor. There was a thick carpet underfoot, which was being cleaned by a servant down the hall. Each of the doors was made of the same exquisite dark wood as the ballroom below, and had a gold plated number in front of it.

They stopped in front of room three hundred fifteen and Lyssa looked to Vel expectantly.

"I don't have a key or anything—"

"Why would it be locked?" Vel said, opening the door.

Lyssa suddenly felt as if she was in a time warp, stepping into a room that looked exactly the same as it did the last time she was here. The white four-poster bed was neatly made with a pink comforter neatly folded over crisp pillows. White bookshelves lined the pink-striped wallpaper walls, filled with teddy bears and other knick-knacks. A white desk and chair were in the corner, a stack of notebooks and other books neatly placed on top.

"Are we in the right room?" Vel asked, looking around, dubiously. "Seems a little...girly, don't you think?"

Lyssa walked over to the desk and picked up one of the books, *History of Planetary Exploration, Volume 3*, and smiled at him. "Definitely my room."

"Pink?" Vel said, looking at the wallpaper.

"Not my choice," Lyssa said, flipping through books on the desk. She came across a half-completed book of number pattern games, remembering how Sostas would buy these in bulk to keep her busy. "I didn't know half of this stuff was here. Looks like they just shipped all of my belongings here after each semester."

"You didn't even come home once?" Vel said, watching her thumb through her books.

"Well, when you have a pirate's gun to your head and your mother doesn't do anything, kind of cements your desire to never set foot here again," she smirked, wryly. "Not as if I spent much time here before that happened, either."

"Where were you?" Vel asked, sitting down on the bed.

"With Sostas," Lyssa said, distractedly thumbing through a book. "Down in his lab."

"So when are you going to go talk to Mother?" Vel asked, looking at her curiously.

"Do I still have to do that?" Lyssa asked, closing the book and rolling her eyes. "It's obvious she's uninterested in doing anything other than murdering me."

"Lucky for you, you took down Dal Jamus," Vel smirked. "You know, if she tries."

Lyssa paused for a moment, letting the full scope of Vel's comment sink in, before she turned to look at him impressed.

***

Lyssa found herself lying awake in her childhood bed, unable to sleep. Although it probably had something to do with the leftover adrenaline from sparring with her many siblings, it was more likely due to the blue glow from Leveman's Vortex in the night sky.

She rolled on her side away from the light, but found herself staring at a set of murderous-looking dolls that had never been touched. She flipped onto her back and covered her face with her pillow—but the smell of the dust was too much and she had to sit up.

Damn that Leveman's Vortex, she thought, moodily.

Angrily, she kicked the covers off of her and padded to the door, hoping that maybe a nighttime stroll would help clear her mind and help her sleep. After all, she had another full day of backstabbing, evil sibling fun—she needed her rest.

Her bare feet made no noise on the carpet as she walked down the silent hall with shut doors. She wondered which room was Vel's—he'd all but disappeared after a while. But then again, he did enjoy being here, so maybe that's what it was.

She came to the end of the hall and the spiral staircase, and began walking slowly down the hall, counting in her mind the many times she would walk up and down these stairs. Most of the time, she was in a hurry—quickly changing out a set of clothes or grabbing a book Sostas wanted her to read on their next trip.

She came to the bottom of the stairs and paused; the transition from soft carpet to stone tile was always jarring. Carefully, she placed one foot on the floor, wincing at the coldness, before placing both feet on the ground. She padded out into the ballroom, the giant paintings eerily lit by candlelight. The decorations for the party were nearly complete—and already tables had been set up along the sides to hold food and drink.

Sostas was never one for parties, and it was rare that his wife would coerce him into attending one. When he did attend, he would sit in the corner wearing whatever he had been wearing that day, covered in dirt or oil from tinkering with machines, scowling and daring anyone at the party to come talk to him. Lyssa was always by his side, cross-legged on the floor,

166

watching the ladies and gentlemen dance.

She continued walking across the tile floor, illuminated by the candelabras near the pictures and also by the looming Leveman's Vortex, which seemed to follow her through the house. Off to the right of the room was another hall, this one leading to the kitchens. Much like the rest of the ghostly house, they were empty, but she could see giant ovens and pantries stocked with food, just waiting to be prepared for the party tomorrow.

She continued on her midnight stroll, until she found herself in front of a large metal door, with a glowing red keypad. She stood in front of it for a moment, hesitating and wondering if it would be a better idea to turn around and go back to bed. Instead, she reached her fingers up and pressed the buttons, the soft tones of the keys combining into a familiar, comforting melody.

With a small click the door unlatched and she pushed it open revealing nothing but darkness. Her fingers searched along the wall until they slid over the light switch, illuminating a long staircase and a man hastily scribbling in a black, leather bound journal.

"You're late," he said simply.

"I'm sorry," she replied, slowly walking down the stairs.

"Lock the door, Lyssandra, I swear to the Great Creator," he muttered, without looking up.

She turned around and locked the door behind her, and walked down the stairs. The lab was filled with machines and books, and the walls were covered in chalkboards, with hastily scribbled notes and mathematical equations all over the walls. His desk, though, was the center of his universe, covered with stacks of papers and maps, but always a little space for his journals.

He didn't speak to her as she took her spot at her own table, textbooks about Deep Space Exploration that she wouldn't get to until she was three or four years into the Academy. Her eyes were locked on him, focused on the journal in front of him, and the scraps of paper from some observation about Leveman's Vortex that he was trying to parlay into some other discovery.

"Quit staring at me and get to work," he barked, his back still turned to her.

"I finished this book already," Lyssa said quietly, before realizing, "I graduated from the Academy two years ago."

"Yet you still can't remember to lock the door behind you," he grunted, turning the page. "Look and see what you've brought."

Lyssa turned to look behind her and was up in a flash, as three unwelcome guests came strutting down the stairs. Mrs. Dr. Sostas Peate, wearing her finest afternoon dress, followed by Priest Helmsley in his floor length frock, and Sera, who trailed farther behind, in a simple sky blue dress.

"M-Mother," she whispered, turning to look for protection from her father, but finding him gone. In fact, the lab was devoid of most of his things—save for the scraps of paper on the desks and her books in the table. Lyssa turned to face the three of them, her heart beating out of her chest.

"So this is where the two of you have been hiding, hm?" Priest Helmsley said, superiorly looking about the room. "Filthy in here."

"Lyssandra, it has been three months," Sera said, trying to keep her emotions in check. "We are concerned about him—where has he gone?"

"I don't know," Lyssa said, for what felt like the hundredth time. "He just left one morning and he hasn't called and—"

"This is pointless," Mrs. Dr. Sostas Peate said, giving her a look. "She's nothing but a liar. Jukin is searching for him, I know that he will help—"

"He didn't!" Lyssa cried, feeling a firm hand on her shoulder and a cold barrel against her temple. Her mother was staring at her through a video screen, looking rather unimpressed with her predicament. Behind her, Helmsley looked even less concerned.

"Jukin didn't help, please Mother!" she pleaded, her voice shaking from terror. "Please don't let them kill me."

"Well, then I suppose you had better contact someone else for help," Mrs. Dr. Sostas Peate smiled, although her eyes were daggers. "Perhaps your father thinks you are worth saving."

"MOTHER!" Lyssa screamed as the gun clicked against her head. "MOTHER PLEASE!"

"You see, child?" Helmsley replied. "There are consequences for your actions."

"But I didn't do anything wrong," she cried, falling to her knees. "I've never done anything wrong."

She watched a tear fall to the ground—and then, as if it was melting the floor itself – it fell straight through. The floor began to heat up, and smell of sulfur filled her nostrils. Looking up sharply, she found herself in front of the Arch of Eron, the silver curtain slowly turning an inky black, and the sky growing fiery red.

"Oh, but child, you have been wrong since the day you were born," Helmsley continued, walking around her. The ground around her began to crumble and fall into a river of fire beneath her.

She looked up to Helmsley, petrified, but found it wasn't him—it was Sostas.

"You were supposed to be good," he said, bending down to look at her.

"I tried!" Lyssa sobbed. "I tried to be good! Please! Please....please don't leave me..."

He paused and turned to look at her once more, his brown eyes staring directly into hers.

"I have no use for a rotten soul."

And with that, she felt the ground give way underneath her.

CHAPTER FIFTEEN

"NO!"

She shot upright, her whole body shaking.

It took her a moment to remember where she was—to recognize she wasn't falling to her death. She covered her eyes with her sweaty hands, taking deep, gulping breaths to try and calm her thumping heart. The entire dream had been so real.

"Lyss?" Vel said, poking his head in. "Are you okay? I heard screaming."

"Fine," she said, unable to look at him.

"You look white as a sheet," Vel said curiously, before smirking. "You didn't dream about another cliff, did ya?"

"No," she whispered, heading straight into the bathroom to splash water on her face. "What are you doing here anyway?"

"Well, you missed breakfast," Vel said, proffering a napkin. "Brought you a biscuit."

"Thanks," Lyssa muttered. "Why was breakfast so damned early?"

"Duh," Vel said, looking at her through the mirror. To Lyssa's stumped reaction, he replied, "We have Temple this morning."

"Oh," Lyssa said, shades of her dream coming back to her. "Enjoy."

"Thought you might like to go," Vel smiled, waving the biscuit around.

"Why?" Lyssa grunted, wiping down her face.

"Because it seems to me like you could use some time to reflect," Vel said, as she took the biscuit from him.

"I don't need to reflect on anything," Lyssa said, brushing past him. "I've been to a Helmsley sermon before. All he does is take whatever has pissed Mother off that week and turn it into an hour-long diatribe."

"That's not true at all," Vel sighed. "He has very insightful and very thoughtful presentations about how we can look at ourselves and make sure we're doing what is required to ascend to heaven—"

"Oh, well," Lyssa said, pulling on a clean shirt. "Maybe it's just when I attend that he spends the whole time not-so-subtly hinting about how terrible I am."

"Or maybe," Vel smiled, offering the biscuit again. "His words ring so close to home that you can't help but feel like he's talking about you."

"No, I actually think Mother tells him to target me," Lyssa smirked.

"Come with me," Vel said. "I'm going to prove you wrong."

"Fine," Lyssa said, slipping her mini-computer into her pocket. If anything, she could do some bounty hunting while she was stuck in there.

The sun was already hot, as evidenced by the waving fans fanning the faces of women in at least ten different layers of dress, between petticoats, slips, and the intricate outer dress. Each one gave her a disapproving (perhaps jealous) look as she waltzed by, arm in arm with Vel wearing a pair of wrinkled pants and a wrinkled shirt.

The Temple at the Manor was the very first building constructed on the planet. The spot was chosen because Leveman's Vortex was visible through the giant open window during the entire sermon, providing real incentive for the attendees to pay attention.

The Vortex caught Lyssa's eye as she walked into the Chapel, the rows of pews already filled with people milling about. Vel pulled her into the center of an empty pew near the front.

"No, I'd rather not be so close," Lyssa muttered.

"Nonsense, this is the best spot to see the Vortex," Vel replied.

"I've seen it enough," she muttered, helplessly looking around. Her eyes danced across the murals painted on the walls, depictions of ancient travelers to the Vortex who had tried to use trickery to get around the soul weighing. Mercurious stood behind his younger, more pious brother during the treacherous journey through Lethe, until his brother passed beyond the arch. Rongo used magic to transform himself into a child, but his soul was weighed just the same. Others that Lyssa couldn't remember lined the rest of the wall, each making it far enough to the soul weighing.

All of them had the same fate—falling into for Plegethon, the terrible river of fire.

Just like her.

Lyssa's attention was drawn from the murals as Priest Helmsley came to the podium, shuffling about papers. Right next to him came Mrs. Dr. Sostas Peate, dressed in her very best temple outfit, exquisite green silk and a giant hat. She daintily (as she could) sat down in her ordinate chair next to Priest Helmsley and darted her small eyes out across the audience.

Lyssa watched with dread as they landed squarely on her and a smug smile grew on her face. She tutted to Helmsley, who leaned over to hear what she was whispering to him. He looked up and caught site of Lyssa, then reshuffled his papers.

"Good morning, all," he began, his voice echoing in the suddenly quiet temple.

"Good morning," a chorus of voices responded back.

"Blessed be our matriarch on this anniversary of the day her soul left the Great Vortex," he began, looking out in the crowd. "Blessings to the beautiful family she has created in her years since, a family that has dedicated themselves to the Great Creator and serving piously in His vision."

"Here we go," Lyssa muttered.

"Oh stop," Vel said, nudging her. "Not everything is about you."

"But some among us," he continued, "some among us have strayed from the teachings of the scriptures. Some of us are living lives of falsehoods, of evil purpose. And no evil is more vile than that of perpetrating lies—especially to those who love us most of all."

Lyssa turned and gave Vel a pointed look. He intentionally ignored her and continued to listen to the sermon, a forced happy look on his face.

"There is no shortcut to eternal bliss," Helmsley continued, his eyes continuing to sweep over in Lyssa's general area. "Mercurious found this to be true. We recall how he followed behind his brother—his pious, good brother, who lived a life we could all envy—through the white fields of Lethe to Eron's Arch."

Lyssa nudged Vel, "Oh, is that supposed to be a dig at you? You haven't been living a very pious life lately—"

"Shut up!" Vel hissed back. "I love this story."

"You know how it ends," Lyssa said, looking at the man falling to his death in a fiery river.

"You know, you could at least try to be a little bit respectful," Vel snapped.

"The both of you had better quiet down or I will make you be quiet!" Sera hissed from in front of them.

Lyssa responded by sticking her tongue out.

"You are such a child," she heard Sera mutter before turning around.

"Mercurious—" Helmsley continued, giving the three of them a look. "Thought that he had outsmarted the Great Creator, as he had crossed the white fields of Lethe, and could even see the Arch of Eron—touch it almost. The moment his brother's soul passed beyond…"

"He fell to his doom into Plegethon," Lyssa muttered, as Helmsley boomed across the audience. She felt the buzz of her mini-computer. Looking around, she quietly pulled it out, looking at the missed video call she had received from Sage. Knowing he would continue to bug her, she sent him a message:

Can't talk. What do you want?

After a few moments, he responded:

Where ya been?

She looked around to see if anyone was watching her—they all had rapt attention to Helmsley's detailed story about how this Moronious or whatever-his-name-was burned for all eternity. She turned back to her mini-computer and responded:

Got dragged to Manor. Why?

She waited for a moment and then received another message from him.

The Manor-Manor?

As in your Mother's house?

As in the place you swore you would never go to again?

She pursed her lips, annoyed.

Yes, the Manor. What do you want?

You turned in the top bounty then disappeared from radar. Thought you'd strut around, seeing as your bounty just went up another 5M.

	17) (No last name listed), Razia
Wanted For	Engagement in piracy, bounty hunting, kidnapping, aggravated assault, resisting arrest
Reward	15,000,500C
Known Alias	None
Known Accomplices	Tauron Ball, Sage Teon
Pirate Web affiliation	Dissident

She quickly switched applications to look at her bounty profile:

A smile grew on her face—this was it! This was the kind of thing she was looking for. Turn in a bounty—immediate increase in hers. Finally, people were-

"Quit looking at that thing in Temple," Vel hissed.

Lyssa made a face at him and turned back to her messages:

Dissident was sooo happy Journot was captured.

Lyssa frowned typing back:

He told me I'd embarrassed the web, said he regretted taking me off probation.

Bullshit. I've never seen him so happy. But you know him—he's too stubborn to admit when he's wrong.

Lyssa bit her lip and replied:

Meaning what?

She waited with bated breath for his response:

Meaning he knows you're a damned good bounty hunter.

"YES!" she hissed, louder than she meant to. Helmsley, in the middle of describing the horrible pain that comes with burning in an eternal hellfire, stared at her with his mouth open, and Mrs. Dr. Sostas Peate looked about ready to slaughter her.

Vel, on the other hand, simply plucked the mini-computer out of her hand and tucked it under his arm, smiling back at the two of them, as if the problem was now solved.

Lyssa sat back with her arms folded across her chest, but couldn't bring herself to be upset.

Dissident thought Razia was a good bounty hunter. And it was only a matter of time before she proved it to the rest of them.

***

	2) Hardrict, Cree
Wanted For	Engagement in piracy, bounty hunting, hijacking, grand larceny
Reward	47,589,524C
Known Alias	Bobby Kayden, Farrell Tadeusz, Brooks Henry, Knox Camron
Known Accomplices	Finn Widemann, Warren Reiley, Bandit Scout, Kae Glenn
Pirate Web affiliation	Contestant

	3) Loeb, Jarvis
Wanted For	Engagement in piracy, bounty hunting, hijacking, grand larceny
Reward	45,746,852C

Known Alias	Arlo Gavigan, Robert Lee, Levon Gere, Roman Gibson
Known Accomplices	Sebastian Wheldon, Terrell Willis, Kassian McCarrell, Axel Kayse
Pirate Web affiliation	Protestor

	4) Lee, Linro
Wanted For	Engagement in piracy, bounty hunting, hijacking, grand larceny
Reward	41,054,500C
Known Alias	Ed Maxwell, Libertad Lark, Mika Castro, Joseph Cavanaugh
Known Accomplices	Royden Relleck, Enzo Rossi, James Rock
Pirate Web affiliation	Contestant

She scrolled through the different bounty profiles of the top ten—eager to take her pick of any of them. After rescuing her mini-computer from the clutches of Vel, who would only relent once Helmsley was completed with his long-winded sermon, she trotted out into the intricately designed gardens of the Manor. She found herself a shady tree far away from the loud screaming of the spawn of her siblings, near one of the many artificial ponds that dotted the landscape. She had been here for what seemed like hours, enjoying the nice breeze and the occasional bird that landed on the lake.

"Here you are!" she heard a voice behind her, but she didn't bother to turn around. Vel plopped down beside her, wearing his running clothes and shoes, and began sucking down his water. "I've been looking for you all afternoon."

"Why didn't you get me if you were going for a run?" Lyssa pouted.

"'Cause you disappeared after Temple," Vel said, his breath labored. "I've been running all over the place looking for you. Tried your ship, tried Father's lab—"

"It was unlocked?" Lyssa said, eyebrows raised, remembering her dream again. She couldn't figure out why it kept popping into the forefront of her mind, but it was starting to get old.

"No," Vel said, shaking his head. "But I knocked on the door for a few minutes before I realized you weren't in there."

"Nobody knows the code," Lyssa mumbled.

Vel sighed, sitting back against the tree and resting. "Beautiful day," he panted.

"Yup," Lyssa said, looking out into the pond. "So apparently Dissident was actually happy that I had captured Journot."

"What?" Vel smiled, looking over to her. "Really?"

"That's what Sage said," Lyssa nodded, a smile tugging at the corners of her mouth.

"That's awesome," Vel grinned, gently nudging her.

"It's a relief, to be honest," Lyssa said, looking down at her mini-computer. "I was starting to question myself there…"

"Well," Vel said, looking at her curiously. "You can't actually think that the Great Creator wants you to be a bounty hunter….do you?"

Lyssa looked up sharply, but not because she was angry at Vel. Yet again, she was reminded of her dream, and what Sostas said to her right before she woke up.

"I know you don't believe in the Great Creator, but—" Vel started.

"I believe in Him," Lyssa whispered sincerely.

"You….you do?" Vel said, sitting up to look at her.

"I've been inside, Vel," she said, looking out over the pond. "Inside-inside. As in… through the white fields of Lethe to the Arch of Eron."

Vel was silent, his mouth open and his eyes wide, mouthing words, but unable to form them.

"Sostas was doing experiments there," Lyssa continued, staring firmly ahead. "Trying to figure out what it all meant, where it all came from."

"Hang on," Vel blinked, his mind processing what she had just said. "Hang. On. You have been *inside Leveman's Vortex?!*"

She nodded solemnly.

"HOW?!" Vel screamed, probably louder than he meant to.

"Sostas figured out a mathematical equation for entry," Lyssa said quietly. "And, obviously, exit. It's this complex thing—weight of the ship, proximity to other celestial bodies, all that junk. There's a very specific calculation that—"

"I'm sorry," Vel said, looking at her as if she had three heads. "You have been inside Leveman's Vortex?"

"About once a month since I was four years old," Lyssa smiled at him, before it faded slightly. "Until Sostas left, of course…"

"So….it's all real?" Vel whispered.

"Look at you, Mr. Non-believer," Lyssa chided him gently.

"I mean it's one thing to go on pure faith," Vel swallowed, sitting back against the tree with a shocked look still on his face. "But quite another...you are sure you've been there?"

She nodded, unable to wipe the image of the world crumbling from her mind.

"What's it like?" Vel asked.

"It's weird," Lyssa said, eager to talk about anything other than what she was imagining. "There's a fluctuating magnetic field that scrambles your brain a bit, if I remember correctly. But it's just this big white place that you just wander around for a while until you come across the arch."

"The Arch of Eron is real?" Vel whispered.

She nodded. "Sostas would make me sit in front of it while he puttered on his experiments."

"That's...that seems kind of wrong to be experimenting there," Vel shook his head. "That place is holy—"

"It was damned boring is what it was," Lyssa chuckled.

"Do you think...do you think that's where he is?" Vel asked, quietly.

"Why in Leveman's Vortex do you want to meet him so badly?" Lyssa asked, rather than answering his question. "Why do all this? Why this internship? Why work with Pymus, of all people?"

"Lyssa, I'm sixteen years old, and I've never met my father," Vel said, sadly.

Lyssa still didn't understand. "Why is it so important to meet him?"

"He's my father," Vel shrugged, now looking out into the pond as Lyssa had done before. "I mean, sure, I had older brothers. But none of them were my actual father. He's always been this ghost in this house—never spoken about, but still there. Everyone always talked about how he doted on you—so I thought, well...maybe if he was still alive..." he trailed off, sadly.

"And what if he was alive?" Lyssa whispered.

"Maybe we could have the relationship I've always dreamed about?" Vel smiled, hopefully. "Maybe he'd pat me on the shoulder and say, 'Atta boy, Vel, you're doing great.' Maybe he'd...I don't know," he trailed off, blushing slightly.

Lyssa stared at him for a minute. It had never occurred to her that in the absence of knowing the real man, Vel might have fabricated this romantic notion of Sostas. She knew in her heart that, given the chance, Sostas wouldn't give Vel the time of day. Sostas couldn't even make time for his eldest son, no matter how hard he tried or how much he did to impress him.

But as she watched Vel, so young and innocent, she found herself feeling the need to lie to him.

"I think he would have really liked you," she smiled.

***

"So how long do I have to stay here?" Lyssa grumbled, angrily crossing her hands over her chest.

"I really wish you would have worn a dress," Vel sighed, adjusting his white tie and long black suit coat. "You look like a heathen."

"I don't wear dresses," Lyssa smiled, smoothing out the wrinkles on her nicest DSE-appropriate pants. "You didn't answer my question—how long do I have to stay here?"

"You have to have one conversation with Mother," Vel said, looping his arm through hers. "Lasting at least five minutes. And it has to be civil."

"Define civil."

"You know what I mean," Vel said, leading her out into the ballroom—now filled with people. Ladies wearing full dresses of silk and lace, curled hair and painted faces. Men with long black waistcoats and high socks—some even sporting white wigs, although it was considered woefully out of fashion. They were swirling about the floor much like Lyssa remembered them to be when she used to sit in the corner with Sostas.

"Let's get this over with," Lyssa muttered, spotting the guest of honor. Mrs. Dr. Sostas Peate was dressed in her most beautiful green silk dress, complete with a petticoat nearly large enough to offset her already large frame. She was surrounded by her sisters, each as rotund as her, and Sera, who looked much like a twig next to them. It was obvious that the three elder women had been drinking, as Sera was watching Lyssa like a hawk.

"Well look at who we have here!" Mrs. Dr. Sostas Peate said, her glass filled with her signature drink—brandy.

"Be nice," Vel hissed before turning to smile. "Mother, you look beautiful."

"Yes, son," she said dismissively, turning to look at Lyssa up and down. "Great Creator in Leveman's Vortex, do you even own a dress, or are you perfectly fine with walking around looking like you were raised by wolves?"

"Mother, please be nice," Vel said, watching Lyssa's eyes narrow.

"Well, I supposed she practically was," one of the sisters, wearing a rather odd shade of pink for a dress, swirled around her brandy. "After all, Eleonora, you barely had a hand in her rearing."

One of the other sisters giggled like a woman half her age. "Tell me, dear Lyssandra, how is your father?"

"Mother," Vel interrupted, feeling Lyssa stiffen next to him. "May we have a private chat?"

"Oh, Lyssandra continues to maintain that she has no idea where her

178

father has run off to," Mrs. Dr. Sostas Peate laughed, ignoring Vel completely. Her sisters twittered amusedly as they daintily sipped their drinks.

"Lyssandra, you honestly expect us to believe that Sostas would leave behind his darling little ragamuffin assistant? Why, he doted on you so!" One of the women cooed poisonously. "Ignored all of his other children just to spend time with you?"

"Oh, don't bother," Mrs. Dr. Sostas Peate said. "Lyssandra doesn't care for her siblings—didn't even lift a finger when her own intern was kidnapped by a pirate underneath her very nose—"

"Oh my!"

"Oh my goodness!" they twittered.

"Mother, I was fine—" Vel said, looking between Lyssa and Mrs. Dr. Sostas Peate. "Lyssa—"

"Well, Mother, I guess I learned from the best, didn't I?"

The twittering stopped, and Vel turned to look at Lyssa sharply.

"Excuse me?" Mrs. Dr. Sostas Peate smiled, her glass refilled with brandy by a passing servant.

"Please don't," Vel whispered. "Just let it go. We can get out of here—deal is done."

"Yes, Mother, why don't you tell everyone what happened when I was kidnapped?" Lyssa seethed, angrily tearing her arm from Vel's and facing her mother full on. "And what you said when I had a gun to my head?"

"I'm sure I don't remember what you're talking about," she laughed, but Lyssa could see the nerves behind her jovial eyes.

"Then let me help you remember, *you stupid bitch*," Lyssa said, her blood pulsing in her ears. Everyone and everything in the room suddenly stopped—the music, the conversations. Every eye in the room was now trained on them.

"Lyssa," Vel said, placing his hand on her arm again. She angrily tossed it away.

"You said, 'Why don't you call your father, Lyssandra,'" she said, her voice trembling. "You said, 'Maybe he thinks you are worthy of being saved.'"

"I'm sure that—" Mrs. Dr. Sostas Peate laughed nervously.

"I HAD A GUN AGAINST MY HEAD!" Lyssa screamed, her words echoing in the hall. "I begged you to save me, and you just….left me to die."

"Obviously not," Mrs. Dr. Sostas Peate said, taking a sip of her brandy. "As you're still here."

"You…you actually…" She stammered for a moment, almost not believing her own ears. "Is that why you let Sostas take me?" she continued,

179

ignoring everything in the universe except for the woman standing in front of her. "Is that why you let him leave me on planets for days at a time and drag me to the damn near end of the universe? Why you let him put me in unimaginable danger? Because you...you'd rather....?"

Mrs. Dr. Sostas Peate didn't respond, but a small blush was finally visible beneath her caked make up.

"What did I do to you?" Lyssa asked, her voice high. "What could I have possibly done to have—"

"You were *born*," her mother replied, before taking another gulp of brandy.

A gasp arose from the collective audience.

"*Mother!*" Vel hissed.

Lyssa was stunned silent, her eyes wide with hurt, and her mouth open in shock. Her ears rang dully, but her mind was numb—repeating over and over what she had just heard. More voices joined in the chorus, a symphony of screaming in her head. They were chanting the same thing:

She had been born evil, damaged. Nothing she did would ever change that The Great Creator had given her a preview of what was to come, and kept haunting her dreams with reminders. Her fate was sealed, and there was nothing she could do about it.

But she wasn't dead yet.

She wouldn't give these people in the ballroom the satisfaction of defeating her.

Scrapping together the last bit of dignity that she had, Lyssa raised her chin and stared squarely at her mother.

"Fine," she smiled, her voice no higher than a whisper, but audible to everyone in the room. "You wish I was dead? That I had never been born? That's fine. You're gonna get your wish. Because this is the *last time* you will ever see Lyssa Peate."

And with that, she turned around and walked out of the silent ballroom.

CHAPTER SIXTEEN

"UNCLE! UNCLE! UNCLE!"

Razia kicked him once more in the side for good measure. Methodologically, she bound his hands and feet, and kicked him onto her floating canvas. She actually wasn't sure what he was worth—maybe a couple thousand credits. What she did know about him was that he looked at her funny at the bar where she was sitting, and that meant he needed to get his ass kicked.

This was her fifth bounty in half as many days, and she was starting to feel it as she walked out into the dying sunlight in the afternoon from the bounty office. Her arms ached, her legs ached, and her head was throbbing from too little sleep and too much thinking. Stuffing her hands in her pockets, she strolled down the street, more focused on the way her boots kicked up the dust than what was in front of her.

She had everything she wanted now. She was free of Lyssa Peate—free from hateful mothers, disappearing fathers, jealous siblings. Free of Pymus and his obnoxious questions. Free from having to excavate planets, free from having to bite her tongue when she was weaseled out of thousands of credits. Free from stupid interns and their stupid questions and their stupid ideas to drag her to the Manor.

Not completely free, she thought moodily, ignoring the buzz from her mini-computer. He had been calling her non-stop for days now, she was sure to have a chat about what had happened. She was uninterested in hashing it out—what was done was done, and all that she needed to know was that she had been right all along. Lyssa Peate was better off disappearing forever—nobody cared about her anyways.

She continued walking down the street, lost in her own thoughts. It would be better for him if he just interned with Dorst. Dorst could teach him all about how to be a good scientist, the proper way to excavate a planet, without all of the machines and dangerous rock creatures. They would probably having a great time bonding—Peate to Peate. Vel would be happier, not having to worry about pirates, hunting bounties, or sisters whose souls were damned to...

She sighed audibly before becoming cross with herself for moping. She just hadn't been sleeping well is all; every time she closed her eyes she was back at the Manor standing in the middle of the ballroom, and usually ended in the world disintegrating from under her feet.

After a few minutes of rambling down the streets, she found herself walking into Harms' bar, quite unsure of how she got there, but quietly relieved to see him sitting there.

"You look rough," he smiled, as she sleepily slid into his bar. "Want a coffee?"

"Yes please," she mumbled, placing her head down on her hands.

"What's up?" he said, cocking his head at her. "You okay?"

"'m fine," she mumbled, as a coffee appeared in front of her. "Just haven't been sleeping well."

"Probably because you've been capturing pirates left and right lately," Harms smiled, watching her gulp down the coffee. "You can take a break you know..."

"Nah," she said, cupping the coffee in her hands. "This is what I've been waiting for, finally able to focus on work."

"And what have you been doing since you got off probation? Not working?" Harms asked, amusedly.

"I've been distracted by other stuff," she said, placing the coffee cup down.

"What kind of stuff?" Harms asked.

She shrugged, noncommittally.

"I'm going to tell you something, and I don't want you to get mad at me," Harms began.

Immediately, her eyes skewered him with an icy glare. "Why does everyone think that I just get mad at—"

Harms gave her a knowing look and she deflated.

"I haven't slept," she mumbled.

"I know, and that's why I'm going to tell you to take a break," Harms finished. "Seriously, you've been working non-stop for the past two weeks—you've turned in five top bounties and at least ten mid-to-low level bounties."

"So?" Lyssa snapped, moodily before blinking at him. "Wait...it's been two weeks?"

"See, you don't even know what day it is," Harms chuckled. "Take a breather. Go hang out on a beach for a week, or wherever it is that you disappear to."

"I'm not disappearing anymore," she growled, feeling irrationally angry at the thought of having to slink back to the Academy, or that she in any way needed Lyssa Peate. Didn't he know? Lyssa Peate was damaged goods—the farther away she got from her the better. Even her own mother thought she'd be better off dead.

"I'm telling you that you should," Harms said, firmly. "And you need to—"

"The only thing I need to do is find another bounty," she snapped. "Quit telling me how to live my life."

"Wow," Harms sighed, sitting back and looking at her. "Really?"

"Yes, really," she glared. "I'm fine."

"Okay then," he shook his head, sounding as if she was going to regret it. "What do you want to know?"

"Linro Lee," she said, pulling the first name that came to mind. She had been looking at his profile last night, or maybe it was a few days ago. He was in Contestant's web; and since Relleck was still the most wanted in the universe, he would be a fair consolation prize. "Does he have a crew?"

"No," Harms said simply, without expanding.

She blinked at him, feeling his animosity from across the table. To be perfectly honest, she hadn't really come here to ask him about Lee (she wasn't really sure why she was here in the first place), so she didn't have a list of questions to ask him. And her mind, slowed by exhaustion and non-stop activity, was coming up blank with other questions to ask him.

The only thing she really wanted to talk about was why she kept dreaming about Leveman's Vortex, and how much she wanted to knock her mother into next week. But, as usual, she couldn't talk about that with Harms. And from the way he was looking at her, she wasn't sure he'd be receptive even if she could.

"Anything else, Razia?" he asked, superiorly. "I have a busy day telling other people how to live their lives."

"Oh don't be an ass," Razia rolled her eyes. "I was just—"

"Payment please?" Harms said, holding out his hand.

"What, for that?" Razia blinked. "You barely gave me anything."

"You didn't ask anything, and I'm on the clock the moment you sit down," Harms said, looking at his tablet. "Not to mention all the freebees over the years."

"Fine then," she said, slamming her C-card down on the table, angrily watching him swipe it. "Take your damned money."

"Pleasure doing business with you, Razia," Harms said, pulling his tablet up in front of his face and ignoring her.

"Well...well screw you too!" she snapped, standing up and snatching her C-card away from him. "Maybe I'll just go find me another informant."

"Good luck finding someone who'll work with a woman."

Her eyes widened slightly and her mouth fell open.

"Excuse me."

"It's the truth," he responded simply, dragging his finger along the tablet as he continued to work. "Now run along and go find this bounty you are so eager to go find."

"Fine, I will," she said, but with much less gumption than before, his words stinging more than she cared to admit.

***

She sat in the bridge of her ship, several windows open across her dashboard with Linro Lee's information. To be honest, she should have asked Harms a little bit more, but she couldn't call him now.

The *nerve* of him, saying that other informants wouldn't talk to her because she was a woman. She was in the top twenty! She had turned in major pirates—Santos Journot, even. She had to have made some kind of an impression.

Instinctively, she turned to look behind her to whine, but again, she was reminded that she was completely alone on her ship. She couldn't believe she was so wrapped up in not having Vel here—she'd done perfectly fine being alone for two years. What did she need of anyone to talk to, when she could be bounty hunting?

She looked up at Lee's info in the pirate intraweb.

	4) Lee, Linro
Wanted For	Engagement in piracy, bounty hunting, hijacking, grand larceny
Reward	41,054,500C
Known Alias	Ed Maxwell, Libertad Lark, Mika Castro, Joseph Cavanaugh
Known Accomplices	Royden Relleck, Enzo Rossi, James Rock
Pirate Web affiliation	Contestant

The three aliases that she had discovered earlier had been used recently, although sparingly. Between the three, she could see gaps in parking, in food, and in—

Her eyes traveled over to her mini-computer, as it lit up again. She reached over and ignored the call.

IN, she corrected herself, other incidentals. She might be able to find him just based on the three, but it would be easier if she could figure out if he had a fourth alias. It was, of course, entirely possible that he had just not spent any money for the times where—

Her eyes darted to her mini-computer again, as he was calling her once more.

WHERE there was a gap.

"God in Leveman's Vortex," she sighed, rubbing her face to wake up. She was on her second cup of coffee, but her scattered mind was unable to focus on the task at hand. What she really could have used was a good, long run on a planet.

But she was no longer excavating planets, so that was out. So was sleeping, which was more tossing and turning than actually sleep.

Her mini-computer lit up once more, and she reached over and turned it off.

***

Because of all her prep work, Lee was actually fairly easy to find—using one alias exclusively on M-6899. She assumed that he must be on vacation—it was a popular planet to plan a get-away. The planet itself was mostly water, with some small islands (most likely the tips of huge mountains from the surface floor). These islands were encompassed by all-inclusive resorts, but smaller cities were built on top of massive wooden docks. It was in one of these smaller cities—just the kind of place a pirate would be found—that Linro Lee was spending his time.

She lazily looked through the available parking decks, happy to find most of them wide open. She chose her spot from the numerous available and swiped her Lyssa C-card on the dashboard to pay.

Insufficient funds.

She stared at the pop-up on her dashboard, the words making sense but not computing at the same time. Insufficient funds? Was there some kind of an account minimum for this parking account? She could have sworn that she had tons of money in her Lyssa Peate account.

Swallowing, she quickly turned to the Universal Bank to check her account balance.

Less than one hundred credits.

She sat back in shock.

She had finally run out money.

That wasn't entirely true, she countered. She had plenty of money—millions in fact—in her Razia account. But by swiping her Razia card, she would let any pirate who was hunting for her know exactly where she was.

185

The smart and mature thing to do would be to turn her ship around, excavate a planet, sell it, and then capture Linro Lee.

But the stubborn voice inside her head was having none of that, and promptly slid the Razia C-card in her dashboard to pay for parking.

***

She was feeling rather paranoid and exposed as she walked along the rickety streets. Indeed, there was nothing but warped wooden planks as far as she could see. Beneath the slats, she could see, hear, and smell salty water sloshing against the pillars that extended down into the sea floor below. This planet, she mused, was probably a gold mine for some prospector— they probably paid a couple thousand credits for it, and now it was a major destination for vacationers. It was probably someone like that smartly-dressed prospector, who'd weaseled some poor DSE out of a huge profit.

Wait a second, she thought, annoyed with herself. Why did she keep thinking about things that were no longer a part of her life?

She pulled out her mini-computer, opening Lee's profile again. He was still making purchases at a bar down the street. Still, she mused, scrolling down his recent transactions, even with a secret alias, he didn't appear like he was hiding very well.

Five drinks today at the same bar.

Three nights at the same hotel—same room.

Breakfast, lunch, dinner—all within a two block radius.

And this same pattern had gone on for the past three days.

Stuffing her mini-computer back in her pocket, she wondered why he could possibly have gotten so sloppy. Maybe in the absence of Santos Journot (*You're welcome*, she thought bitterly), pirates were feeling a bit freer to be a bit less concerned with hiding. Or maybe he had just gotten so cocky—not many pirates left D-882.

Her thoughts were halted by the sight of someone familiar standing in front of the bar she was about to walk into. In her muddled thoughts, she could have sworn that she had been in this situation before.

"Hi friend," Sage smiled at her, his arms crossed in front of his chest.

"Ugh," she rolled her eyes. "What do you want?"

"Couple things," Sage grinned. "First, you need to apologize to Harms."

"He needs to apologize to—" she snapped before her mind caught up. "Wait… what are you doing here? How did you find me? And why were you talking to Harms in the first place?"

"The answer to that second question is that I know both your aliases," Sage smiled. "So I can always find you."

"I only have one alias now," Razia snapped, trying to get around him.

"I noticed," Sage nodded, stepping in front of her. "Pretty unlike you to have such a low balance. Don't you have a thing for that?"

"I'm not doing that anymore," Razia growled. "Move."

"You know," he pressed. "Maybe you should take a week off. You're looking rough—"

"You know that's exactly what Harms said!" she narrowed her eyes at him. "Why does everyone seem to want to have a say in my life—"

"Come on, Lyss—"

"DON'T CALL ME THAT!" she screamed, reacting without thinking. "I am done with her."

"Fine, whatever you want to call yourself," Sage said, grabbing her by the arm gently. "I'm telling you—"

"Get off," she said, shoving him away and marching into the bar.

"Seriously," Sage said, following behind her closely and looking around nervously. "This is not—"

"Go. Away." She growled, turning just as a drink was placed in front of her. She looked at the bartender curiously. "I didn't order this."

"He did," he said, pointing behind her.

Razia looked behind her and, to her utter surprise, Relleck was standing there with seven of his goons.

And Linro Lee.

"What the..." Razia gaped, looking around confused.

"That's why," Sage snapped in a whisper. "Maybe next time you should take the hint when Harms is trying to help—"

"Harms wouldn't sell me..." She trailed off in realization. "Oh…yeah he would."

"He was trying to get you to take a break so he wouldn't have to," Sage growled. "But, as usual, you had to be a real bitch when anyone tries to help you—"

"How *dare* you," she hissed, turning on him.

"Hate to interrupt the date," Relleck smiled. "Should we do this the easy way, or do we have to endure another one of your pathetic attempts at defending yourselves?"

"Do you really think I'd be dumb enough to come here without my crew?" Sage said, as a group of seven rose from a table in the corner.

"Of course not," Relleck said, motioning to the other side of the bar. At least ten men rose from their seats and joined them.

"Oh come on," Sage sighed.

"Now, as I was saying," Relleck said as his goons closed in around them.

"HOLD ON." Razia screamed. "Just...hold on a second."

Relleck and the room looked at her expectantly.

"Who are you hunting, really?" Razia said.

"That doesn't matter," Relleck said, stepping forward.

"YES IT DOES," Razia screamed again. "Yes it does." She stepped forward and poked her finger at Relleck's chest. "Who are you after?"

Behind her, Sage made a gesture towards Relleck, mouthing something.

"Well, obviously, I'm after Teon, but-."

Razia stood back, blinking for a moment before balling her fist and lunging with a, "You son of a—"

When her fist hit his chin, the melee started. She found herself roughly being shoved and pushed between different fist fights, ducking and bobbing as fists and jaws went flying all over the place.

OOF.

CRASH.

And then, out of no where, an elbow came backwards and knocked her right in the stomach. She fell down to her knees, and found herself looking up at a fast moving gaggle of men, all focused on everything except her on the ground. And she found if she scooted ever so slightly, she could wriggle her way out of the tangle of legs and feet.

Out of the brawl, she took stock of the sight. Nearly twenty men—the entire populous of the bar—were beating the crap out of each other.

And although she could easily slip out the door to safety, she had unfinished business to attend to.

Putting her fingers in her mouth, she whistled loud enough to get everyone's attention, as she readied her feet to run.

She caught eyes with her target and smiled devilishly.

"Hey Relleck," she smirked. "Come get me."

She hung around long enough to see him untangle himself before twisting around and breaking out into a planet-worthy sprint down the wooden street.

She could see him chasing her out of the corner of her eye, and was glad to see no one else following him. She could feel him getting close, and she broke out into an all-out, creature-fleeing run, putting some distance between the two of them. She avoided the cracks and warped slats in the ground, years of running on uneven planet undergrowth having trained her muscles.

When she felt he was far enough behind her, she suddenly ducked between two buildings, holding herself flat against the wall and waiting with a quiet, excited pant.

She heard the footsteps and readied herself, instinctively reaching out and grabbing the back of his shirt, using his inertia to throw him into the alley. He landed with a heap, winded and dazed from the chase, but she could see the angry fire in his eyes.

"Now," Razia said, cracking her knuckles. "Let's see how good you are without your-UGH!"

He lunged at her, without warning, and they went tumbling to the ground, the rough, uneven ground digging into her back as he lay on top of her. His sweaty palms connected with her wrists and pressed them hard into the ground. She paused in her struggling to look up at him, his face inches from hers, and his breath, still heavy from the struggle, was warm on her face.

"Got you," Relleck smiled, his eyes connecting with hers.

She stared back, defiantly. There was no way he was taking her back without a fight.

"You know," he said, his eyes still searching hers and a smile growing on his face. "I don't have to take you to the bounty office."

She stopped struggling and looked up at him, confused. "You what now?"

"Contestant and I were talking," he said, sliding his hands up from her wrists to take hold of her hands. "And I think that you'd make an excellent addition to our web."

"You want me to join your web?" She became acutely aware that he was completely on top her, and she started to feel very uncomfortable.

"Well," Relleck said, and Razia felt him move—if possible—closer in. "I mean, Contestant wasn't completely sold on the idea....but I'm pretty sure I could convince him....if I were convinced."

"Yeah, and how am I supposed to do that?" she snapped, really hoping that what she was feeling was something on his utility belt and not something else entirely.

Relleck smiled lasciviously as he moved his hips against hers—just enough that she could connect her knee with his groin. Hard.

He rolled off of her with a loud cry, rolling around in a ball with tears streaming down his face.

"First of all," Razia said, so angry that he had just said that to her that she wanted to watch him writhe in pain. "How could you even think that I'd ever want to—UGH!"

He continued to cry, his face red, as he rolled from side to side.

"And second of all, I would never, never leave Dissident's web," she growled defiantly. "Not for you, not for anybody."

She unhooked her floating canvas bag and glared at him. "And third of all, have fun in jail tonight."

He lay on her canvas, writhing in pain, but not struggling to get away, as she trotted down the wooden streets, focused on getting him off this planet before any of his minions realized he was missing. He was going to make such a good story—Dissident couldn't be mad at her for this one. But even so—just the pure joy of finally having something on Relleck. No more of having to listen to his stupid jabs, his sexism. She had finally proven she was better than he was.

She hopped off of the lift on the station, and her heart dropped to her stomach.

Her ship was open.

Panic in her chest, she ran over, dragging Relleck behind her, a thousand nervous scenarios playing in her head. What if someone had broken into her ship? What if someone was lying in wait to capture her? What if someone had stolen all of her equipment? What if-

Her nerves switched to annoyance when she realized Vel was standing in front of her ship.

"You son of a bitch," she sighed, knocking him slowly in the shoulder. "You scared the shit out of me. What are you doing here?"

"I…um…." he whispered, looking at something behind her.

"What is it?" she said, nudging him. Out of the corner of her eye, she could see someone standing behind her.

"Razia, I presume?" Pymus sneered.

CHAPTER SEVENTEEN

She stared at Vel for a moment, wondering if she had imagined what she had just heard. Maybe she was having a dream, or Relleck had knocked her out. Slowly, deliberately, she turned around, her whole body tensed.

It was indeed Dr. Pymus was standing in the middle of this docking station, wearing his DSE lab coat and glasses. She stared at him as he examined her catch, amusedly looking between the man bound and gagged and her, mouth open, eyes wide, unable to speak.

"Why don't you release that poor man and we can have a little chat, hm?" he said, replacing his glasses on his slimy nose.

"I…" she stammered.

"I suppose you wouldn't want him to hear more of this conversation, hm?" Pymus smiled. "Razia."

She swallowed, understanding his intent. Almost instinctively, she reached down and began to untie Relleck. He watched her with shocked eyes as she pulled the gag out of his mouth.

"Go," Razia said, her voice hollow. So much for her great plans.

"What?" Relleck said.

"Go, you idiot!" Razia snapped.

Without another word, Relleck stumbled off the gurney and began running away down the street as fast as his legs and sore crotch would let him. She watched him go with a silent anger, and turned to look at Pymus with the meanest glare she could muster.

"What are you doing here, Pymus?" she said, folding her arms over her chest.

"Dr. Pymus, my dear," he corrected. "I'm here for a little chat. And since it seems you are rarely at the Academy, I thought I might come find you out in your….other pursuits."

"How long have you known?" she said, racking her brain to come up with some reason why he would be here—or worse, what he could want from her to blackmail her.

"Oh, since your brother here was 'kidnapped,'" Pymus said, smiling at Vel, who didn't smile back. She suddenly wondered what he was doing here. "I'm rather surprised that no one has ever caught on."

"I don't usually run in the same circles," she smiled.

"I think I am most surprised that your eldest brother hasn't noticed," Pymus continued, watching her face. "Jukin would be awfully interested to know what you've been up to."

"What do you want?" she repeated, bracing herself for the worst.

"I'd like to know about Leveman's Vortex," Pymus said predictably.

"It's this big swirly thing in space that destroys everything," Lyssa deadpanned.

"Yes, but what I would like to know is how you get inside," Pymus smiled. "I hear you have the mathematical angle for entry, after all."

Her heart fell into her stomach and she immediately looked to Vel, unable to hide her emotions. Shock and hurt immediately turned to rage— more at herself for believing for even a second that Vel wasn't like the rest of them. He was a Peate after all—a backstabbing, selfish lineage that cared more for themselves than the welfare of anyone else—most especially her. She should never have trusted him from the moment she found him looking up Sostas' transaction history.

"You see," Pymus continued, satisfactorily, "I would, in fact, like to see the inside for myself. Do my own experiments—make my own observations."

"Have a good trip," she responded. There was no way, nothing he could ever offer her or threaten her with that would ever make her set foot—pre-death—in that place ever again.

"I thought you might say that," Pymus sighed, sadly. "So, if you don't take me to the Great Vortex, I shall have no other choice but to cancel the bounty on your head."

"Bounty?" she laughed, shaking her head. "What bounty?"

"The bounty that propelled you from near obscurity to a number that I assumed would have resulted in your capture," he sighed. "What are you, twenty five? Thirty?"

"You...?" Her eyes widened again. She'd assumed that her bounty shot up so high because she'd kidnapped Vel—other pirates maybe chipping in as a sign of solidarity, or perhaps her Mother in an attempt to save Vel.

But it was Pymus.

"I even added to it, five million, ten million," Pymus continued, gleefully watching her face. "I contacted your runner—Dissident, is it?—to see who I could get to finally capture you for myself. He put me in contact with that Relleck fellow who promised me he could capture you within the week—if I paid him an additional fifteen million."

Her head was spinning, waterfall realization that the past few weeks had just been a sham. The only person with money on her head was Pymus. But not only that, Dissident had set her up—and told Pymus who would be the best to take her down.

Harms was right. She was a joke.

A chocolate-fetching joke.

"An investment, it would seem, that was wasted in the end, because your dear brother here was able to find you in just a few hours," Pymus said, turning to look at Vel. "You must have taught him very well this bounty hunting trade. I daresay when he is expelled from the Academy, he will have a bright future in piracy."

Vel looked to him sharply, but said nothing.

"So, shall we go?" Pymus smiled. "Or do I have to go through the trouble of canceling your bounty and then letting your eldest brother know exactly where to find you. From the way that Dissident fellow talked, it seems he would be happy to be rid of you. As, apparently, would the rest of your family."

She could feel the world crashing around her, and could take no more. Defeated at last, she quietly walked past him before pausing and whispering.

"Let's just hope it's in better shape than when I left it."

***

Lyssa lay on her bed, her eyes on the ceiling but her mind somewhere else. Outside, the stars were whirring by, as the ship sped towards the Great Vortex.

She thought she had gotten so far. She thought that once she had finally broken into the top fifty that she would finally get the respect and adoration that she deserved.

She found her mind floating back to standing in that diner, staring at Evet Delmur. Perhaps she should have just taken the hint then and saved herself the pain and trouble of thinking that she could ever be anything more than Lyssa Peate. Perhaps it was time to just accept the fact that she was to be punished for the rest of her life, because perhaps she did, in fact, deserve to be.

She wondered what kind of world she was going to come upon when they landed.

She wondered how far she could take them before it blew apart again.

She wondered if he was there.

Her thoughts were rudely interrupted when she heard the sounds of her door opening. She shook her head and rolled over away from the door so she didn't have to look at him. She felt him sit down on the bed next to her. After a few quiet minutes, he began talking.

"Three months ago, I started asking around the Manor to see if any of our older brothers had spoken to you about Sostas," he began, quietly. "Somehow Pymus got wind of it and worked out a deal to get me this internship in exchange for sharing anything I found. I never..." he sighed. "I never planned on actually telling him anything. I just wanted to find out about Father."

She shifted, but didn't respond.

"Then...well, you know, the kidnapping thing," Vel sighed. "After you dropped me off at the Manor, I went to Pymus, and I told him that I didn't want to work for you anymore." She heard him laugh quietly. "I had a whole story, even tears ready. But he stopped me before I got one word out, and told me he knew."

She continued to stare at the wall.

"He said that he no longer needed me, actually," Vel continued. "Said that he put this huge bounty on your head, and he was going to 'let the law figure it out.' I thought he was going to turn you into Jukin, so I told him that I could find out more if I..." He swallowed nervously. "If I got you to trust me."

Her mouth tightened, but she continued to say nothing.

"My goal though, was to get him enough so he would leave you alone, without you having to know," he said, quickly. "When you said that you could find anyone using their bank account, I thought...I thought I could find out everything, but..." He sighed. "I found nothing in his bank account."

She shifted again, but said nothing.

"When we returned to the Academy, I tried to give him the sensors, I thought that was what he really wanted. I mean, I told him to forget the damned vortex, he could make billions with these things," Vel said. "But he didn't want that. So when you told me about Sostas taking you to the center—but I told him that the calculations were lost..." he trailed off. "But he didn't believe me."

"Imagine that," Lyssa responded, dryly.

"I was going to leave it alone, by that point, I knew you could take care of yourself. But then Sage told me that Harms had caught wind of some guy offering a 15 million credit bonus for anyone who captured you, and that Relleck had taken the job," Vel said. "I knew that he'd be gunning for you, so I told Pymus that I could find you. And...well..."

She heard him sigh.

"And that, Lyssa, is the truth," Vel sighed, standing up. He walked over to the door before stopping again. "Actually, there is one more thing."

"Of course," Lyssa snapped.

"I want you to know that from the bottom of my heart, with every single fiber of my being, and from the depths of my soul, how very sorry I am," he whispered. "I never wanted to...I just wanted to know....I..."

The ship began to tremble slightly.

"Guess it's time," she whispered, brushing by him without another word.

She walked onto the bridge with Vel in tow, ignoring Pymus, who was sitting in one of the jump seats happily. She kneeled down in front of her dashboard and began tapping on the sides.

"What are you doing?" he drawled.

"Getting our way in," she snapped, as the hidden door swung open. Inside was a single, worn black journal, which she pulled out and began flipping through.

"Is that?!" Pymus gasped.

"Not yours," Lyssa responded, pausing on the page covered in a long string of numbers and equation symbols. She opened her green-red application, switching the view from the green-red dot to a display of the back-end computer code. Slowly, she compared the code on the screen to the numbers on the page, changing a number here and there.

"Are you sure you got it right?" Pymus snorted.

"You'd better hope so," she snapped. "Otherwise it'll be a short trip."

That seemed to shut him up as she finished her comparison. Then, hearing her father in her ear about how sloppy she could be, she checked the code again. Satisfied, she switched the code back to the red-green, currently showing green.

The tremors were increasing, as was the pressure. She sat down, tossing an unwelcome look back to Vel to make sure he was strapped in, before tightening her own belt.

"It is going to get a bit rough," she said, watching the debris fly by faster and faster. Her eyes were glued on the green, her hands on the joystick was starting to feel heavier—everything was starting to feel heavier. Bits and pieces of space debris clouded the window, but disintegrated from the sheer force of the vortex. Lyssa double-checked her numbers again and swallowed nervously, trying to not second-guess herself.

Outside of the ship, comets and space debris disintegrated, and she could hear Vel whimper, The green was still green—

And then it suddenly went blank, displaying a weird code error.

"What does that mean?" She heard Pymus say.

She couldn't respond—but she started to feel the familiar push and pull of the gravity as they approached the center. Her body would at once feel heavy and then light as air, and then feel like it was going to be crushed into nothingness. Now there was nothing outside the window—the comets and meteors and other debris having been pulverized to a white dust that surrounded them. Very slowly she began to realize that the push and pull of the gravity was gone, replaced by the sense of...nothingness.

Looking up at her dashboard, her instruments were showing completely different readings from each other. Out in front, it was hard to even tell they were moving—it was just white outside her window.

"Are we here?" She heard Pymus call from the back.

"Yes...we're here," she whispered.

***

She opened the hatch of her ship, but didn't step off, staring out into the white landscape in front of her. Somehow she found herself searching the plain for anything—any sign of a ship, or even a person. But all her eyes could see was the emptiness. She never expected to be back here again.

"Well?" Pymus said behind her. "We're waiting..."

She rolled her eyes, and stepped off the edge of the plank...

...and immediately found herself standing in the basement hallway at the Manor.

She stepped back on the ship, nervously, the world turning white again.

"Lyss?" Vel said, concerned. "What's wrong?"

"No, nothing's wrong," Lyssa murmured.

"Then shall we get a move on? I don't have all day," Pymus asked.

She turned to give him a dirty look, but then faced the whiteness again; taking a deep breath and stepping off her ship.

Again, she found herself standing in the basement of the Manor.

"Son of a bitch," she whispered, stepping back onto her ship. Again, she could see whiteness.

"Is this your way of trying to be cute, because it's not working," Pymus said impatiently.

"Can it," Lyssa snapped, nervously biting her thumb and thinking. She knew this was a vision—a hallucination brought on by the intense magnetic field. So why did the sight of being in the Manor cause her such panic?

Seriously, she told herself. *Stop being ridiculous.*

With a determined glare out into the Vortex, she firmly placed both feet into the hallway of the Manor. She closed her eyes, telling herself that this wasn't real—she wasn't about to run into her Mother again.

Opening her eyes, she wondered why that thought jumped into her head.

Slowly, she began to walk, passing the kitchen, empty of servants and the smells of the upcoming meal. It was as empty as the night she was at the Manor.

No, she told herself. She had dreamed that. It was as real as what she was seeing right now. Because this wasn't real. She was in Leveman's

Vortex.

She could hear her footsteps echoing off of the walls, and saw her reflection in the shiny marble floor. Her heart was beating out of her chest, but she tried to keep her face emotionless.

She stopped, standing in front of her father's laboratory door.

In the back of her mind, she could hear voices, but all she could see was the door in front of her. Slowly, she reached up to type in the access code—again, finding comfort in that familiar combination of tones.

The door didn't open, but a peculiarly familiar voice echoed through the hallway.

Deep Space Exploration Vehicle Z-633, please identify yourself.

Lyssa blinked, shocked.

"What?" she found herself saying.

You are requesting access to a Planetary and System Science location. Please enter your authorization code.

Dumbly, she typed in her Academy identification code—9448639—and was surprised when the door clicked open. Gently, she pushed her way inside...

And found herself standing in the middle of Harms' bar.

"What the..." she whispered, taking a moment to look around. The dusty streets of D-882 were empty outside the bar, and the room itself was silent except for the sound of whirring fans above. And voices—some in the distance, but some close by.

She was overcome by the feeling of guilt at the way she had treated Harms. He was only trying to protect her—only trying to keep her from herself. He deserved better than the way she spoke to him.

Smiling, she saw him in his normal spot, talking with someone. But when she got closer, she realized that it wasn't Harms at all.

"D....Dorst? Sera?" she stammered, looking between the two of them. Indeed, just as normal as Harms would be with some pirate, here were Dorst and Sera, he wearing a lab coat, and she wearing her simple sky blue dress.

They were talking to her.

"You are so stubborn," Sera sighed, dabbing the corners of her mouth with her napkin. "You have never listened to anyone who ever tried to help you. Not to me, when I tried to keep you on the right path, not to Harms, when he tries to warn you about dangerous bounties! All you do is push people away!"

"W-what?" she spat, nervously. How did Sera know she was a bounty hunter? Or Harms for that matter?!

"You are reckless, too, always have been," Dorst sighed. "It's like you don't care for your own safety sometimes! Following Relleck like that, when you knew he was probably up to something. Dal Jamus, as well—he could have really hurt you. You have forgotten everything Tauron taught you!"

"How did you you..." she trailed off, stopping herself. This was the most ridiculous thing she had ever seen. Sera and Dorst would never be on D-882, let alone in Harm's bar. They also would never know that she was really Razia, or know about Tauron, or any of this.

It was the magnetic fields—this was a hallucination. She used to have them when she was a little girl; although less odd than this one. She closed her eyes, using all of her mental strength to focus and overcome this hallucination. When she opened her eyes, she would be in the middle of a white field, Vel and Pymus would be behind her and-

She opened her eyes to the inside of the Planetary and System Science Academy.

Annoyed, she began walking down the hall with purpose, angry that she was being so easily swayed by these magnetic fields. Or maybe she was just angry to be back here, in this place that she had sworn she would never set foot again. Hallucination or not, the anger in her chest was real.

She turned a corner and found herself in a queue of people, lined up near the cafeteria.

Except it wasn't scientists in the line.

It was pirates.

She could pick them out, there was Santos Journot, Zolet Obalone, Dalton Burk. Even Dal Jamus, holding a tiny tray, ready to eat, as if this was completely normal. And standing at the front of the line was Sage and Relleck.

Somehow she felt like she had been here before—at the back of the line, Sage and Relleck at the front. Everything had been handed to them, and she was here, fighting to even be in line. Instead of lining up at the back of the line, she purposefully marched her way to the front, intent on giving Relleck and Sage a piece of her mind.

"You can't cut to the top pirates," Relleck sneered, looking her up and down. "This spot is for the most wanted pirates only."

"What?" Lyssa said. "This line is for—"

"Top twenty pirates," Relleck continued, looking forward. "God in Leveman's Vortex, why are you always trying to prove you belong where you don't? Over-compensate much?"

"Leave her alone, Relleck," Sage said, as usual, stepping in to save her when she didn't need it.

"I can handle this," she snapped.

"I know you can," he smiled at her. "You've always been able to handle yourself. Must have been all those nights you were left on the planet by your father. Taught you to be self-sufficient, to survive."

Lyssa's eyes widened. She had never told Sage a word about her father—deciding very early that she was much better off keeping as much of that to herself. Besides, she was going to be Razia—what good was it sharing Lyssa for.

"How did you know that I—"

And suddenly she found herself in the middle of a dark jungle. Panic bubbled in in her chest—she had been here before. He had left her again, he was off in Leveman's Vortex doing research and left her here to do his dirty work. She was all alone on this lonely planet, and she was going to die here, probably.

She trudged through the darkness, jumping at every sound or movement out of the corner of her eye. This place was teeming with life, and she, just a little girl, was just ripe for the eating.

She hurried out of the jungle and onto the banks of a wide river. There was a bright moon overhead, illuminating the river with an eerie white glow. Or was she staring at the glow from Leveman's Vortex? That damn spiral was always following her around, it seemed.

She fell to her knees, feeling emotionally and mentally spent, just waiting for the bottom to fall out, as it always did. It didn't matter how much she tried to run from it—deep down, she would never be able to escape the darkness and the evil that she was.

She opened her eyes and caught sight of her reflection in the water. It was Lyssa—hair tied in a bun, thick glasses, lab coat. And she looked so...defeated, so abandoned.

She couldn't help but feel sad for the girl looking back at her. She had been kicked around and left behind by everyone she had ever loved. Her father didn't want her, her mother thought she was better off dead. Her siblings ignored her—or worse.

Even she didn't want herself.

After all, she was the one who was trying to be rid of Lyssa, the one who disparaged her and thought she was worthless. But looking at this other part of herself in the water, she began to realize how wrong she had been.

Lyssa wasn't worthless—she was strong, she had survived abandonment by her father and family. Razia could have never had the courage to stand in front of Dal Jamus and taken him down if Lyssa hadn't been fighting for herself since the day she was born. Razia never would have been able to stand up for herself if not for Lyssa's years of torture at the hands of the Peate siblings.

Lyssa was brilliant—years of being kept quiet with pattern and number games had primed her brain to keep small details organized in her brain like a catalogue. Razia would never have been allowed to stay with Tauron and become a bounty hunter, had it not been for Lyssa's curiosity and intelligence and dogged obsessions with solving complex puzzles.

Lyssa was a safe haven, a place to escape to when things got too rough. Razia would have had no where to hide after Relleck nearly captured her. No where to reflect and realize where she could do better. Razia might have been captured by now if it wasn't for Lyssa.

Without Lyssa, Razia would never have amounted to anything more than a low-ranked bounty hunter who captured petty purse thieves.

Without Lyssa, Razia was nothing.

The reflection faded, and she began to feel cool rock under her hand where sand had been. Her eyes shifted upwards to take in the sight of an old, weathered arch.

She was kneeling at the dais of the Arch of Eron.

How she got here, she had no idea.

Slowly, she pushed herself off of her knees, a feeling of serenity and calm coming over her as she had never felt it before. For a few blessed moments, she relished in the tranquility that had finally settled in the pit of her stomach, until she heard footfalls and the sound of her name.

"Lyss!" she heard Vel call after her. "Lyssa, can you hear me."

"Yeah," she nodded, turning to him. He was looking her up and down as if she had completely lost her mind.

"What happened to you?" he gaped, his hands grasping her shoulders. "You just started walking around in circles mumbling about—"

"Nothing," she smiled, gently pushing his arms off. "It's the magnetic fields, they can cause severe hallucinations."

"What did you hallucinate about—" Vel said, curiously watching her.

"Not important," she said, watching Pymus slowly walk up to the two of them.

"It's real," Pymus breathed. "The arch....it's...it's real."

"Of course it's real," Lyssa snapped, keeping her eyes glued on him.

"Okay, so does this mean we can leave now?" Vel said, nervously looking around. "I don't feel right being here."

"My boy, I have work to do," Pymus scoffed, lifting one of her sensors out of his satchel.

"Those aren't going to work here," Lyssa said pointedly. "The magnetic fields are too strong."

"Pardon me if I don't want to take the word of a girl who just hallucinated her way here," Pymus said, waving the machine in the air.

"Right, or maybe the Great Creator doesn't want us in his business," Vel said edgily, as if he was expecting the Great Creator Himself to walk out of the Arch and chide them for being so sacrilegious. "So how about we get on out of here. Or, better yet, Lyss and I can get out of here. And you can stay here."

"You're right," Pymus said, putting the sensor away and pulling out a gun. "I think it would be best if the two of you went away."

"Pymus, what are you doing?" Lyssa said, grabbing Vel protectively.

"Oh, don't worry, your souls won't have that far to travel," Pymus smiled. "Vel, I'm quite sure that the Great Creator has something lovely planned for you. Dr. Peate, I...." he shrugged. "I guess you'll just have to find out."

"You don't have to do this," Vel said, sliding closer to Lyssa, who tightened her grip on his arm.

"I do, unfortunately," Pymus said, pointing his gun at Vel and pulling the trigger.

Before she could even think, Lyssa shoved both herself and Vel out of the way. The two of them tumbled to the ground beside the Arch.

"Lyssa!" Vel said, looking to her.

"He didn't get me," Lyssa said, searching her body.

"Oh, well," Pymus said, leveling the gun at them again. "Let me try that again."

Before he could pull the trigger, there was a loud crack that echoed across the white plains.

Lyssa's heart dropped into her stomach. She turned back behind them to look at the Arch of Eron. The silvery wisps that hung from the stone had turned an inky black—in fact the entire world was starting to darken every second. Pieces of the arch began to crumble, small pebbles falling down the dais.

"Vel...." she whispered, instinctively unhooking her utility belt from her hips and snapping it securely around Vel's. "You're gonna have to run."

They heard another loud crack; a large bolder had broken off of the arch, tumbling down the hill and then falling straight through the ground, a red-tinted steam rising from the ground beneath them.

"What did you do?!" Pymus yelled, just as a crack appeared beneath his feet.

And without another word, he disappeared through the ground.

"Lyss?" Vel said, knowing exactly what was happening, his eyes transfixed on the fiery river flowing far beneath their feet.

"RUN VEL!" Lyssa screamed, grabbing his hand and yanking him forward.

Cracks were appearing all around them, and big chunks of the ground disintegrated to the inferno below. Keeping Vel in the corner of her eye, Lyssa deftly dodged the cracks, first left then right then right again, running only so fast as to keep Vel close enough. In the distance, she could see her ship.

"THERE!" she screamed, momentarily distracted. She felt her foot land on a crumbling ground, and froze.

"LYSSA!" she heard Vel say, grabbing her hand as the world gave way.

She was falling, still holding onto Vel's hand. He was screaming beside her, and the river of fire was coming closer and closer and closer.

She closed her eyes, ready for the pain.

It didn't matter now, none of it mattered.

She still had a terrible soul and now poor Vel was yet another casualty of it.

Her body jerked roughly, and she wondered why the fire didn't feel so painful. In fact, it didn't feel like anything at all.

If anything, it was getting less hot.

"I GOT YOU!" she heard him say.

She opened her eyes and all she saw was a burning river. Forcing herself to look upwards, she finally registered the death vice Vel had around her forearm with his hand. Vel, slowly being reeled up to her ship, attached to the magnetic clip on the utility belt that she had given him, was smiling at her, relieved.

"I got you," he repeated, looking down at her. "I'm not gonna let go, I promise."

He tossed her up onto the open hatch, her fingers connecting with the hot metal. She pulled herself up and sat on the edge of the ship, feeling the fire and smelling the sulfur and wondering why the Great Creator didn't just put her out of her misery already.

"Are you okay?" Vel asked, as he pulled himself up to safety.

"Let's just get out of here," she whispered, standing up and heading to her bridge.

CHAPTER EIGHTEEN

Dr. Lyssa Peate stepped off of her ship in the dock of the Planetary and System Science Academy, wearing her signature white collared shirt and dull gray dress pants. She had just come from a planet excavation, a far away, habitable planet with huge fields just ripe for running. Her legs were still achy from the twenty miler she stuck in there.

Her eyes, hidden behind her thick rimmed glasses, were scanning the dock for anyone who looked like they recognized her. It was an odd hour to arrive at the Academy, but there were still dock hands and young DSEs milling about, removing cargo and loading it. Two U-POL officers were strolling the docks, but they paid her no attention. They weren't the Special Forces anyway.

She locked up her ship, confident the coast was clear and headed for the lifts.

The ride to her lab was uneventful, although they had changed all the advertisements in the cab to those advocating the current president of the UBU for re-election. Lyssa thought the entire political process was stupid—how could one person speak for a universe full of different creatures—and the ads were worse. It was early too—the next election wasn't for another six months.

She arrived at her level and stepped off, stuffing her hands in her pockets and walking down the empty hall. Most of the labs were closed, but a few doctors were working, eyes glued to a microscope, or watching the reactions of their chemical experiments.

She arrived at her lab and gently typed in the access code, when she felt a presence behind her. In the reflection, she saw blonde hair and a white lab coat, with a slightly shorter intern next to him.

"Dorst, I'm not—"

"Oh no. No, no, no, dear Lyssa," she heard a familiar voice say. Whirling around, she momentarily thought she was having another hallucination, because Sage Teon, replete with official badge and white lab coat, was standing in the middle of the Planetary and System Science

Academy. But more curious was the fact that his face was covered in purple bruises and his lip was slit down the middle.

"What in Leveman's Vortex happened to you?" she gaped.

"Oh, you know," Sage shrugged, his thin layer of composure barely covering a boiling river of rage. "Me and my crew thought it would be fun to engage in a good ol' fashioned bar brawl with a pirate and his crew that I WASN'T EVEN AFTER."

Lyssa swallowed, realizing in the excitement of capturing Relleck, and then Pymus, that she had completely forgotten that Sage and his crew had stayed behind to fight Linro's and Relleck's crews.

And from the looks of it, it was a hard fought battle.

"A pirate, whom, I find out later, that YOU LET GO," Sage said, his face turning red with anger. "I cannot FATHOM why you would do this."

"I...uh..." she said.

"So do you know what I did?" Sage said, a slight mad look in his eye. "I TURNED IN LINRO LEE." He nodded. "Yeah, that's right, I turned in the pirate you were hunting."

She didn't dare look annoyed.

"DOES THAT PISS YOU OFF, LYSSA?" Sage barked at her, now completely in her face. She could see that he was really badly bruised, and the split in his lip had reopened from his ranting and raving.

She realized he was waiting for her to respond, his chest heaving in rage, and quickly shook her head.

"AND MY BOUNTY IS NOW NUMBER SIX IN THE UNIVERSE," Sage screamed. "DOES THAT PISS YOU OFF?"

Lyssa bit her lip, trying her best not to burst out laughing at the way he had very uncharacteristically lost his mind. All she could do was shake her head.

"SO I THOUGHT, WHAT WOULD REALLY PISS YOU OFF. AND THEN, LUCKY FOR ME, YOUR BROTHER CALLED."

Vel, who was watching the spectacle amusedly, shot her a quick look.

"SO I KNEW THAT WOULD REALLY PISS YOU OFF!" Sage screamed, not caring that several passersby were watching them oddly. "DOES THAT PISS YOU OFF LYSSA?"

She realized that he was looking for a yes here, and nodded fervently.

"GOOD, I'M GLAD," Sage barked at her. "HERE'S YOUR DAMNED BROTHER. NOW I'M GOING TO THE DAMNED DOCTOR TO MAKE SURE I DON'T HAVE A CONCUSSION."

And with that he turned around and huffed off, hands in the lab coat pockets.

"Man, that guy is crazy about you," Vel observed, casually.

"Oh get sucked into Leveman's," she hissed at him, walking into the lab.

"Been there, done that," Vel grinned, following her inside. "Wouldn't recommend it."

"Why are you here?" Lyssa asked, sitting down at the old computer and firing it up.

"Because you and I nearly died at Leveman's Vortex last week. Then you drop me off at the Manor without two words and disappear."

"I was excavating a planet," she muttered, syncing her mini-computer.

"Which, and I don't know if you recall, but I'm supposed to do with you?" Vel asked, matter-of-factly. "As I am still your intern."

"I thought the deal was that if I went home that you'd ask Dorst to be your teacher," Lyssa responded without looking at him. "Or was that a lie, too?"

"Do you honestly expect me to believe that you wanted to be rid of me?" Vel retorted.

"Pymus is gone, so no need to keep you on as my intern," she muttered, still unwilling to look at him.

"You're just mad because I saw something you didn't want me to see," Vel shrugged.

The color drained from her face. She was sure those were hallucinations.

"You... saw?" she whispered, finally looking at him.

"I didn't have to," Vel said, quietly reaching over and turning off the monitor so she would talk to him. "You were done—truly, utterly, and completely done. But something happened at Leveman's Vortex—"

"NOTHING happened," Lyssa growled, sitting back and turning on the monitor.

Vel reached over and turned it off again. "Liar."

"Oh good, you've finally figured it out," Lyssa said, turning it back on.

"Quit deflecting," Vel snapped back. "Tell me what you saw."

She stared at him.

He stared back with the same level of intensity.

She narrowed her eyes.

He narrowed his back at her.

"UGH!" she said, finally giving in. "It was....nothing," she sighed. "Nothing that matters anyways."

"Why do you say that?" Vel asked.

"Because you saw what happened?" Lyssa shook her head. "It's the same thing that happened with Sostas."

"W-what?" Vel blinked. "What are you talking about?"

"The last time I went to Leveman's Vortex with him," Lyssa sighed, staring at the dark computer screen. "Sostas was being a real asshole. Yelling at me for nothing. And he, and mother, and everyone had always made me feel like I was wrong, or bad, or whatever. So I thought...I thought I could ask Him."

"Oh, Lyssa," Vel sighed.

"And before you know it, the same damned thing was happening," she whispered, trying to swallow the lump in her throat. "The world just disintegrated. The Great Creator gave me my answer. I have a bad soul—I am a bad person. It doesn't matter what I call myself—I'm going to burn. Mother knows it, Helmsley knows it. Father even…saw it firsthand…"

"Did he…fall?" Vel asked.

"No," she said. "Worse. He was so angry with me he couldn't even look at me. The next morning…" she swallowed. "He was gone. He had no use for a rotten soul."

"Why were you his assistant anyways?" Vel asked.

"Because I was the only kid that Mother would let him take," Lyssa replied darkly. "As you saw, she obviously didn't care if I lived or died."

"That or…" Vel said, thoughtfully. "He was using theology to his advantage."

"How do you figure?" Lyssa asked, annoyed.

"Do you remember the story of Mercurious?" Vel asked.

"Who?" Lyssa asked.

"It's a story in the scriptures—you would know if you weren't playing on your damned mini-computer at Temple," Vel snapped, knowingly. "About two brothers, one who was good and one who was not so good. The good brother died and the evil brother followed his soul back through the fields of Lethe all the way to the Arch of Eron."

"Is there a point to this story?" she said, folding her arms over her chest.

"The point is that I would wager Father needed you so he wouldn't suffer from those same hallucinations. They probably are only brought on when a person's soul is not good enough to pass through the Arch, so if he brought you with him…"

"So you're saying he needed me because I had a *good* soul?" she asked, incredulously.

"I'm saying it makes sense—" Vel said.

"No, it doesn't," she insisted stubbornly. "If I have such a good soul, how come I still had hallucinations? I mean, I saw Dorst and Sera at Harms' bar for crying out loud."

"What'd they say?" Vel asked, amused.

"Stuff," Lyssa muttered. "They were wrong anyways."

"What'd they say?" Vel repeated.

"They said I was stubborn, and too reckless, and I push people away," she snapped.

"Seems pretty accurate," Vel observed, watching the predictable glare arise on her face. "You are, and you do."

"Well Relleck and Sage said that I was over-compensating and...and can take care of myself," she trailed off, realizing that Sage wasn't actually saying anything she disagreed with.

"Yes, you do," Vel nodded. "And you can."

"And..." She clammed up. Her self-reflection wasn't something she really wanted to share with him.

"Some scriptures," Vel noted, watching her face as she withheld from him. "Say that the Fields of Lethe are there to help wayward souls figure out their truth and atone before they can reach the Arch of Eron," he paused, smiling. "You looked pretty content when you finally came back to reality. And I didn't see the Arch until you did."

She shifted uncomfortably, remembering the warmth and clarity she felt. It was true, the hallucinations stopped when she came to realize how wrongly she had been thinking about herself.

"Didn't matter what I saw or didn't see," she said, angrily. "I obviously failed the judgment. As Pymus can attest..."

"If I recall, Pymus was the one standing closest to the Arch when the judgment was passed, not you," Vel pointed out, smiling. "Per the story of Mercurious, that means that *his* soul was being judged, and not yours. So if you ask me, perhaps he got what he deserved."

Lyssa looked up at her blank computer screen, wheels turning in her head. Pymus *was* closer to the Arch when everything changed. When she was a little girl, she had stepped up to the Arch to ask the Great Creator what he thought of her, and her father had pulled her away...

"If anything, I think that proves how good your soul is," Vel smiled, knowing that he had finally gotten through to her. "A little wayward, perhaps, but you found your way."

His words rung in her ear – and she suddenly felt very uncomfortable.

"Ugh," Lyssa snapped, turning back on her computer. "Can it with the mushy shit."

"God in Leveman's Vortex, you are so predictable," Vel smiled. "See? The Great Creator was right. The moment someone gets even remotely close to you, you just shut down and start with the sass."

"Why are you so *annoying* today?" she whined, hoping they would move on soon.

"Because I—"

They were both interrupted by the sound of her mini-computer buzzing. To her surprise and slight horror, it was Dissident.

He had been calling her for days now, but she didn't want to respond. She knew he was probably going to kick her out of his web for good. She was still stinging from the news from Pymus that he had hired Relleck to capture her—she didn't know what kind of verbal abuse he was going to lay her way this time-

"Are you gonna take that?" Vel asked.

She looked up at him, hearing his words, but taking a different meaning from them. For some reason – maybe it was Vel, maybe she was just tired of getting kicked around—she felt like finally standing up for herself with this guy.

"No, I'm not," she smiled, gently pulling off her glasses and hair band.

"What is wrong with you?" Dissident seethed, his face inches away from the camera. "Why didn't you turn him in when you had the chance, you stupid girl? I could have been rid of him for—"

"Well, I was gonna," Razia responded, tossing a look to Vel. "But you know, I was just so damned pissed at the fact that he was hired to capture me."

She saw Dissident's face change slightly.

"And, it turns out, my own runner actually set me up," she continued, watching his face. "Funny story, huh?"

"Well, you see, I—"

"Can it," she snapped, her voice full of fire and confidence that it had rarely had with him. "Here's the deal, asshole: I'm in your damned web, and if you ever pull a bitch move like that again, or even so much as hint that you want to kick me out, I will drag your sorry ass out of that rat hole of an apartment that you live in and I will leave you so black and blue that you will be pissing blood for a month."

"You don't—" he sputtered, his face pale with fear.

"You live five blocks from Harms' bar, sixth floor, apartment B," she smiled, watching his eyes widen. "Have a nice afternoon."

And with that, she hung up on him.

"That was epic," Vel grinned.

She dropped her confident face momentarily. "Was it too much?"

"Just enough," Vel said, pulling up a chair to sit next to her. "So tell me about this planet you excavated?"

"No," Lyssa snapped, pulling her glasses back on. "Go bother Dorst."

"So...about that..." Vel laughed nervously and began scratching the back of his head. "After you stormed out of the Manor, I may have told Mother that she was an unbelievably selfish, hypocritical cow who was going to burn in Plethegon for the way she had forsaken her own daughter."

Lyssa swiveled her head to stare at him, impressed.

"So....I'm not sure I would be welcome on Dorst's team right now anyways," Vel said, trying to keep the smile off his face.

Lyssa turned back to the computer and mumbled, "Well, I guess you can stay a little longer. Just stay outta my way."

"Wow, don't sound too excited," Vel laughed. "Your air of mystery will be shattered if anyone thought you actually liked spending time with me."

"I'm not, whatever, you're stupid," she muttered, quickly looking back at the computer in front of her with a blush rising on her cheeks. "I don't care. Asshole. Get sucked."

"I'm sure," Vel smiled, knowingly, gently nudging her. "I love you too."

"Whatever," she rolled her eyes. But as her little brother sat down next to her, she couldn't help the small smile that tugged at the corner of her mouth as they put together her planet presentation.

ACKNOWLEDGEMENTS

First and foremost, thank you, Dear Reader, for picking up my book and reading it to the end. You are my Sunshine and make me happy when skies are gray. I do hope you'll take a moment to follow me on social media, and, if you enjoyed the book, please consider writing a review on Amazon or Goodreads.

The publication of this book—and the subsequent publication of the sequels, short stories, and umpteen thousand blog posts—is a dream nearly fifteen years in the making. It took my own journey through Leveman's Vortex to realize that the person I am is the person I've been hiding for a very long time. And you have the product of that realization in your hands.

I do want to thank my beta-readers, Becky and Kristin, for giving me the sanity check to push forward with publication, as well as the untold thousands who read my work in the varying stages of completion since I first started writing all those years ago.

ABOUT THE AUTHOR

S. Usher Evans is an author, blogger, and witty banter aficionado. Born in a small, suburban town in northwest Florida, she was seventeen before she realized that not all beach sand is white. From a young age, she has always been a long-winded individual, first verbally (to the chagrin of her ever-loving parents) and then eventually channeled into the many novels that dotted her Windows 98 computer in the early 2000's. After high school, she got the hell outta dodge and went to school near the nation's capital, where she somehow landed jobs at National Geographic, Discovery Channel, and the British Broadcasting Corporation, capping off her educational career with delivering the commencement address to 20,000 of her closest friends. She determined she'd goofed off long enough with that television nonsense and got a "real job" as an IT consultant. Yet she continued to write, developing twenty page standard operating procedures and then coming home to write novels about badass bounty hunters, teenage magic users, and other nonsense. After a severe quarter life crisis at age twenty-seven, she decided to finally get a move on and share those novels with the world in hopes that she will never have to write another SOP again.

Be sure to follow her on Twitter (@s_usherevans) for more on Razia's adventures.

ALSO BY S. USHER EVANS

Sage Teon and the Fake Diamond Heist (Razia #1.1)
Sage Teon and the L Word (Razia #1.2)
Alliances (Razia #2)

Empath (Coming June 2015)

17386643R00125

Made in the USA
Middletown, DE
21 January 2015

THE REBUSQUEST WEBSITE ©

Bringing Back the Spirit of Saturday Mornings.

www.therebusquestwebsite.com

Welcome to the world of Rebusquest. Webcomics created by Cullen Pittman that have the style of classic Saturday Morning cartoons. Rebusquest is about an average 12 year old boy named Carson who finds and solves a magic rebus that transports him to the weird and surreal world of Rebusquest where rebuses puzzles are a way of life. With the help of a sassy teenage elf named Reba, Carson must travel the strange lands gathering clues that will form rebuses hoping that one of those rebuses will help Carson return home someday. Other webcomics on this site include; X.O. Seal, a cyborg seal from the future who fights crime. And Skelroy and Bonus, he story of two skeletons who love injuring themselves doing crazy motorcycle stunts.

I hope you'll have fun!

Cullen Pittman Productions